"The ranch work, the cattle, the riding… This is what I left the Amish world for."

"And the other freedoms...right?" Wilder asked.

"This was the freedom I wanted," Sue said. "To be a cattlewoman."

Wilder paused, surprised. "Driving cars, watching TV, flicking on a light?"

"Don't get me wrong, I don't want to give those up, either," she said. "But I don't want to just go back to town, get a job in a grocery store, and... live my life. I got a taste of the work I really love, but having a baby in the mix isn't going to be easy."

"I wish I could keep you on after my brother gets back," he said.

She smiled faintly. "You don't have to worry about me. I'll be fine. When I'm a mother, everything will be different. It won't be all about what I want anymore—it will be about my child. And that's the way it's supposed to be."

"What if you stayed here with me?"

Dear Reader,

Strong mothers raise strong daughters—it's the way the world works. My mother and I are both strong women, and it's a beautiful thing. But strong women sometimes end up on opposite ends of an issue.

In this book I wanted to look at mothers and daughters and how love overcomes in those precious relationships, too. Love is always stronger than whatever differences or disagreements might come up.

If you enjoy this book, I hope you'll come find me on my website at patriciajohns.com or on social media. I also invite you to sign up for my monthly newsletter, which has giveaways and provides a little glimpse into this writer's world.

If you check out my book page on my website, you'll see that I have a pretty lengthy backlist. If you like cowboys, Amish or even small-town stories, I have something for you. You never know—you might find your next read!

Patricia Johns

HEARTWARMING

A Cowboy in Amish Country

—

Patricia Johns

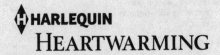

HARLEQUIN
HEARTWARMING

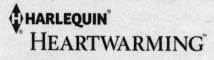

ISBN-13: 978-1-335-58459-5

Recycling programs
for this product may
not exist in your area.

A Cowboy in Amish Country

For questions and comments about the quality of this book,
please contact us at CustomerService@Harlequin.com.

Harlequin Enterprises ULC
22 Adelaide St. West, 41st Floor
Toronto, Ontario M5H 4E3, Canada
www.Harlequin.com

Printed in U.S.A.

Patricia Johns is a *Publishers Weekly* bestselling author who writes from Alberta, Canada, where she lives with her husband and son. She writes Amish romances that will leave you yearning for a simpler life. You can find her at patriciajohns.com and on social media, where she loves to connect with her readers. Drop by her website and you might find your next read!

Visit the Author Profile page
at Harlequin.com for more titles.

This book is for my mom.

She's a strong woman who raised a strong daughter.

Thank you for raising me to be the woman I am.

I love you!

CHAPTER ONE

THE SUN HUNG low in the sky, spilling golden light over Amish Country. Here in the heart of Ohio, almost all of the farms were Amish owned and operated, except for the Westhouse ranch.

Shadows stretched long across the farmyard, and there was a chill in the evening air, the smell of a bonfire in the distance. Wilder Westhouse leaned back against the fence, watching the job applicant's technique.

Sue Schmidt had applied to work on the ranch for a couple of months until Wilder's brother, Conrad, and his wife, Annabelle, got back from a well-deserved vacation. Anyone Wilder hired had better know the work—he wouldn't have time to teach that much—and Sue's résumé was downright impressive. In addition to her general competence, she was attractive in a way that had caught his eye. It shouldn't matter—it didn't really—but he'd noticed.

She was slim, with long auburn hair pulled back into a sleek ponytail. She wore a snug pair of jeans and a formfitting pink T-shirt that had a streak of dust down the side. She had a long-sleeved shirt tied around her waist, and when the calf jogged off to the other end of the corral, she didn't chase it. That was good instinct right there—a cowhand never won if she was stuck chasing down a calf. She paused, then changed her direction, moving slowly, calmly, confidently. She slid the hook smoothly behind the calf's hind leg and pulled it steadily backward.

The calf struggled, but Sue put her weight behind the hook, and Wilder took the prepared ear-tag punch and quickly straddled the calf. He punched the tag in place. The calf jerked and balked, and when Wilder swung his leg free of the animal, Sue expertly released the hook hold. The calf ran back to its mother's side.

Wilder looked over his shoulder at the pretty job applicant. She arched an eyebrow at him, and he noticed—not for the first time—her sparkling blue eyes.

"You seem to know the work," Wilder said. And she was a far sight better than the other applicants.

"I've worked ranches since I was a child," Sue replied. "I like cows. I understand them."

"It's just me on the ranch right now, and whoever takes the job will be staying in the ranch house. I don't know if that would be uncomfortable for you," Wilder said.

It might be mildly narrow-minded of him, but he'd expected to hire a man for this position. However, he wasn't opposed to taking on a woman. Whoever could do the work was what mattered most to him.

"I'd have my own room?" Sue asked.

"Of course. But everything else is shared— bathroom, kitchen, TV."

"I can live with that," she replied.

"It's dawn to dusk work," Wilder added. "Room and board is free. I pay a daily rate."

He outlined the money he could offer, and she nodded. "Sounds fair."

"Okay, well…" Wilder shrugged. "If you want the job, you're hired."

A smile lit up her face. "Thank you. I appreciate it. I suppose I should mention that my brother lives right next door to you."

"What?" Wilder shot a look over the fence toward the Amish farm next door. Wollie Schmidt was a good neighbor, and they often helped each other out. "Wait…you're *that* Sue Schmidt?"

"You've heard of me?"

Wilder opened the corral gate and secured it behind them. "Yeah, I've heard of you. You're the sister who—how do they say it?—'jumped the fence' and left the Amish life. They talk about you like you died."

"I didn't die," she replied. "I just couldn't live Amish. But if you leave, it's almost like you do die to them. There's Amish and there's everything else. They don't see any gray area."

"I'm not Amish, and I get along with your brother just fine," Wilder said. He had a good relationship with his Amish neighbors on both sides, but especially with Wollie Schmidt. It had taken some time to gain the Amish man's trust, and in a community like this one, those relationships mattered. Ranchers needed their neighbors.

"My brother has considerably lower expectations for you," she replied, but she shot him a disarming grin. "No offense."

"None taken." He shook his head. "So why are you here—as in, next door to your brother? Are you thinking of going home?"

"Not exactly," she replied. "First of all, I never went that far. I've been living in Wooster. I was doing some assisting for a local large animal vet."

"Right…" That was part of her impressive résumé, her last job listed. "So why are you leaving that job? It sounds like a great gig."

"His nephew just graduated with his vet tech diploma, and I stepped aside. I could see the writing on the wall," she replied. "And looking for work, I came across your ad. Do you believe in things happening for a reason? Well, yours was the only job I was qualified for, and right next door to my family. I thought it might be one of those serendipity things."

Wilder followed her gaze toward the farm next door. A little girl came out of the house wielding a shovel, and tramped out to the garden. Sue's gaze locked on the girl.

"Who is that?" she asked softly.

"Jane—your brother's daughter. You've never met her?"

Sue shook her head. "*Mamm* mentions her, but I've never seen her in person."

Wilder fell silent, and he noticed the conflicted emotion flickering across her face. Then she dragged her gaze back to Wilder and forced a smile.

"Are you sure you want to work this close to home?" Wilder asked.

She nodded. "I'll be honest. I need the job. And I won't let any personal issues affect my work. I promise."

"Is this going to be a problem for Wollie?" Wilder asked.

"You'd have to ask Wollie." Her composure was back. "But I can tell you this much—I know ranching, I'm good at it and you can trust me to get the job done right the first time. If you think you can get that from anyone else, then feel free to hire them instead."

It wasn't really an option.

"Honestly, you're the only one who was qualified," Wilder said. "And not drunk."

She met his gaze uncertainly as if wondering if he was joking, then a smile tickled her lips. "Another point in my favor. I don't drink."

As a recovering alcoholic himself, her

being a teetotaler was actually a point in her favor. He didn't have any booze on-site, and he wouldn't allow it. He needed help for two months on the ranch, and Sue was not only capable, but willing to do the short-term job.

"Let's give it a try," Wilder said. "If it doesn't work for you being this close to your family, you can let me know and I'll keep looking for someone else. But for the time being, I'd be happy to work with you."

Sue nodded. "Thanks."

"Did you want to see the house?" he asked.

Sue followed him as they walked from the corral to the house. Little Jane seemed to be digging up some potatoes, and she stopped her work and shaded her eyes, watching them. She wouldn't recognize her aunt, but Jane was a curious child who made the Westhouse ranch her personal business. Wilder had always thought it was because they were "English," and the differences intrigued the girl.

"Your niece comes over to visit pretty often," Wilder said.

"Does she?"

"She likes to watch TV. She pretends she isn't, but she'll stand right where she can see it from the kitchen, and then freezes there."

Sue smiled faintly. "Does my brother mind?"

"He'd prefer she didn't. But we have a pretty cordial relationship, and I think they just explain how wicked we are from a distance."

Sue chuckled. "They don't think technology is wicked."

"No?" Wilder frowned.

"No," she said. "It has to do with maintaining the Plain lifestyle. Technology pulls people away from the things Amish people feel are most important, like family and community. So TV isn't evil, it's just not conducive to families actually talking to each other in an evening. It doesn't help people stay connected."

"I can't argue with you there," Wilder said. "Parents everywhere complain about their kids being glued to screens."

"Exactly," she said. "So the Amish follow the rules called the *Ordnung* in order to preserve their way of life. It's not about *Englishers* being evil. It's about being..." She shook her head. "It's about being Amish."

"So you don't think Wollie warns Jane about our dangerous lifestyle over here?" Wilder teased.

"Oh, he definitely does." Sue laughed, though, softening the words. "But he'd never say you were evil. He'd say your way of life has dangerous temptations. I know it's a fine line, but I think it matters."

Sue seemed to care about the way the Amish were understood, and he cast her an evaluating look. She did look a little bit like Wollie around the eyes. And Wilder could see a bit of Linda, her mother, in her, too. But somehow, he couldn't see her dressed in those modest, Amish clothes—blocks of color with a white apron on top. Sue had too much sass about her, and if Amish women had sass, they hid it under a layer of decorum.

"Do you think you'll ever go back?" Wilder asked.

"Not unless forced," she replied softly, and her gaze flickered in the direction of the farm next door.

"Would they force you?" he asked uncertainly.

"What?" Sue laughed breathily and shook her head. "Sorry, I didn't mean forced by them. Everyone has a choice, and the Amish believe very deeply in a person's right to choose. No one is going to come drag me back. I meant forced by circumstances, you know? But no. I don't see myself ever going back to the Amish life. I left for a reason, and nothing has changed."

Once at the house, Wilder took a quick look at her red Chevy pickup. Call it professional curiosity. Wilder liked tinkering with vehicles, and her vehicle was an older model, with a fair amount of rust. He'd be curious to get a look under the hood. Those old Chevys could stand up to a lot. He glanced back in the direction of the Schmidt farm, and Jane waved enthusiastically from the garden. Wilder waved back to the little girl, then opened the side door for Sue.

"Come on in," he said.

Sue came inside, and as she shut the door behind her, he noticed how she deflated just a little bit.

"How long since you've seen your family?" Wilder asked.

"My mother?" Sue shrugged. "Probably three years. My brother? About fifteen years. I never did see him when he was married, and I certainly didn't meet his daughter. I was long gone before all of that."

"So… Are you going to try to keep yourself a secret, or…"

"A secret?" Sue smiled faintly. "That wouldn't really be possible. I'll go over and let them know where I am. Hopefully, it won't be too awkward for you."

"For me? Nah." Wilder grinned. "I'm already the outsider around here. Don't worry about me."

So long as Wollie was okay with his sister living in Wilder's house. He had a sudden image of the tall, gentle man next door stomping over here with a few strong opinions to share. But Wilder and Wollie knew each other quite well, and they had a great deal of respect for each other. The fact that she was willing to go face her brother was rather impressive. She had a backbone, that was for sure.

"Do you want the tour?" Wilder asked.

"Sure."

"Okay, well, this is the kitchen." He gestured behind him, and he tried not to notice just how pretty his new ranch hand was. Not only was she his employee, which would make any kind of flirting inappropriate, she was also his neighbor's younger sister. Men had a certain protective streak when it came to their sisters, and Wilder had heard enough about Sue to know that she was special. So pretty or not, he'd just have to pretend he didn't notice it.

What had he just gotten himself into?

THE TOUR OF the ranch house was a short one. There was the kitchen done in dark browns from the eighties, a sitting room with a TV, a couch and some bookshelves, and three bedrooms down one hallway. The one that would be hers overlooked a nicely kept vegetable garden that seemed to have some potatoes still left in the ground and orange pumpkins sitting under large, yellowing leaves. The rest had been hoed under.

She'd noticed a little addition to the house when she'd driven up. It was newly painted white with the even Amish trim around a generous window, and a chimney coming up out of the roof. In the kitchen, she saw the new, solid door that led into the addition.

"That looks like a *dawdie hus*—an in-law suite," she said, nodding toward the door.

"Yeah, we added it on when my brother got married," Wilder said. "Conrad and his wife, Annabelle, are going to build their own house out past the barns, but that will take a bit of time. Until then, this'll give them some privacy."

Wilder's dark gaze moved over her face in a friendly way, but she felt her face warming all the same. He was good-looking—tall, lanky, strong. And she liked the way he talked easily, opening up. Just the type of man she found herself most drawn to.

"It looks Amish built," she said.

"It was a really generous wedding gift from the local Amish farmers," Wilder replied. "Your brother and the other neighbors. Conrad arrested some cattle rustlers that were causing a lot of trouble for the Amish farms, and it was their way of saying thank you."

Sue nodded. "They would do that, wouldn't they…"

The Amish didn't stay in anyone's debt, and she'd always liked that about her upbringing. They helped each other, always paying it back when they received help.

Wilder opened the fridge and pulled out a can of Coke. He passed it over, and she accepted it with a smile of thanks.

"Can I ask you something?" That dark gaze landed on her again.

"Sure."

"Why did you leave the Amish life?"

That was the question everyone asked. And even after all these years, she didn't have an easy answer for that.

She said quietly, "I just couldn't live by the rules anymore. I wanted to be able to drive a car, own a computer, watch TV… I just didn't believe in the Amish life the way you need to in order to commit to it. I know all the beautiful things I left behind, but I couldn't be happy while I was feeling trapped."

Wilder nodded. "I get it. Do you regret leaving ever?"

There was something about this cowboy that made her want to answer more honestly than she normally did. People idealized the Amish, romanticized them. But for her, it was just…life, albeit under different rules.

"Sometimes. When I'm lonely, or when I'm struggling to make ends meet, I think that if I'd stayed Amish, I wouldn't have those problems because I'd have a close knit community to lean back on. But I also wouldn't be able to live my life the way I want to."

"I get it." He nodded. "I don't think I could live by those rules, either. I always was a bit of a rebel deep down."

"Me, too." She met his smile. "It's ironic when my rebellion looks like electricity and working a ranch, though. For everyone else, I'm incredibly tame. For the Amish, I'm scandalous."

They both chuckled, and as she glanced around the kitchen, she felt the hominess of this little house. It reflected the relaxed man in front of her. She wasn't normally very comfortable talking about her history, but with Wilder it felt different. She didn't sense any judgment there, maybe just because he understood better living out here in Amish Country.

"When do you want me to start working with you?" she asked.

"When can you start?" he asked.

"I'll have to pack a bag," she said. "Day after tomorrow?"

"That sounds fair to me."

"Thanks." She pressed her lips together. "Since that's hammered out, I should probably go next door and let my family know what's happening."

"I'd appreciate that," he said with a rueful smile. "I've got to get along with my Amish neighbors, so the fewer misunderstandings the better."

She'd need to get along with her Amish family, too. Sue was here to work, and she intended to make good on that. While she'd told him she was back because she'd lost her job with the vet, that wasn't the only reason.

She was pregnant—just not visibly yet—and she needed to sort out a future for herself and her child. How would she take care of herself with a newborn? Would her family be willing to help her out? She wasn't sure. At fourteen weeks along, to look at her, no one could tell yet that she was expecting. The doctor said that since she was taller that she'd take a bit longer to "pop." She could feel the baby, though—a flutter inside her that gave her a rush of secret joy every time she felt it…

Sue's pregnant figure would arrive, and probably soon. She had maternity jeans and T-shirts packed with her other clothes. It was only a matter of time now before she needed them, and hopefully she'd have already proved her value to Wilder before he found out about her pregnancy. She *needed* this job.

A baby was coming, and while Sue didn't want to return to the Amish life, she might not have a choice.

SUE SAT IN the front seat of her Chevy and pulled a comb through her hair. She let the tendrils fall loose around her shoulders. Back when she was a teen, having her hair down was considered the height of rebellion. Now in her thirties, she just wanted to look nice. No one would expect Amish modesty from her anymore. She smoothed on a bit of lip gloss and added some powder to her face. The Amish didn't wear any makeup, so wearing something even this subtle was almost like war paint as she prepared to head over to her brother's house to announce her presence.

What kind of reaction could she expect?

Sue hopped out of the truck and headed across the short stretch of field, her heart hovering in her chest. Not so long ago, this was the home where Sue had grown up. It was the same, but different now. The apple tree she used to climb as a little girl in the front yard was gone. The seedling she'd left behind at the side of the house was now a mature tree. And the house that once seemed so big looked smaller to her adult eyes.

The front door opened, and the little girl she'd seen earlier came outside. That would be Jane, her niece.

"Hello!" Jane called. "Are you coming over to visit?"

Sue waved weakly.

"Sue?" An older woman appeared behind the girl. Sue's mother. Linda Schmidt slipped past the little girl and hurried down the front steps. "Sue? Is that you?"

Linda didn't seem to need an answer, lifting her skirt and running in Sue's direction. When she got to her, Linda flung her arms around Sue's neck and pulled her down into a fierce hug.

Sue closed her eyes, her mother's familiar embrace feeling like a homecoming all its own. She smelled of baking and baby powder. She was older now—her hair completely gray, and her figure a little rounder. When Linda released her, Linda wiped tears off her weathered cheeks.

"Where did you come from?" Linda looked around. "Where did you park?"

"I'm actually staying next door at the *English* ranch," Sue said. "I took a job there."

Linda frowned. "Cooking?"

"Ranch work," Sue said with a low laugh.

"Oh, Sue…you're a woman, you know," Linda said, shaking her head. "Come inside. I'm sure you're hungry. You're awfully thin. You should eat more."

Sue wasn't actually all that thin, but her mother's love language was food, and everyone looked too thin for Linda. Sue followed her mother up the steps and she looked down at Jane whose eyes were round.

"Are you Aunt Sue?" Jane asked. She'd obviously overheard.

"That's me," Sue said with a smile. "You must be Jane."

Jane nodded soberly but didn't answer, and the three of them went into the house together. They passed through the sitting room, and Sue saw that the furniture had changed, with a newer blue couch replacing the old brown one. But the smell of the house was the same family combination of wood wax and baking.

"Come sit down at the table," Linda said. "I've made an apricot and apple crisp, if you'd like."

"That sounds great, *Mamm*."

Linda slid a plate in front of her, and another in front of Jane. The little girl's intense, blue gaze hadn't left Sue yet.

"Hi," Sue said quietly. "I imagine your *daet* talks about me sometimes."

Jane nodded.

"Am I scary?" Sue asked.

"No," Jane said. "You're very bad, though. You *left*."

Even though it was a child's understanding of things, it stung a little.

"Well, I've come to visit," Sue said. "Your *mammi* told me all about you, and I've been wanting to meet you for a long time."

Linda sat down opposite them, and she gave Jane a reassuring smile.

"So why work a ranch?" Linda asked. "I thought you had a good job with the vet."

"I did, but the boss's nephew needed work, and you know how that can be." Sue shrugged. "But I love working with the cattle. You know that."

"I know. You always did," Linda said. "And

I suppose Wilder must need the extra help. You could stay here with us, you know. You don't have to stay next door with a stranger."

"You might want me here, but I'm not sure Wollie will."

"Why not?" Linda demanded. "All he wants is for you to come home."

"He wants me home for good," Sue replied. "Not like this. I have no intention of spending the next two months arguing the finer points of Amish beliefs with him." She looked down to find Jane still watching her, and Sue's stomach sank. "I'm sorry, Jane. I don't mean to say anything bad about your *daet*. I love him very much, but sometimes we argue."

"Oh." Jane dropped her gaze. That must have offended the girl, or at least caused some distrust of her aunt. Sue cast her mother a helpless look.

"Aunt Sue and your *daet* are brother and sister," Linda said, brightening her tone. "Think of your friends, Joel and Tabitha. You know how they tangle and argue? Well, that used to be your *daet* and your aunt."

"Tabitha sits on him," Jane said with a mischievous smile.

"Is she the older sister?" Sue asked.

"No, she's just meaner," Jane said with an impish grin.

Sue couldn't help but chuckle. "How are Amanda and Jake? And Rose and Noah?"

For the next few minutes, they discussed family gossip—her sisters and their families who were in different parts of the country now, her cousins, second cousins, third cousins… And she pretended that this was nothing more than a visit. But she couldn't help wondering if she'd need to find a way to fit back into this Amish life again.

Other single women in Wooster had babies and took them to day care. There was government support if they needed extra help. They could even sue the father for child support. When she told Chaney she was pregnant, he'd demanded she get an abortion and they'd fought about it and broken up. He was moving to Utah for work anyway, and while she could track him down and demand money, she didn't have the heart to do it.

She heard boots on the short staircase that led to the kitchen's side door, where her brother appeared. Wollie looked different with his married beard, but she'd still recognize him anywhere. He met her gaze with friendly good humor, but then his eyes widened.

"Hi, Wollie," she said. "How are you?"

"You're...back?" Wollie sounded strangled.

"Not, exactly." She gave the quick explanation of her job next door.

"I'm here for a little while," she concluded.

He scrubbed a hand through his hair.

"Can't we just...visit? It's not like I'm shunned, Wollie!"

She'd never been baptized into the church, which meant that the most severe community punishment didn't apply to her. Every teenager had a choice before baptism, and she'd made hers.

"Jane, come with me," Wollie said curtly. "You're going to help me with chores."

"But I want to stay with *Mammi* and Aunt Sue," Jane said.

"Jane, now." His tone brooked no argument, and the girl got up and went to the door. Wollie headed back out, his daughter in tow, and the screen door slammed behind them.

Sue looked at her mother. "See? Wollie obviously thinks I'm a bad influence."

"Never mind him," Linda said with a sigh. "He's spent the entirety of Jane's life making you into a walking morality lesson on what not to do. Seeing you in the flesh is going to ruin a lot of that."

"You think so?" Sue asked with a weak smile. When they found out about the baby, the power of those lessons might come swooping back for her family.

"My dear girl," Linda said, putting a hand over hers. "You and your brother have always bickered. And I think it's high time the two of you made some peace. If you don't want to stay under this roof, well, I suppose I understand that. And there might be some wisdom to it. I'm glad you're next door for a long while. It'll give you and your brother a chance to patch things up. An afternoon of intense disagreement never seems to work. But a few weeks of being next door to each other might calm everything down enough for you to talk."

"You're very reasonable, *Mamm*," Sue said.

"And who knows?" Linda said with a smile. "Maybe you'll find your way home yet."

Maybe she would, but it wouldn't be the way her mother had been hoping for. If Sue ended up home again, it would be out of desperation.

CHAPTER TWO

WILDER COULD SEE the kerosene light glowing cheerily from the Schmidt kitchen as he came in from the barn that evening. Sue had said she wanted to do the job, but now, remembering her conflicted expression when she left to go see her family a few hours earlier, he had to wonder if anything was going to change. Maybe her family wouldn't be so keen on this…or maybe whatever family dynamic had driven her away the first time would do it again. He did hope that he'd get a chance to work with her, though. She was skilled, and pretty, and…whatever. Was it so wrong to like her company?

Wilder pulled off his hat and removed the stray piece of straw that had been tickling him. It had been a long day, and he was looking forward to getting some extra help around the place without his brother here. Normally, he at least had some help in the evening or morning, depending on his brother's work schedule with the sheriff's department.

He'd texted Conrad with the details about their new hire. Wilder wasn't going to try to get anything past his brother, even if it did make his own life easier for the short term. He'd spent too many years being selfish when he was drinking, and this was a fresh start. Conrad had replied almost immediately.

Sue... like, the Sue they all talk about?

That's the one. She's good at the job. The other guy smelled like booze.

Whiskey to be precise. Give Wilder more time with him, and he probably could have guessed the brand and year.

His brother knew just how tough it would be for Wilder to be around someone who drank.

I think you made the right choice. I trust your instinct. But be careful with our neighbors. We need their good opinion.

That was reassuring, the fact that even after years of letting his family down, Conrad would trust his instincts on anything. But Wilder was a changed man, and none knew it quite so well as his brother did.

All the same, fitting in here mattered for more than just Wilder. This was Conrad's ranch, too, and their future here depended upon their neighbors.

Even with his brother's support, had he been stupid to hire on Wollie's sister? She was the most qualified of the lot—he stood by that. But she was probably the most complicated, too.

The Amish didn't have pictures, so he'd never seen what Sue looked like. No one had mentioned how beautiful she was, or that easy way she had about her that put everyone around her at ease, too. No one had mentioned her being a skilled cattlewoman, although Wollie had talked about his sister quite a bit lately. Sue wasn't anything like Wilder had expected.

"Wilder!"

Wollie was heading across the farmyard. He ambled with that easy rolling gate that Wilder had learned to expect from his neighbor, but his face had the look of granite.

"Everything okay?" Wilder asked.

"My sister says she's staying with you," Wollie said curtly.

Okay, right to the point.

"I've hired her," Wilder said. "She starts day after tomorrow. She only told me after I offered her the job that she was your sister."

Wollie pulled off his hat and slapped it against his leg. "What kind of job is this?"

"Ranch work." Wilder shrugged. "There isn't much else I'd hire for. But I have to tell you, she's good at it."

"Good or not, she's a woman," Wollie said irritably.

"I hate to break it to you, man, but women are capable of working a ranch. Our women do it all the time. And when I looked at the applicants, Sue was the best. She's skilled with cattle, she knows the work and I won't have to train her on anything."

"I believe a woman belongs in a home," Wollie said. "We protect our women. Sure, they work hard, but it's more appropriate that it happens from the house where they are safe."

"I don't know what to say. She applied, I hired her. I didn't seek her out. I didn't twist her arm."

"She could come home," Wollie said curtly. "That is an option for her, you know. She's always been welcome to come back."

Wilder sighed. "That's a family issue. If you have a problem with her working here, you've got to take it up with her. Besides, if I don't hire her and she leaves, you're no further ahead in sorting things out with her, are you?"

The argument for her staying popped out before he'd even thought it through all the way. He didn't want to get into the middle of Schmidt family drama, but he felt the need to defend himself.

"At least you know me," Wilder added. "If she gets a job elsewhere, you won't know her boss."

"That's a good point." Wollie scrubbed his hand over his beard. "What did she say to you?"

"Not much," Wilder admitted.

"Did she mention why she left?" Wollie looked up at him uncertainly.

"I asked," Wilder admitted. "She said she knows what she gave up, but she just couldn't live the Amish life."

Wollie sighed. "*Yah*. That doesn't make it easier. I can't fix that, can I?"

"Family can be complicated," Wilder said. "But is living like me really so bad? You've gotten to know me and my brother over the last few years. We're good people. We've stood by you as our neighbor. You've seen who we are. It's not so terrible."

"You wouldn't understand," Wollie said, but his tone was softer now. He intended no offense.

"What do you want me to do? Tell her that you don't want her working with me?" Wilder asked.

"No," Wollie said. "That would just make her mad. She hated it when I used to meddle in her life."

"So what am I supposed to do?" Wilder pressed. "I put out an ad, and she replied. This is all aboveboard."

"I can't demand anything of her," Wollie said. "But I don't mind telling you that I don't like the idea of a woman doing men's work. A woman isn't as strong as a man. She's more vulnerable."

"In this case, she's more skilled, too," Wilder

said. "This just isn't just about strength. It's about knowing cattle, and working smarter."

"Where is she staying?" Wollie asked.

"In the spare bedroom."

"In your house."

"Do you want her in a shed?" Wilder laughed.

Wollie didn't look amused.

"Look," Wilder said, sobering. "She's got a room to herself, and you have my personal promise that I'm going to respect that. Okay? She works for me. I don't toy with those lines, and her privacy is paramount."

Wollie sighed. "Just remember that she's a woman when it comes to work, and when it comes to respecting her."

As if Wilder could forget.

"I won't ask too much of her," Wilder said. "That's a promise. I'm really just grateful to have someone as skilled as she is to help me out."

Wollie nodded. "It'll have to do. But if I find out—"

"Wollie, it's me!" Wilder shot him a smile. "Come on, you're worrying for nothing. I'm nothing if not a gentleman. Okay?"

"Okay." But Wollie didn't seem terribly comforted. "Anyway, before my sister showed up and threw everything into a spin, I was going to tell you that I'm getting married again."

"What?" Wilder shot his friend a look of surprise. "You're serious?"

"Who jokes about marriage?" Wollie asked. "Yes, I'm serious. It's high time I gave Jane a mother. And I…missed being married."

"Well, congratulations," Wilder said. "I'm truly happy for you."

"Thank you."

"Who is she?" Wilder asked.

"Her name is Jerusha Lapp, and she's never been married before," Wollie said. "She's a very good woman—kind, hardworking, a great cook."

"How did you meet her?" Wilder asked.

"Well, I've known her for a long time. We've been friends. We've talked… And I suppose when I started thinking that marriage might be in my future again, we warmed up to each other."

"The timing was just right," Wilder said. "How does Jane feel about it all?"

Jane had loved all the wedding festivities when Conrad got married last year. She was a bouncy, rambunctious girl. But she was also six. She'd have an opinion about her father's remarriage, no doubt.

"She doesn't know yet," Wilder replied. "I'm telling her tonight. Jerusha is coming for dinner tomorrow, and Jane will meet her properly then."

"You nervous?" Wilder asked.

Wollie sucked in a breath then paused. "*Yah*. I am."

Wilder slapped him on the shoulder. "The best things in life are terrifying. I'm truly happy for you. I'm sure Jane will love her, too. If I can help you out in any way, let me know."

Maybe Wollie would need a hand with his cattle while he was focused on matrimony.

"Are you really willing to pitch in?" Wollie asked. "It's okay if you were just being polite."

"No, yeah... I mean..." Wilder floundered. "I wouldn't say it if I didn't mean it. You're my friend, Wollie. Of course, I want to help."

"Thanks. I do appreciate it. I'll take you up on that."

What were neighbors for?

Wollie looked toward his own property,

and shaded his eyes. Jane's small form was by the chicken coop, and Wilder could make out her fiddling with the door.

"Jane!" Wollie shouted. "Leave that rooster alone!"

"But, *Daet*, I want to give him a treat!" Jane hollered back.

Wollie muttered something in Pennsylvania Dutch, but Jane stepped back from the coop.

"I'd better get over there," Wollie said. "That rooster is a mean old bird, and she loves it like a puppy. She'll be the death of me."

"Talk to you later." Wilder watched as his neighbor headed back toward his daughter, and he had to admit, there was a bit more of a spring in the man's step than he'd seen before. Sober, serious Wollie Schmidt was getting married again…

Well, good for him. Wilder could see how his neighbor might need a wife again. Wollie's mother might soften his home up, but a wife was something different all together.

She might actually loosen the man up!

Two days later, Wilder was up, dressed and ready to start his day when Sue's truck rumbled up to the house. He opened the side door and watched as she hopped out of the vehicle and pulled a duffel bag out behind her. He couldn't quite imagine her in Amish clothes. There was something so appealingly cowgirl about her, from her scuffed boots to her worn black T-shirt displaying a tractor logo, to the hoodie she wore unzipped over it. Layers—it was the best way to get through chores on days like this one that would start out chilly and end up thick with heat.

Sue greeted him with a smile as she came up to the side door.

"Come on in," he said.

"I was afraid I'd be late," she said.

"Nah, I'm just having my coffee," he said. "Do you want a mug?"

"No, thanks," she said. "I'm trying to quit coffee."

"Really?" He poured himself a mug, doctored it up with cream and sugar and took a sip. Her gaze followed him with a look of longing on her face. "You sure you want to quit?"

She turned away. "Yep. I'm positive."

He chuckled. "Because you looked like you

might want a mug of your own there for a second."

"It doesn't matter if I want it," she replied. "It's all about self-control."

"What's the benefit?" he asked.

"I don't remember," she said with a low laugh. "Quit tempting me."

"Let me show you to your room," he said, leading the way to the bedroom he'd prepared for her. It was clean, a little sparse, but comfortable enough. The window was propped open with a wedge of wood, and a finger of cool, morning breeze worked its way inside. Her brother's warning about her privacy was still echoing in his mind, and he stayed at the doorway, giving her space.

Sue deposited her duffel bag on the end of the bed.

"This will be great," she said. "Thank you."

"No problem."

They headed back toward the kitchen, and he asked, "So how do you feel about your brother's upcoming wedding?"

"What?"

Wilder looked over at her in surprise. "Wollie's wedding?"

"He's getting married again?" Her eyebrows climbed.

"Oh—" He swilled the last of his coffee and deposited the mug in the sink. "Sorry, I thought that would have been a big topic of conversation over there. I just found out."

"No one mentioned a word of it to me," she said. "Not even my mother..."

"She keeps a good secret, does she?" Wilder asked with a small smile.

"I didn't think she did, but I guess I'm wrong." Sue pulled a hand through her hair, then pulled it back into an impromptu ponytail. "Who is Wollie marrying?"

Wilder shook his head. "I'm sorry. I don't remember her name. It was something different."

"It's okay." But he could see the tumble of emotions in her gaze. "Look, from my limited experience, weddings bring out the best and worst in families. Just hold your breath until it's past."

"That's how your family deals with milestones?" she asked with a faint smile.

"It's how I do it," he said with a shrug. "My brother got married last year. It was really nice, but by the time you get two people in a chapel, the families on both sides have had a chance to get completely worked up. There are hurt feeling over tiny things, people who mean well but trample boundaries… Actually, the calmest person there was Wollie."

"My brother at an *Englisher* wedding?"

"Yep. Your mom and niece, too."

"Wow… They've come a long way."

"Is that so shocking?" he asked.

"For my brother, yes. He must have really respected your brother a lot. That's all I can say."

"The point is, if your brother's getting married, there's going to be all sorts of adjustment," Wilder said. "I know that from experience. It helps if you just refuse to get offended over anything at all."

Sue might not take that advice, he thought ruefully.

"Yeah, well, first things first," she said. "It would be nice to be told about it."

Wilder stepped into his cowboy boots, and they headed outside into the morning chill. September days were still warm, but the mornings were cold, and a brisk breeze made him hunch his shoulders and pick up his pace to get warm. Sue did the same, and they walked close enough to each other that their sleeves brushed. The morning was dusky still, and he noticed her gaze move toward her brother's house across the field. A light winked on in the Schmidt kitchen.

"You miss them, huh?" Wilder said.

Sue snapped her gaze forward.

"It's okay to admit it," he said.

"It's not really home anymore," she said.

"There might come a time when you need them," he said. "My brother and I are really different. He's the by-the-books cop, and I'm the ne'er-do-well cowboy."

"Ne'er-do-well?" She shot him a grin. "Who even says that anymore?"

"People say that!" He chuckled. "In books, anyway. Hey, I might have a terrible attitude, but I do read. The point is, you need family. They're the only ones who understand your unique kind of dysfunction."

Sue smiled. "My brother isn't quite so accommodating as yours."

"We went through a stretch where we didn't talk at all," Wilder said. "When we inherited this place together, we decided it was time to patch things up. My uncle never had kids, so he left the family land to my brother and me. He and our dad didn't speak for decades. We didn't even know my uncle was sick. It's so easy to fall into family patterns, and repeat old mistakes. I didn't want to find out my own brother was dead with a lawyer's phone call, you know?"

"How about finding out he's getting married?" she said.

"Well… Same idea, I guess," he agreed. "There's still time for Wollie to tell you. Maybe he wanted to do it right."

"Telling your sister you're getting married doesn't require atmosphere," she said ruefully. "If he held back telling me, it wasn't about timing. The thing with an Amish family is, you're either Amish, or you're not. And if you're not, well…they either tough-love you back into the fold, or you stop coming around."

"There's no in between?" Wilder asked.

"Not for Amish. My brother might not have any intention of telling me. I wouldn't put it past him."

"Yeah, but they're *human*," Wilder said. "So they disagree with you. Are you shunned?"

"No. I left during my *Rumspringa*. So it's not a shunnable offence."

"That's a good thing," he said. "There have to be families that have figured out some sort of balance."

"Of course, there are," she said. "Just not mine."

Wilder chuckled. "Okay, okay. I understand. It's complicated."

They arrived at the barn, and he pulled open the door to let her go inside first, then entered and flicked on the light. Inside were the cows that were recovering from injury—one had been bitten by a snake and developed an infection in her leg. Another had a gut problem and was on some special feed while it sorted out. And then there was the bottle calf that had been rejected by its mother. "If you could start with a bottle feed for the calf," Wilder said, nodding toward the little animal. "I'll take care of the other cows. Then we can muck out stalls."

"Sure. Where's the calf formula?"

"In that white cupboard over there."

Wilder felt reassured at the way Sue moved with confidence around the barn. He headed over to the cow with the snake bite. He worked quickly to remove the bandage, then he headed over to the cupboard next to the sink, where Sue stood getting a bottle ready.

"Do you know what I found difficult living *English*?" she asked.

"What?" He grabbed the medicated ointment from the shelf.

"Knowing what was realistic to expect out there in the regular world, and what was just a holdover from my Amish upbringing," she said.

"I could see that being a challenge," he said. "What sorts of things weren't you sure about?"

"Marriage, for example," she said. "I was raised to look forward to being a wife. It's still lodged in there. But people don't approach relationships in the same way outside the Amish community. There's a lot of space between dating and married, you know? And with the Amish, if two people have feelings for each other, they're married pretty quickly. I don't know how long it took my brother and his fiancée to decide to get married, but I'm willing to bet it happened fast. And for Amish, there certainly isn't any living together before marriage. I tried living with my ex—he was very persuasive. He said marriage didn't make a difference. It was only a piece of paper. He pointed out that I was past thirty and still single, so maybe I shouldn't be quite so demanding."

"He sounds like an ass," Wilder retorted. Classic manipulation—get her to do something she didn't want to do by making her feel bad about herself.

"Yeah, he is." Sue shook up the bottle, and when she didn't say anything more after a couple of beats, he headed back toward the injured cow. He inspected her leg. The swelling had gone down quite a bit, but he wouldn't be satisfied until the wound had healed over. Infection was too easy to set in out there in the field.

He looked over at Sue again, her back to him, and felt an unexpected wave of tenderness. Maybe Wollie was protective for a reason. Sounded to him like she hadn't met the right kind of man yet.

"I'm not crazy to want that, am I?" She raised her voice so he could hear her across the stalls. "People still get married out there in the *English* world."

He found himself touching his left ring finger with his thumb without even thinking, and when he noticed it, he stopped.

"Of course," he said. "All the time. Heck, I was married once."

"Really?" She shot him a curious look over her shoulder. "What happened?"

This had suddenly swerved into personal territory again, but he'd brought it up, hadn't he?

"I met Misty in high school," he said. "We got married when we were both twenty. By the time we turned thirty, it was over."

"That's it?" she asked.

He shrugged. "It was a bad idea from the start."

"You weren't well matched?" she asked.

"I don't know..." He wrapped a fresh bandage around the cow's leg. "It turned out we were too different, after all. She liked to flirt. We'd go out dancing, and she felt like she was still attractive if she could get other men interested. She thought it was fun to get me jealous."

"Oh... That's mean," she said.

He hadn't behaved in a way he was proud of, either, though. He'd get jealous and yell. She'd yell back, and they'd sleep in separate bedrooms for a few days. It was a mess, and thinking back on it, he was embarrassed. He didn't like who he'd been back then—always hoping for something he never got, feeling empty, feeling lonely. And then acting like a jerk.

"I wasn't the most mature guy, either," he admitted.

Sue held the bottle for the calf, but when he caught her eye, she shot him a sympathetic look.

"I'm not proud of how I acted every minute of my relationship, either," she said.

"I think when you aren't getting your needs met, you find yourself… I don't know…less than you know you can be," Wilder said.

"Yeah. Exactly!" She smiled. "For me, the thing I wanted and couldn't drop was marriage and kids. It's something I've always wanted. Chaney had me convinced it wasn't possible for me anymore—my chance at that was past. I was too old, he said, and most men didn't want to be locked down like that. He said I should just be happy with what he was offering. I really tried, but Chaney… I felt like maybe I didn't love him enough. I don't know. Sorry, I don't mean to ramble about that, but long story short, I still wanted marriage and kids. I couldn't shake it."

"You shouldn't give up on it," Wilder said. "And for the record—any man who'd try to get you to settle for less by insulting you? You don't want him. You can do so much better than that. I don't like this Chaney guy much on principle."

And the very thought of that guy driving her down in order to convince her to stay for less—he'd like ten minutes alone with him. Although he'd probably regret that and end up in trouble.

"He's in the past," Sue replied.

"How far in the past?" he asked.

"I left him a couple of weeks ago."

"Oh…" It was clicking into place now. "Is that why you took a live-in position—you had to move out?"

"I was staying with my friend Becky. But that couldn't be long term, obviously. She's a good friend, but she's got her own life. I'll find something else when this job is over. Don't worry."

"Where's the rest of your stuff?" he asked.

"Chaney kept it." The calf finished with the bottle, and she scratched its head. "But that's okay. It wasn't like we were living in the lap of luxury. And he's moving to Utah for another job."

"You don't want your things?" he asked. This guy just keeping her stuff sounded pretty unfair and heavy-handed. Maybe she needed a friend to march down there and get it back for her.

"The Amish part of me packs pretty light," she said. "I never did have too much to my name—some dishes, some linens, a few changes of clothes, a couch. I mean, he can keep the couch, and the dishes and linens are replaceable."

Wilder nodded. "I guess that's a positive thing."

"It is." She winced. "I'm embarrassed to even be talking about it."

Wilder was silent for a moment. He headed over to the other stall with the cow working through the special feed. Her belly was down to a normal size again, and she looked up at him with her liquid eyes, chewing her cud.

"You know, we're going to be working to-gether pretty closely." Wilder looked over to where Sue stood. "And if you were another guy, we'd talk about all sorts of things before the job was done. We'd cover trucks, politics, family life, ex-wives, the whole gambit. I think it's normal for people who work together to talk. To...open up a bit."

"I'm just another guy?" she asked with a laugh. Her blue eyes glittered with humor, but when she laughed, her face split into a gorgeous smile that made his heart stutter in his chest.

"Your brother made it very clear that you are not," he said, meeting her grin. "And I'd never be dumb enough to refer to a woman as just another guy. But we're working together, and that's a different dynamic. We can either be distant and formal for eight weeks, or get to know each other...get to be friends."

"I think I'd prefer the friendship," she said.

"Me, too. You never know—you might run into me if you visit home more often."

"Maybe so." Her smile lit her face, and his heart skipped a beat.

Dang. He'd have to control his reactions to her...

Stupid as it might be, Wilder was looking forward to this. He was a cowboy who'd get a beautiful, interesting woman at his side while they worked the herd. He wasn't stupid enough to think she was just another cattle-woman, but he'd appreciate both her expertise and her company for the next two months. It could definitely be worse.

CHAPTER THREE

THERE WAS SOMETHING about getting back into a barn again that felt right to Sue. Working with the vet had brought her onto multiple farms and ranches, but it wasn't the same as actually working a herd. She and Wilder mucked out stalls together, and they had a good rhythm. Once the barn was done, they came back to the stable, cleaning out stalls, brushing down the horses and sending them out to pasture. It felt good to get moving, to breathe in the animal-scented air and see labors result in neatly turned out stalls.

"You're a real pleasure to work with," Wilder said. "I mean, you think the way I do when it comes to getting the work done. That's pretty rare."

"Thanks," she said with a small smile. "To me it's just the logic of getting the job done. You have to think it through to the very end before you start."

"Yeah, exactly." He nodded a couple of times. "Don't feel like you have to overdo it, though. I'm already properly impressed."

"Who says I'm pushing myself all that hard?" she asked with a low laugh. She meant it as a challenge, and she waited to see how he'd react. Was this some manly cowboy thing where he was afraid of her breaking her fragile, female self on the work?

Wilder eyed her for a moment, then his face colored slightly. "Your brother was concerned that I might overwork you," he said.

"He's still the same..." She shook her head. "He's always been like that. He figures women belong in the kitchen."

"I think he said the house," he replied with a rueful smile.

"Same difference." She returned his smile, though. "I'm fine."

"Okay," he said, "but just so you know, if you get injured, he'll never forgive me."

"Then I'll have to stay in one piece." She shot him a grin, trying not to roll her eyes. That was Wollie, though. He was the most earnest man on the planet who truly believed he was doing the honorable thing by keeping women safely tucked away. She'd never agreed with him, and they'd fought about it for years. It was oddly comforting to come back to find nothing had changed.

They finished with the last horse stall and headed for the door. Sue was getting hungry now, and she was hoping that Wilder was feeling it, too, because she was up for some eggs and toast. As they came back outside, the sun was rising above the horizon, casting golden rays across the dew laden grass. And across that field between the farms, she spotted her brother walking back toward his house. Wollie saw her at the same time.

Maybe it was time to talk a few things out with Wollie—this didn't have to take long.

"I'll meet you inside," Sue said, and without waiting for a response, she headed across the narrow field in her brother's direction.

Wollie paused, looking uncertain. Sue was sick of this. Was her brother really going to try to hide something as public as his wedding from her? And what made her such a disappointment, anyway? That she wasn't Amish? How tragic. Wait until he found out she was pregnant to boot! Not that she would be announcing that yet.

"Wollie!" she called.

Her brother rubbed a hand over his beard and started in her direction, loping along with the same stride she remembered from their teen years. He was bigger now, older, with the full, thick beard that married or widowed men wore, but he hadn't changed that much. She could still get under his skin, it seemed. They met in the center of the field, and she planted her hands on her hips.

"Morning," he said. "Everything okay over there?"

"Everything's fine," she said. "You?"

"Yah." He glanced over his shoulder toward the house where his breakfast would be waiting. "Is he going to feed you?"

"Of course," she said. "I just want to know if you were going to tell me that you're getting married."

Wollie met her gaze with a look of mild surprise, then he pulled off his straw hat and scrubbed a hand through his hair. "I was going to."

"The day before yesterday would have been a great time," she said. "When I said, 'Hi, Wollie, how are you?' You could have said, 'Just great, Sue! I should tell you, I'm getting married!'"

Wollie rolled his eyes at her sarcasm. "You show up after how many years and expect me to act in a certain way? You show up in blue jeans that are immodestly tight, clothes that look insultingly *English* and you're staying with the neighbor, not even with your family."

"I've got a job, Wollie." She sighed. "You might actually understand that."

"You could still sleep under my roof," he said curtly.

"I don't want to." It was the truth. "I'm not exactly welcome, am I? You saw me, grabbed your daughter and marched off, as if I'm some sort of danger to her. I'm her aunt!"

"We haven't seen you in fifteen years!" he retorted.

"I haven't seen *you* in fifteen years," she said. "I've seen *Mamm*."

Wollie's eyebrows rose and he stared at her. Behind her, Sue heard the horses nicker. There was good reason why their mother had never told Wollie about their chats. Wollie was so inflexible that he would have made *Mamm*'s life miserable over it.

"Really." Wollie shook his head. "Okay, so *Mamm* was keeping her own council."

"Yeah, and that goes for your secrets, too,

apparently. She never told me about your wedding, either."

Wollie sighed. "She wanted me to tell you myself. I was going to, Sue. Today, probably."

That did mollify her a little. With Amish families, there was no telephone to pick up to keep people in the loop. They learned about things in person, or by written correspondence.

"Oh." She swallowed. "So who is it?"

"Jerusha Lapp."

Sue knew Jerusha from her school days. She was a couple of years younger than Sue was, but she'd been a nice enough girl.

"Are you going to be her first husband?" Sue asked.

"*Yah*, she never did marry." Wollie cleared his throat. "She's kind, though. And she can love my daughter. She's a good cook."

"Do you *love* her?"

Wollie nodded. *"Yah."*

"You could have led with that." She sighed. Wollie would always be Wollie. "Well, regardless of how you feel about me, I'm happy for you, Wollie. You deserve a good wife."

"Thank you."

"I'm going to be around for two months,"

she said. "Since you're still keeping it pretty quiet, I'll probably be gone by the wedding."

"It's in three weeks," he said woodenly.

"Three weeks?" It was her turn to stare at him in shock. "Okay, well… I'll definitely still be here, then. Am I going to be invited to the wedding?"

He swallowed. "Of course. Everyone is coming."

So she was lumped in with everyone. "Am I allowed to know my niece at all?"

"I don't think that's a good idea," he replied. "She's at a very impressionable age."

"And I'm…dangerous?" she asked.

"You're *Englisher* now," he said.

"Apparently, she visits the *Englisher* neighbors all the time!" she shot back. "How am I so different?"

"You're family!" Wollie said, his voice rising like a wave. "You're held to a higher standard than the *Englisher* neighbors are! I don't want her turning out like—"

He bit off the last word, but the meaning sank into Sue's heart. Truth be told, she wanted better for little Jane, too. But life could be a whole lot harder and more complicated than anyone anticipated.

Sue wouldn't take the bait. She could see her brother's self-righteous indignation taking root, and he was no different now than when he was a teen—not at heart.

"So what's this about not wanting Wilder to work me too hard?" she asked.

"You know you shouldn't be out there with him."

"Me?" She couldn't help the full smile that spread across her face. "Wollie, I'm good with cattle. I was better than you were, and I'm willing to bet that I can still outride you, and outwrangle you. Even now."

Even pregnant.

Wollie blinked. "We don't bet. It's wrong."

"It's a figure of speech!" She rubbed her hands over her face. "Wollie, you drive me crazy. I'm not actually putting money on this. I'm saying, you hate that I'm better than you."

"You shouldn't be competing with men," he said shortly.

"So you admit that I am." She shot her brother a teasing smile. "Oh, come on. You know what? I don't have to compete with Wilder. He appreciates what I can do, and it's not a competition. Some men like that I'm competent."

"He's not your brother," Wollie said curtly. "You always did like to act like a tomboy."

"The ironic thing is," she said, "with the *Englishers*, I'm not even considered a tomboy. I'm just a woman who's good at her job. And that doesn't *touch* my femininity."

Her brother looked at her with a mildly confused look on his face. He didn't get it. He couldn't. All he knew was the Amish life, the Amish ways. And Amish women took care of the home and let the men be men in the fields. Wollie kicked at a tuft of grass with his boot.

"If you came back, we could find you a nice Amish husband," her brother said.

"Oh, Wollie," she said with a low laugh. "I'd eat him for breakfast. You know it."

Wollie's lips turned up into a smile, and for the first time he laughed. "*Yah*, I know."

"Can we at least try to get along?" she asked. "I won't ruin anything for you. I promise you that."

Her brother nodded. *"Yah."*

"And can you not treat me like your fragile little sister when it comes to Wilder? I need this job, and he cares what you think."

"You *are* my little sister," Wollie said, his

voice softening. "*Englisher* or not, you have a family. You didn't hatch from an egg."

"I know. But I'm not made of glass, either."

Wollie nodded. "Fine. I'll leave Wilder alone."

"Thank you." Because even as an Amish man who was pacifist to his very soul, she knew that her brother could be intimidating.

The farmhouse door opened and a little form appeared on the porch. Jane was waiting for her *daet* to come in for breakfast. And Sue's stomach rumbled. She was hungry, too.

"I'd better get inside," Wollie said.

"*Yah,*" Sue said, reverting to her Pennsylvania Dutch accent. "Me, too."

Sue gave her brother a nod, and they both headed off in opposite directions. She glanced over her shoulder once, but he didn't look back. He was going to his own home, where *Mamm* would have his breakfast ready, and he had a little girl who'd be excited to see him. She envied him the family life. Soon enough she'd have a little one of her own, but it wouldn't be quite the same. Wollie's situation was socially acceptable, and hers wouldn't be. At least not for the Amish.

Sue could smell the frying bacon from outside the house, and her mouth watered as she headed inside.

"Hey," Wilder said, looking up from the stove.

"Hi," she said. "Sorry about that."

"That looked pretty intense," Wilder said.

"Wollie and I are always like that," she said. "But I think I made some headway. I promised not to ruin anything with his wedding, and he promised to stop intimidating you."

"Me?" He caught her gaze, and for a moment, her heart seemed to stop in her chest. "I'm not intimidated."

His dark gaze held hers, and she could tell that she'd pricked his pride there.

"No?" she said.

"Not much." He chuckled, the moment breaking and he turned back to the stove. "So does that mean you're invited to the wedding?"

"Oh, everyone is invited to the wedding," she replied. "The whole community will be there, plus extended family and probably friends from outlying communities. If his wedding is like the other ones from our area, there will be at least five hundred people."

"What?" Wilder pulled some French toast from the pan and put it on a plate, sliding it across the table in her direction. "I thought the Amish liked things plain and simple. I thought it would be a pretty low-stress wedding."

"Plain. Capital P," she said. "It means something different to the Amish. It's about keeping to a certain rule book. About living without modern conveniences, even when it means more work for everyone… It's certainly not easier! There will be five hundred people to feed and entertain without any electricity, internet, or automobiles. There's nothing low stress about that kind of wedding."

"Huh." Wilder turned his attention to dipping bread into egg and laying each slice, sizzling, into the pan. "I offered to pitch in and help out if Wollie needed me. I was thinking he might want me to help him out with chores the morning of the wedding or something, but I'm getting the sense here it might be bigger than that."

"What did he say?" she asked.

"He appreciated it. He said he'd take me up on it," he replied.

Sue met his gaze and laughed. "Oh, Wilder. Did you really?"

He nodded, and when he looked over again, she saw worry in his dark gaze. If he wasn't intimidated before, he certainly looked it now. "What did I get myself into?"

"That's really decent of you," she said, a smile tickling her lips. "I'd say this will definitely help you bond with the local Amish farmers. Weddings are a huge affair. I guess you're about to find out."

WILDER SLID THE French toast out of the pan and onto a waiting plate. He wasn't a guy who liked weddings and formal affairs. He'd been supportive for his brother Conrad's wedding. In fact, he'd been the best man, but he couldn't say that he enjoyed it much. He could be happy for his brother without enjoying all the formality of a wedding, and it looked like he might have just waded into another one. There probably wasn't a polite way out of it, especially if he wanted to maintain a good relationship with his Amish neighbors.

Wilder brought the food over to the table. A bottle of maple syrup was waiting for them, as well as a jar of canned peaches.

"This looks great," Sue said. She looked closer at the lid of the canned peaches where there was a little circular sticker. "Did my mom make these?"

"Yeah, she did. Your family has been really good to us since we moved here."

She nodded. "That's good. I'm glad."

"How did you know?" he asked.

"She color codes her jars with these stickers," she said. "Then she knows which jars are newest, and which need to be eaten up right away."

"Oh…" He opened the jar, then pulled out his key ring where he had a bottle opener, and he used it to pop the seal. "Well, let's eat hearty. This morning, I want to get started on the garage roof. There's a place I need to reshingle."

"Sure."

For the next few minutes, Wilder and Sue were silent, focused on the food in front of them. He was hungry, and he was gratified to see that Sue was, too. They ate French toast with fruit and syrup on top with a side of bacon. Wilder had a big mug of coffee with his, and Sue had a glass of milk.

"I have a hard time imagining you in

Amish clothes, putting laundry on a line or something," he said, reaching for another piece of bacon.

Sue smiled, her eyes glittering with humor. "I never did play by the rules very well."

"It doesn't seem like a bad way to grow up, though," he said. "Life on a ranch, close family connections, lots of good food… I mean, there are worse childhoods."

She took another bite, then nodded thoughtfully. "Hmm. True."

"Your niece seems to have a pretty great life over there," Wilder went on. "She runs and plays, comes to visit us, helps your mother in the kitchen, and goes out with your brother sometimes when he works in the barn… I mean, I grew up in a city. We visited my grandfather before he passed, and then it was all concrete and sidewalks ever after. I can appreciate a nice country upbringing for kids."

"As a parent, you do your best," she replied.

Her response was an odd one, and he met her gaze curiously, but she didn't say anything more. He heard the sound of small shoes on the step, the squeak of the screen door and a little tap.

"That's Jane," Wilder said.

"Yeah?" Sue put down her fork and headed for the door. She opened it, and stepped back as the little girl marched past her into the kitchen. She was wearing a blue cape dress and a pair of purple running shoes, and in her hand she held a small suitcase. Perhaps she'd used it for spending a few days with an aunt or something, because Amish children didn't tend to travel much. Wilder eyed it uncomfortably.

"Hi, Jane," Sue said.

"What are you up to?" Wilder asked.

Jane looked up at Sue, then over at Wilder. "Hello. I've jumped the fence."

"You mean you squeezed through the rails," Wilder chuckled. "I don't think you'd get over it with a suitcase."

And he knew exactly what she meant by jumping the fence, but he was hoping that he could downplay it enough that the girl would relent. The last thing he needed was to be explaining to Wollie what his daughter was doing at his place. He was in a prickly enough position with Wollie as it was.

"*Yah*, I went under the fence to get here..." Jane shrugged, not seeming to grasp his humor. "But I've run away from home. I'm never going back. I'm going to be an *Englisher* like you, Aunt Sue."

Wilder raised his eyebrows, and Sue shot him an alarmed look.

"You can't do that," Sue said.

"You did it," Jane countered.

"*Yah*, but—" Sue sighed. "Your *daet* will miss you, Jane. What will he do without you?"

"My *daet* is getting a new wife," Jane retorted. "He just told me. And I don't like that. So I've run away."

"That's a very serious thing to do," Sue said quietly.

"I know." Jane looked longingly toward the plate of French toast. "And running away has made me hungry."

"Do you want to eat with us?" Wilder asked.

"*Yah*. I really do." She put her suitcase down in the middle of the floor and climbed up onto a chair at the table. Wilder went to fetch her a plate, and when he looked over at Sue and Jane, he could see the family resemblance.

"So you don't want your father to get married?" Wilder asked, placing a plate with a fluffy piece of French toast before her.

"Nope." Jane reached for the syrup and Sue caught it before Jane did, then poured some syrup onto her toast for her.

"Why not?" Sue asked. "Do you know Jerusha?"

"*Yah*, I know her." Jane's knife scraped against the plate. "And I don't like her. Not one bit."

"Is she nice to you?" Sue asked cautiously, and her gaze flickered toward Wilder. He could read the worry there. Did Amish people end up with wicked stepmothers?

"*Yah*, she's very nice," Jane said. "She gives me cookies, and she tells me my hair is pretty, and she smiles at me all the time. And now I know *why*!"

Wilder couldn't help but chuckle. It could be so much worse, but he wasn't going to enlighten the girl about that.

"Bacon?" Wilder murmured, nudging the plate toward Jane.

"Yes, please." Jane took a strip and took a bite out of it before dropping the rest onto her plate.

"But Jane, she sounds like she wants to be your new mother," Sue said.

"I don't want a new mother," Jane retorted, spearing a bite of French toast with her fork.

"She'll help your *daet* to be happy," Sue said.

"Oh, she doesn't need to worry about that," Jane said, stuffing the toast into her mouth. "I do it already."

Wilder caught Sue's eye and they shared a rueful smile. Sue was about to get a taste of Jane Schmidt's strong will, which Wilder and Conrad were very familiar with.

"But you won't be making your father happy if you run away and turn *English*," Wilder said.

"Oh..." Jane frowned, chewing. And for a moment, she seemed to be considering this. "Well, I'll go home again if *Daet* promises not to marry her. Then we can go back to being just me and *Daet* and *Mammi*, the way we're supposed to be."

"And your *daet* will never have a wife again?" Sue asked.

"He doesn't need one," Jane said seriously. "What will he do with a wife? Me and *Mammi* cook and clean and we do the laundry, and we make him lemonade when it's hot out, and we mend his shirts when he gets holes in them."

"But a wife is more than just someone who cooks and cleans," Sue said.

"*Yah*, the holes in the shirts need fixing, too," Jane said irritably. "I said that."

"Okay, a wife is also more than someone who fixes shirts," Sue went on. "A wife is a partner in life. She's a best friend. She'll help your *daet* when he feels sad, or when he's grumpy, even."

"I don't like that," Jane said. "I don't want a new *mamm*. I have a *mamm*, and she's dead, and I don't want another one. I'm not going home if he's going to get married."

"I think you'll miss your *daet*," Sue said softly.

"I think he'll miss me more!" Jane's eyes flashed with determination, and Wilder barked out a laugh.

"She's probably right," Wilder said.

"Don't encourage this!" Sue said, shooting him an annoyed look, and Wilder put his hands up.

"I'm not encouraging it," Wilder said, still

chuckling. "Jane, your *daet* will be very mad at me if I keep you here and don't send you home. If nothing else, you should think about me in all of this. What am I supposed to tell him?"

Wilder stood up to bring his plate to the sink, and he glanced out the side window to see Wollie heading over in their direction, marching through the long grass at a brisk pace. Speak of the devil...

"You can tell him that I won't change my mind," Jane said past another mouthful of food.

"Your father is coming now," Wilder said. "I'm sorry, kiddo, but I'm going to have to rat you out."

Jane's chewing slowed, and her blue eyes turned toward the door. Wilder headed over to pull it open, waving to Wollie.

"She's here!" Wilder called.

"Thank you." Wollie's tone was dry. "Sorry about that."

"She's just having some breakfast," Wilder said. "I think she wanted to visit her aunt."

Wilder didn't mention the suitcase. If he seemed not to take it seriously, maybe no one else would, either. Including Jane. Wollie didn't look mollified with that explanation, and when he came up the steps and into the house, he fixed his daughter with a no-nonsense look.

"Come on, Jane," he said. "Thank Wilder for your breakfast, and we'll go home now."

Jane didn't answer, and she gulped down her last bite.

"Good morning, Sue," Wollie said, giving his sister a nod.

"Morning, Wollie." She leaned back in her chair and eyed him for a moment. "So how did dinner with Jerusha go?"

"Good." Wollie frowned. "It's a good start. She's a good woman. Jane, come on now. Take your plate to the sink, and let's go home."

Jane shook her head. Wollie's eyebrows went up.

"No," she whispered. "I've jumped the fence."

"Rather, she crawled under it," Wilder said with a chuckle, but Wollie didn't laugh.

"You've jumped the fence, have you?" Wollie said tightly.

"*Yah.*" Jane straightened her shoulders. "I'm going to wear blue jeans like Aunt Sue, and I'm going to live here."

Wilder nearly choked. This joke had gone far enough. Wollie's gaze moved down to the suitcase, and he chewed in the inside of his cheek.

"Why are you jumping the fence, Jane?" Wollie asked gently.

"Because I don't want a new mother, and I want Jerusha to go away," Jane said.

"Jerusha likes you very much," Wollie said.

"I don't like her!"

Wollie's jaw clenched, and he bent to pick up her suitcase. "We'll talk about it at home. Let's go."

"No!" Tears rose in the little girl's eyes.

"Sometimes, Jane," Sue said, leaning down next to her niece, "when you've jumped the fence, you still go home to visit. Your *daet* doesn't stop being your *daet*. So I think it would be okay for you to go home with him for now. I have to go to work, kiddo."

Jane sighed and slid off the chair, then picked up her plate and cutlery and stumped toward the sink. She dropped everything into the sink with a clatter.

Wollie said something to his sister in Pennsylvania Dutch, and Sue answered him in kind. Wilder couldn't understand a word they said, but their tones were low and angry, and the siblings glared at each other. Finally Wollie rolled his eyes and turned to Wilder.

"I'm sorry about this, Wilder," Wollie said. "It won't happen again. Jane!"

The little girl followed her father out the door, and Wilder watched as they stomped together back in the direction of the Schmidt farm. Sue came to the door, too, and he felt the soft warmth of her arm next to his as they watched the pair walk across the field.

"What did Wollie say to you?" Wilder asked.

"That I'm a bad influence on his daughter," she said with a sigh. "And maybe I am."

"I don't know," Wilder said with a shrug. "She's got spunk. I think she'll be okay."

Wilder watched as Wollie held his hand out to his daughter, and Jane seemed to be crossing her arms because Wollie let his hand drop. Wilder needed to keep a cordial relationship with his neighbors, and being stuck in the middle of a family drama was not a great way to do that. Wilder was now the boss of Wollie's sister, and his daughter's destination for running away from home. Wollie was a private man, and if Wilder knew him at all, this was going to grate on him.

"Let's get to work," Wilder said.

CHAPTER FOUR

SUE WORKED ALONGSIDE Wilder all that morning. They worked on the garage roof, replacing some shingles in an area that was incredibly worn. Wilder did most of the work, and she climbed up and down the ladder bringing him tools and shingles as he needed them. She also mucked out some stalls and refilled feeders for when they brought the horses in overnight.

When that work was done, they saddled up the horses and moved out to the east pasture where Wilder said he wanted to check on some fences. The fields were lush this time of year, benefiting from the early September rain. The trees were starting to turn yellow, but the pasture was as green as new spring. Being on horseback again felt like a wild release. It had been some time since she'd been riding. Working with the vet hadn't given her much opportunity to get into the saddle.

Sue rode a gentle mare that seemed more inclined to follow directly behind Wilder than she wanted to listen to Sue, but Sue had been riding her whole life, and she knew how to take a horse in hand. She gave the horse a strong squeeze with her knees and urged her forward until they were beside Wilder.

"I check on this part of the herd more often. We keep them in the pasture that's flanked by a road. I think I mentioned before, but we had some cattle rustling in the area." Wilder rubbed a hand over the back of his neck.

"I heard about that. Cutting fences and making off with Amish cows. It was a big news story in Wooster."

"Yep. My cop brother took it personally, and they arrested the thieves, but once criminals figure out something works, I don't trust them not to try it again. Better safe than sorry."

"True…" Better safe than sorry—she could appreciate that in a new way these days. In her own life, Sue was going to be responsible for more than just herself. There would be a child who'd be affected by every single one of her decisions from here on out. Her life had been about taking the risk up until now.

But safety and security were starting to have a new appeal.

Her choices were affecting Jane already. Little Amish girls didn't declare themselves over the fence and defy their fathers—it wasn't done. It wasn't even thought of! Jane had come up with her plan because of Sue, and Sue felt a tug of responsibility there. She'd left the Amish life for her own reasons, but she had no desire to cause trouble in her brother's home.

"Is Jane a dramatic little girl normally?" Sue asked.

"What?" Wilder looked a little confused by the change in topic.

"Sorry," she said with a low laugh. "I'm thinking about my niece. Is she normally the type to be dramatic and overreact?"

"Not really," Wilder replied. "I mean, she likes to come over and see what we're up to, but she's normally pretty obedient, and she's never refused to leave before."

"So she's really upset about her father getting married again," she said thoughtfully. "Maybe she's not getting the support she needs right now."

"She'll get used to her stepmother," Wilder said. "It'll be fine."

"And if she doesn't?"

"She wouldn't be the first kid to have a stepmom, would she?" he asked quietly. "Amish or *English*, stepmoms are a part of a lot of kids' lives. I mean, is Jerusha a mean person, or..."

"No, she's very sweet," Sue said. "Or she was when I knew her. I mean, mostly it seems that Jane is jealous of her father's attention. But if she's not normally a dramatic kid, I guess I worry a bit. Stepmothers from any culture can be hard on kids...can't they?"

"I suppose," he said. "What are you going to do?"

"I don't know," she said. "Obviously, she's trying to be like me, jumping the fence and all."

"I'd take that as a compliment if I were you," he said.

"It's dangerous for her to imitate me, though," Sue said. "I don't actually want her to be like me. My path hasn't been easy. Do you know what it's like to be between two worlds? I'm Amish born, but I can't live the life. *Englishers* don't really understand me—I don't have the same growing up experiences. I don't have fond memories of TV shows or movies from when I was a certain age. I was raised for a different life, and I never fully fit in in either world." She sucked in a breath. She was saying too much.

"And you want to spare her that," he said.

Teens who ran away from the Amish life didn't know what they were in for...and six-year-old girls knew even less.

"I don't want her to idolize me like that. I left, but it's very lonely out there. My family is in a completely other world from me, and they'll never understand me, any more than the *Englishers* do. In their minds I'll always be the one who needs rescuing. I will never hear my mother tell me that she's proud of me. Ever."

Wilder was silent.

"And I don't want that for Jane."

"What if she can't help it, and as she gets older she realizes she can't live Amish, either?" he asked.

"What if she can, and she just glorifies her rebellious aunt?"

Wilder shrugged. "I'm not saying I want to see her leave her way of life, but I don't see anything so wrong with your way of life, either."

"I appreciate that." She smiled faintly. "More than you know. But my way—jumping the fence, starting out on my own in a completely different culture—is really isolating."

"Turns out my way of doing things is, too," he said quietly. "Sometimes you can't help it."

"Do you mean living out here with the Amish?" she asked.

"Sort of... Actually, it's more than that. I spent a fair amount of my youth fooling around, getting into trouble and hot-wiring cars. As a young man, I drank too much, ended up divorced and had to take stock of who I'd become. I'm not proud of it," he replied. "When you straighten up, that's when you lose friends. You have to stop hanging out with the troublemakers and start living your life in a way that makes decent men— and decent women—trust you. And that process is a long one."

She hadn't realized he had such a checkered past, but somehow she could see it in him—the maturity that came with making some hard decisions.

"But it's worth it, I imagine," she said.

He cast her a lopsided smile. "Yeah, it's worth it. A hundred percent."

That smile seemed like it was for her, and she felt her cheeks heat. He had no idea how charming he was, did he?

A horse-drawn wagon wove its way around a curve and headed down the gravel road in their direction. Two Amish men sat in the front of the wagon, and from what Sue could tell from here, there were a couple of children in the back of it, too.

"So this is a fresh start out here," Sue said.

Wilder was thoughtful for a moment. "Yeah it is, and I don't take it for granted. I've wanted to ranch my whole life, and this is my chance to not only fulfill a dream of mine, but to step up and be the man I always knew I could be."

"I'm impressed," she said. "Not many guys can turn things around like that."

"I only get one life," he said seriously. "I'd rather not waste it."

Her met her gaze for a moment, and then nodded toward the approaching wagon. "I need to talk to Enoch about something. You okay with us going down to say hi?"

"Yeah, of course." Sue shaded her eyes and

looked at the familiar, Amish style of wagon. The wheels were steel—no rubber to cushion the rattle over the gravel road.

Enoch Lapp was a local farmer with a full beard that showed his married status. She'd known him years ago, though. He was a few years older than her, and he'd only been courting his wife when Sue left. She couldn't tell who the other man was at this distance. All the same, they'd have opinions about her, there was no doubt.

Sue heeled her horse into motion, but the animal didn't need much encouragement to follow Wilder's stallion. She hung back, letting Wilder take a significant lead. As she rode, she felt the gentle flutter of the baby inside. She smoothed a hand over her stomach. Wilder had come out here for a fresh start, and maybe she was doing the same thing. She wasn't proud of all of her choices, either, and it was time to get her life going in a better direction—at least relationship-wise. She rode slowly, so that by the time she arrived at the fence, Wilder was already in conversation with the two men.

"It would be a patrol, once every two weeks if we all participate," Wilder was saying. "If you see anything, the point isn't to confront the trespassers. That would be dangerous. What we'd do is go to the nearest phone hut and call the police. If they have calls from locals reporting this behavior, they'll raise the police presence, and that will scare off anyone who means to steal our cattle."

Sue recognized the farmer with Enoch now—it was Elias, his brother, and he had the smooth shaven face of a single man. Elias's eyebrows went up when he spotted her, and she saw the recognition on his face immediately. She gave him a small nod. Behind the men in the wagon, three boys were corralling some puppies in a cardboard box.

"*Yah*, it's a good idea." Enoch's gaze moved in her direction, and he frowned slightly. He turned back to Wilder. "Who's interested in participating?"

"So far, you, Wollie Schmidt and Caleb Hubert," Wilder said. "I don't know all the farmers around here yet, and I was hoping for some help in getting others to participate."

"Hmm." Enoch looked toward Sue again, and suddenly she saw the spark of recognition ignite. "Susan Schmidt?"

"Hi, Enoch." She smiled. "Good to see you. Hi, Elias."

Enoch shook his head. "It's been a long time. Ten years? More?"

"A long time," she confirmed.

The boys in the back of the wagon had turned their attention to her now, staring in wide-eyed silence. They'd realized that she wasn't just another *Englisher*, because they were staring at her with a mixture of curiosity and wariness.

"Are you…coming home again?" Elias asked. "Wollie didn't mention anything."

"No, I'm working here," Sue said.

"Working?" Enoch asked. Both men turned to look at Wilder. "What is she doing for work?"

"I'm a ranch hand," Sue said. She didn't need a man to answer for her.

"So you aren't thinking of coming back?" Elias asked. That seemed like the biggest surprise, but maybe she could understand.

"I'm here to work," Sue repeated.

"Do you need help?" Elias asked. "Do you need a place to stay? Because we can talk to Wollie for you. If you need help in reconciling—"

"It's not like that," Sue replied. "Wilder posted an ad for a ranch hand, and I responded. He just happens to be your neighbor. It's not more than that."

Elias nodded, but she saw his jaw tense and Enoch chewed the side of his cheek. This wasn't the answer they were expecting. The boys still stared at her.

"I see you have puppies," she said in Pennsylvania Dutch.

"Yes," one boy said, the first to break their silence.

"What will you name them?" she asked.

"Spot and Peach," the second boy said, gaining confidence. "But we don't know about the rest."

"I like that." She smiled.

"Have you talked to Wollie about this?" Enoch asked Wilder.

The boys fell silent again, eyeing their father.

"Yep. I have." Wilder's words were clipped.

"Not that it would matter," Sue said. Enoch's question irritated her. Yes, she was Wollie's younger sister, but she was a grown woman capable of running her own life. "I'm an adult. Wollie doesn't make my decisions for me."

"I didn't mean it that way. No one thinks Wollie would run your life," Enoch said quietly. "I'm talking about man to man—understanding each other."

She pressed her lips together.

"You really hurt your family when you left," Elias said. "And Wollie's never gotten over it. People think that when they jump the fence that everything moves on, but it doesn't. Our brother left, if you recall. For the ones left behind, it's a whole lot harder. You don't just get over it. It was tough for Wollie."

"I'm sorry about that," Sue said. "I know it was…complicated. But I need this job, regardless of how my brother feels about it. I'm on my own now. You can understand that, can't you?"

She glanced between the two men, then after a beat, they both nodded.

"*Yah*. For sure and certain," Enoch said. He gave her a weak smile.

The boys were back to wide-eyed stares again.

Wilder sucked in a breath. "So about that community security patrol—"

"We'll think on it," Enoch said quietly, and he gave Wilder a nod.

"Will you bring it up to the other farmers?" Wilder asked. "It's not much use if we aren't all in it together."

"We'll talk to them," Elias said, and he exchanged a look with his brother. But they didn't make eye contact with Wilder this time, and even Sue noticed the cooler response.

Enoch flicked the reins, and the wagon started forward again. The boys stared at her from the back as they rumbled past. She smiled and fluttered her fingers in a wave at the boys. A smile flickered across the smallest boy's face, and she felt vindicated. It was one thing to have a disagreement between adults, but children shouldn't be in the middle of that.

And there was something so pure about a smile from a kid.

WILDER WATCHED THE wagon rattle away, and he frowned. The tone of his cordial relationship with these neighbors had just changed. They'd gone from men who chatted easily with him and laughed at his jokes to…this. They'd been intrigued by his idea, especially since the cattle rustling problem from last year. So what changed? He had a feeling he knew what the problem was... He glanced over at Sue, but she wasn't looking at him. Her gaze seemed to be turned inward.

"Let's head west and keep checking the fence in that direction," Wilder said.

"Sure." Sue roused herself. "No problem. I'm sure I can do this job on my own next time around. I just need to know where your land ends."

Wilder led the way, and when her horse fell in next to his, he looked over his shoulder at the wagon disappearing behind them down the gravel road. Sunlight shone brightly from a clear, blue sky, and the weather was about as perfect as it could get, but his stomach knotted all the same.

"Was it just me, or are Enoch and Elias upset that you're working for me?" he asked.

"It's not just you," she said. "This is delicate territory. Even I didn't realize how they'd be about seeing me again."

The horses' hooves plodded along in a soft rhythm, and Wilder pressed his lips together in a thin, frustrated line. Was this going to be a problem? He'd cleared it all with Wollie, so maybe it was just a matter of Wollie letting them know that this arrangement had his blessing. But still, he could feel the chilly distance that had suddenly opened up between them when they realized that Sue was working on his land.

"Was my brother really..." Sue's voice faded away. "I mean, I know he's angry with me. He has been for fifteen years. But was he really grieving my loss so deeply?"

Wilder glanced over at her again, and he could see the worry in her clear gaze. A tendril of hair had come loose from her ponytail, and it hung down next to her cheek.

"I only got here three years ago, but even as recently as that, your whole family was still grieving the loss of you," Wilder said.

"Oh..."

"I know you don't want to hear that," Wilder said. "But even your niece talked about you. You leaving was like a watershed moment for your family. Nothing was the same again—that's the impression I got. They still talked about you going, still rehashed it, and tried to make sense of it."

"Wollie refused to talk to me about it,"

Sue said. "I wrote him letters when I left. He wouldn't answer them. It isn't like I didn't try."

But it wasn't only her family that had missed her.

"Elias looked a little shaken up to see you, too," he said. The Amish man looked like all sorts of emotions were welling up.

"Elias used to have a crush on me." She smiled faintly. "That was a very long time ago."

Wilder could understand how easy it would have been for anyone to fall for Sue. It didn't surprise him one bit.

"How much am I overstepping with the Amish having you work here?" Wilder asked. "Just…honestly. Cards on the table."

"This is new territory," she said. "It isn't like the *Ordnung* covers this exact situation. I left before I was baptized. That means I was free to make my choice, even if they didn't like what I chose. They can't shun me for it. I can take any job I like, and I could even work at an Amish farm, if I wanted to."

So he wasn't breaking any Amish codes here… "That means it's personal, then."

"I guess," she replied.

"That almost makes it worse. If I was

breaking an Amish ordinance, at least I could plead ignorance. If it's personal, this is an issue between neighbors."

Sue was silent for a moment. "Are you going to find someone else?"

"What?" Wilder barked out a laugh. "Do you see a lineup of available ranch hands banging down my door? I don't have any other options." She didn't smile, though, and he felt a tug of sympathy. "But I'm wondering how many of the local farmers are going to have a problem with this," he said.

"Hopefully not too many."

"Can your brother smooth it out with them?"

"Yeah, he could. I mean…the problem doesn't seem to be what he's saying so much as what he's gone through since I left. I think it's more of an emotional solidarity thing than pulling together over ideals, you know?"

"It seems that way to me, too," he said. "Is this something time will fix?"

"I hope so," she replied. "Because this affects me, too. I need the job, especially now."

There was an urgency in her tone that gave him pause. "What do you mean?" he asked.

"I'd be jobless without it," she said with a small smile, but he sensed there was more to it.

"Right." He paused. "I mean, are you in trouble, or…"

"No, no," she said. "But if I can work with you until your brother comes back, it will give me time to sort out my next step. That's all."

"It's eight weeks," Wilder said. "I'm sure the community can handle this for that long."

Wilder rode along with his horse's rolling gate, and when they got to open pasture, he kicked his horse into a trot and they headed up toward the barn. He reined in when he got a clear view past a line of trees toward the west pasture.

"We'll ride out to the far west end of our property to bring the cattle back in a few days," he said. "How are you with riding herd?"

She paused a moment. "I think I'll be fine."

"You sure?" There was something in her hesitation.

"Yeah. I'm sure," she replied.

He nodded. "I do need the help in getting them back home. That's definitely not a one-man job."

"Hey, it's why I'm here, right?" She pulled her hair away from her face, and he noticed a spray of faint freckles across her nose. "I love this work. I'm glad to do it."

And he was glad for the help. But it was hard not to notice just how beautiful she was.

"What's it like living in the middle of an Amish area and not being Amish?" she asked.

He faced forward again and heeled his horse back into a trot. How much did he want to tell her?

"You really want to know?" he asked.

"I really do," she said. "I'm used to going in the other direction, being the Amish born person out there in the big, wide world, so I'm curious. What's it like for you?"

"Confusing sometimes," he admitted. "Everyone speaks a language I don't understand, so there's that temptation to think that you're missing out on something big. In reality, they're probably chatting about morning oatmeal or something. But it takes some getting used to being that much on the outside of things."

"I could see that," she said.

"And I guess I don't really understand the Amish world all that well. Like, why they dress the way they do, or why they all drive the same kind of buggy, or wear similar clothes…"

He looked over at her, and she shrugged. "The *Ordnung*. It always comes back to the *Ordnung*. That's the set of rules to keep the community old-fashioned."

"You explain things better than your brother does," he said with a grin.

"I know why it all seems so confusing," she said. "He wouldn't really get it. This is all he knows."

"It's different out here, but it's wholesome," he said. "And ever since cleaning up my act, I guess I've realized how rare that is. Just people working hard, being honest, taking care of each other… I mean, I like being around people where if you cuss, they all stare at you, aghast. It's…nice."

He was saying too much. It was a whole different world from the one he'd inhabited for a very long time, and maybe he needed them more than they needed him.

"You want wholesome?" Sue asked.

He didn't want wholesome, he needed it. He craved it.

"I can appreciate a clean, honest life," he said. "It's the kind of life I want—I mean, maybe not to the extreme of casting off electricity and all that, but... They have something the rest of us don't."

They turned uphill, following the fence line, and he looked back again, the wagon just disappearing over a hill. The thing was, he'd kind of hoped that he'd find a way to fit in here with the Amish people. There was something about their calm, steady ways that appealed to him. Maybe it was because he'd had some really rocky periods in his life that it felt like solace. For the last few years, he'd been building relationships with his neighbors, and he was making a little place of his own where he belonged on this ranch.

They were both silent for a while, and Wilder looked over at Sue. She had that odd Amish peace about her, too.

"When I got divorced, I kind of spiraled for a bit," he said quietly.

"It would be really hard," she said.

He was talking too much, and he knew it, but this woman made him want to open up. Maybe it was all the solitude he had lately, or just the feeling of being on the outside around here, but talking to Sue was a strange relief.

"It was a tough time," he said. "The marriage itself was just not working for either of us. We got married young, and we weren't good for each other. Maybe you know what that's like…"

"I think I do." Her smile was reassuring.

"When Misty and I split up, I lost my whole foundation." He cast about for the right words. "We'd dated in high school and got married a couple of years after. I'd grown up with Misty, and suddenly I was on my own. I don't think I dealt with that very well. I was definitely drinking too much, and I'd lost control of my ability to stop. But inheriting this ranch gave me something else to focus on—something that could be all consuming and take up the space that used to be used on drinking."

"That's one of the Amish secrets," she said. "They use work like therapy."

"Yeah?" He squinted at her.

She nodded. "If you work with someone, you're bound to sort out a few of your issues, for example. And some physical work gives you a feeling of having accomplished something. When you sit down after a long day, you feel good."

"Yeah." He caught her eye. "I wonder what

my chances are of sorting out a few of these tensions with local farmers."

"Work with them," she said. "Plow a field. Raise a barn."

"They don't ask me for that help," he said.

She nodded. "They wouldn't. The Amish life has some real beauty to it, but it only stays that way by guarding their boundaries. It's a catch-22. They draw people in, and they push them right back out again."

"Like you?" he asked.

She nodded. "I know all the beautiful parts of the Amish life I left behind. But there isn't room for differences. And that can feel like suffocation, even if the pillow is beautifully embroidered, you know?"

Wilder chuckled at her metaphor and looked back over his shoulder again. The wagon had disappeared from sight. The Amish men were pulling back.

Sue turned in her saddle and looked in the same direction. "The farmers in this community matter to you, don't they?"

Wilder cleared his throat and turned forward again. "I'm making a home here. I'm building a future. That's tough to do all on your own."

She was picking at his loose threads now, trying to make sense of his knots. And he hadn't meant to unload all of this. The horses made their way around the gopher holes as they headed up the slope toward the cow barn.

Most people didn't know what he was trying to do—and he didn't explain himself any more than the Amish did. But running this ranch in the heart of Amish Country was his chance to be the kind of man he wanted to be, where his handshake was as good as cash, and they could count on him when it mattered most. Amish Country seemed like the best place to put down his roots and grow.

CHAPTER FIVE

THE NEXT DAY, Sue spent the morning cutting weeds around the barn while Wilder was dealing with paperwork inside the house. He'd been grumpy about it that morning, stomping around the kitchen as he got the various binders, file folders and his laptop set up for the job ahead of him. She didn't blame him. Paperwork was the price someone paid for owning their own ranch. This morning with the warm sun on her shoulders and a breeze to cool her back, she wouldn't change places with him for the world.

She looked back toward the house where there was a fluttering array of towels and rags on the clothesline. She'd seen a new side to Wilder lately—a gentler, less certain side. He was an outsider just as much as she'd been in the *English* world, and she could sympathize with that. The one thing most people took for granted was a sense of community—until it was taken away, at least. A nosy neighbor that made your business hers could be incredibly trying until you didn't know any of your neighbors at all, and no one would notice if you vanished completely. Even a meddling family could become a sweet memory when she sat by herself out there.

Her cell phone buzzed in her back pocket, and her friend's name appeared on the screen.

"Hi, Becky," she said, picking up the call.

"Hey, Sue! It's great to hear your voice. How are liking the job?"

For the next few minutes, they chatted about ranch work, Sue's family and Becky's boyfriend, who seemed close to proposing. Sue did some easier work while she chatted.

"Oh, I should mention," Becky said, "that Chaney came by my store, and he was looking for your new address. He said you aren't taking his calls."

"I'm not," she said. "I'm tired of fighting with him."

"He misses you."

Sue sighed and rubbed her hand over her eyes. "I put up with his garbage for too long. I hope he does miss me. I was the best thing that ever happened to that man, but it's not mutual."

"Oh…"

"Why?" Sue asked.

"I gave him your address," she said.

"Seriously?" Sue grimaced. "Thanks for the heads-up. But I wish you hadn't."

"I'm sorry," Becky said. "He said that he has your things still, and he needed to give them back to you."

"Of course…" Sue sighed. "It's okay. I'll deal with him."

Chaney wasn't a scary guy, just a toxic one, and the more time she spent with Wilder, the more she realized how much garbage she had put up with.

"Becky, I've got to start mowing some weeds here," Sue said, "so I'd better let you go."

"Of course. Call me whenever you want to chat!"

Sue tucked her phone back into her pocket. What would her boss think of her ex showing up unexpectedly? The last thing she needed was her own personal drama dredged up here. She did care what Wilder thought. He was impressed by her…and she didn't want that to change. Fingers crossed Chaney decided to just let it go and headed out to Utah as was his plan.

Sue pulled the cord and the weed trimmer growled to life. She headed around the back of the barn, the machine buzzing over a thick patch of weeds. When she was done, she turned off the machine and laid it in the grass, then grabbed a rake. For the next few minutes, she put her thought into her work as she gathered the cut weeds and put them into a wheelbarrow. She heard the rumble of another engine, and when she headed around the side of the barn, she saw Wilder driving a red tractor with a bale spear sticking out the front.

What was it about this cowboy that his grin from a tractor's seat could make her heart speed up like that? Sue lifted her gloved hand in a wave, and he touched the rim of his Stetson.

She heaped the last the weeds into a pile before Wilder reached her. He turned off the tractor's engine and passed down a thermos.

"Lemonade," he said.

"Thanks." She twisted off the lid and

poured herself a cup. "I thought you were doing paperwork."

"I got it done," he replied. "Most of it, at least. I want to move a couple of bales out to the west pasture before we bring the rest of the cattle in. They have eaten down the grass there pretty well, and the herd still needs some fattening up before winter."

"Okay," she said. Should she mention Chaney? She considered for a beat, then thought better of it. She already had enough drama surrounding her with her Amish family. She didn't want to add to that. "I've finished with the weeds out here. Let me just toss these into the burn pile, and I can help you out."

Sue picked up the handles of the wheelbarrow and brought it over to the pile of brush that was ready to be burned and tipped the weeds into it. It only took a few minutes to return her tools to the barn, and Wilder started up the tractor again.

"Come on up," he said, holding out an arm. Sue caught his hand and he hoisted her up with one powerful pull. She then stepped onto the runner and grabbed hold of the back of his seat. Wilder started the tractor forward, and she leaned into his shoulder to keep from jostling off the rumbling machine.

Wilder was a strong man, and she could feel it in the way his arm moved against her as he steered the tractor down a gravel drive that led past the barn and melted into scrub grass as they approached an open field.

"Hold on," Wilder said as they bumped over a rut, but it was a bigger bump than she'd anticipated. She felt her grip slip, and suddenly Wilder's arm shot around her waist and tugged her back against him. "It's a bit bumpy here…"

His voice was low and deep, and she held her breath. Wilder's strong hold on her didn't relax. He smelled of musk and hay, and she could feel the place on her side where his fingers splayed. They went down into another trench, and his grip on her tightened, and then they crawled back up. Once the tractor had them on even terrain, Wilder's grip on her loosened and he let go. Her knees felt weak in spite of herself.

"Sorry about that," he said. "Didn't want to bounce you right off."

"No problem." She sounded a little breathless, even to herself, and she couldn't blame it on the bumps. This strong cowboy holding her close had sparked something tender inside her.

Was this the pregnancy hormones? He was her boss, and his gesture hadn't been romantically intended! But still, his steely arm holding her safely against him had reminded her of what she'd been looking for out there with the *Englishers*. She'd wanted a life of her own, *a man* of her own...

Wilder used both hands to turn the steering wheel, and the tractor growled slowly in the direction of the big, round bales of hay that were located in a corner of one field.

"Do you ever think of working on your brother's land?" Wilder asked, raising his voice above the rumble of the engine.

"He'd hate that," she laughed. "He's very stuck on a woman's place being in the home, not out on the land."

"Are you telling me his new wife isn't going to help out at all?" he asked.

"Not in the fields," she replied. "She'll cook, clean, take care of all the food storage and clothes-making... She'll be plenty busy inside, trust me."

"You couldn't live like that, huh?" he asked.

"I like the cattle," she said. "And I'm a middling cook, and a terrible seamstress. So no, I couldn't do it back then."

"Then?" Wilder pushed his hat back to look up at her.

"What can I say?" she said, attempting to joke as she considered her current situation. "I've grown, matured."

Wilder didn't answer that, and she didn't really expect him to. They reached the bales, and Wilder stopped the tractor, turned it around and backed it up until the back bale spear pierced into a round bale of hay. Sue hopped down first.

"Are you saying you wouldn't want me as your neighbor?" she said with a teasing grin.

Wilder didn't smile, but his dark gaze met hers and locked her there. Then he angled his head to one side. "I'd like having you close by, that's for sure."

Her breath caught.

"Are you considering sticking closer to home?" he asked.

"Yeah," she admitted. "I've done it on my own for fifteen years. I think I've proven my point."

"Was that all it was?" he asked. "When you left, I mean."

It had been so much more—a search for her true self, a yearning for freedom that she'd never get if she stayed Amish, and an ability to use her natural talents. It was a long-shot hope that she could find a little nook or cranny where she might fit just right. It hadn't worked out that way.

"No," she said. "It was more than that, but when you grow up, sometimes you have to face facts."

"Like?" He squinted at her, and she shrugged.

"Like life is hard. And there isn't always a perfect little niche for you where your talents are appreciated and you can make a comfortable living," she said.

"I appreciate your talents."

"You're not a long-term position, though, are you?" She'd meant it as a joke, but it came out more seriously than she'd intended. "Sorry, I didn't mean to sound—"

"No, it's fine," he interrupted her. "I don't know why I'm arguing this. I'd love to have you next door. Your brother might even let me hire you in short bursts for cattle drives."

The thought of that gave her heart a little

thrill, and then the baby fluttered inside her, bringing her back to reality.

"I'd be a convenient neighbor," she said.

"I guess I'm wondering if that would make you happy."

Were the last fifteen years of living her life the way she wanted to a waste? Would she come home, admitting defeat?

"I could try to be happy this way," she said. For her baby, she could try. This was a better life for her child than anything else she'd be able to put together right now.

Wilder nodded slowly. "Tell you what. If you think of anything I can do to make that happiness a little more sincere, let me know."

Wilder's gaze was steady, and he didn't drop her gaze.

"That's kind," she said, trying to bat it aside.

"I'm serious," he said. "If you end up being my neighbor, and there's anything I can do, you let me know."

"Anything like what?" she asked, a smile touching her lips. "Are you offering a ride into town or something?"

Because for the Amish who relied upon horses and buggies, a ride into the city to go to Walmart or a big grocery store could be incredibly handy. And she'd miss the speed and convenience of her pickup truck. Actually, she'd miss her pickup truck, period. She was attached to that old rattletrap.

"I'd be happy to be your ride into town," Wilder replied. "Or your place to vent, a friend to share a meal with who won't judge you. I could be your secret electricity."

A smile tugged at his lips. That was a sweeter offer than he might realize, because she'd be facing a whole lot of judgment at home with her family if she stayed.

Sue let her smile go. "Do you mean it?"

"Yep," he said quietly. "You'll find out that I don't say stuff I don't mean. I don't have time for that kind of thing. And I like you, Sue."

His voice was soft, deep, gravelly, and she felt goose bumps rise up on her arms.

"I like you, too," she said.

He shot her a boyish, lopsided smile. "Good."

Then he flicked a lever and the back bale spear lifted the bale off the ground. She watched the progression until it was elevated about six inches.

"Stop," she called.

Wilder flicked a lever and the bale stopped moving. The tractor crept forward again, and turned in a circle to come at the next bale from the front.

The thing with transporting round bales was that they were heavy, and it took two of them to properly balance out a tractor. It was a bigger load, and it took more skill to drive with two bales, but the heavier load was necessary so that you didn't lose balance.

And that was the kind of partnership she'd been dreaming of since girlhood—a man who'd work by her side, who wouldn't insist upon gender roles she'd never excel in, and a man who'd be that counterweight she needed when life was hard. She'd been hoping that taking on the challenge and doing things the "hard way," she'd get that perfect balance.

But that kind of partnership was hard to come by, and it would be harder still with a baby in the mix. She'd left the Amish life in search of something she'd never found...

Was that failure?

WILDER STABBED THE next round bale with the front spear and slowly lifted it. His eye was on the hay, but he could see Sue in his peripheral vision, her hands poked into her back pockets, her blue gaze locked on that bale, too.

"Okay," she said, and he stopped the lift. She came over to the tractor, and he reached down, caught her hand and she climbed back up next to him.

What kind of man did it make him that he liked having her this close? A red-blooded one, probably. She was warm next to him, and her ponytail brushed against his shoulder. The tractor rumbled beneath him as he turned the steering wheel and they headed farther west toward the pasture.

"So, what was your brother like as a kid?" Wilder asked, loud enough to be heard over the engine.

"Serious!" she replied with a laugh. "Very serious, but also reliable."

"Were you close?" he asked.

"Sort of… I was the youngest," she replied. "My sisters were all older and married, and my brother was closest in age, but we drove each other nuts."

"You were too different," he guessed.

"Exactly."

"Yeah, my brother and I were the same," he replied. "He became a cop. He was always very organized, very by the book, you know? We only really started connecting when we inherited this place. Before that…"

"You were the wild one," Sue said ruefully.

"I was back then. I'm working to build a better reputation now…"

"My family thinks you and Conrad are very decent people," she said.

He felt a little swell of pride at that. "That means a lot coming from your family. They're well-respected around here."

"Yeah…" There was something in her tone, though, that made him look over at her again. Her brow was knit, and her jaw was tight.

"Everything okay?" he asked, and he eased off the gas as he reached the gate for the pasture.

"Yeah, fine." She hopped down and headed to open the gate. As she pulled it open, the cows up on the hill started in their direction.

Wilder drove the tractor through, and Sue disappeared behind it to close the gate again. The next few minutes were spent dropping the bales into the big, steel feeders that kept the hay off the grass so it would stay dry. He and Sue cut the plastic mesh that surrounded the bales and hauled the wrap out of the feeders.

The second circular feeder was different from the first one. It split apart on hinges, and as he tried to work the pin free to open it, Sue reached over his shoulder with a little can of WD-40 and gave it a spray.

"Thanks," he said, but he shot her a curious look.

"I never head into a field without it," Sue said.

He gave her an approving look. "That's smart."

"You didn't have any ranching experience when you inherited this place, did you?" she asked.

He shook his head. "I had a couple of friends who did, but not me. I lived in Wooster. Everything I've learned is from friends, local farmers and a whole lot of research online."

"Wow." She cocked her head to one side. "You're doing really well for a relative newbie."

"Newbie, huh?" He barked out a laugh.

They headed back to the tractor as the cattle came to investigate the new food. He hopped up first, and she climbed up behind him without the hand up this time.

He started the engine, and they headed back toward the gate once more. The moos behind them melted into the sound of the engine.

"You know, I'm not too proud to accept some advice from someone who knows what she's doing," Wilder said.

Sue smiled, her face suddenly brightening. "I'd be happy to."

And that was the happiness that had been missing when she'd talked about going back to live Amish with her family again—that brilliance that came to her face at the thought of working a ranch herself.

Back through the gate again, he saw a figure by his house in a straw, Amish hat.

"Is that your brother?" Wilder asked.

"Yeah," she said. "I wonder if he wants to talk to you, or to me?"

Wilder parked the tractor next to the fence, and he and Sue headed over to where Wollie stood waiting for them.

"Hi, Wollie," Sue said.

Her brother gave her a nod. "How are you?"

"Pretty good. Working hard."

Wollie turned to Wilder. "Could I have a word with you privately?"

"Uh—yeah," Wilder replied. He glanced over at Sue, who rolled her eyes.

"I'm going to head inside and get something to drink. I'll be sure to take my time."

Wilder eyed his neighbor curiously as Sue went into the house.

"I think you offended her," Wilder said.

"I'll smooth it out later." Wollie made a motion with his head indicating they should move farther from the house, and they walked a few yards away. "I'll get right to the point, Wilder. My *mamm* and I are worried about Sue."

"You should talk to her, then," Wilder said. "You had the opportunity just now, and you sent her away."

"The thing is, she wouldn't tell us if she needed help," Wilder said. "We have a lot of history, my sister and me. And we're both stubborn. I have my ways, and she has hers. I don't think she'd want to show weakness in front of me. She wants to prove that leaving was the right choice, at all costs. And I don't think she'd tell me if she needed help."

"What makes you so sure something is wrong?" Wilder asked.

"Call it a gut feeling," the other man replied. "I know my sister. She could have found other work. She came here because she needs us. Have you noticed anything?"

"She seems a bit preoccupied," Wilder said. "Maybe a bit worried, but she hasn't said why."

"Well...maybe you could just pass along the message for me—tell her that we'll help if we can. We're her family."

"Yeah, no problem," Wilder said.

"Thank you," Wollie said earnestly. "I appreciate that more than you know." He paused, dug his toe into the grass.

"Is there something else?" Wilder asked.

"You mentioned being willing to help out with the wedding," Wollie said. "And my nephews are pretty busy on their own farms right now, so I hate to drag them away... But there is something we Amish men do when we get ready for a wedding, and I was wondering if you might want to help me with it."

"What is it?" Wilder asked.

"We build an *eck*," Wollie said. "It's a...a corner, translated most literally. We build a decoration that goes behind the bride and groom's table at our wedding reception, and it's the groom's responsibility to build it. My nephews will come by and help me, but I'll have to do a fair amount of sanding and it would help to have another set of hands to get it done in time. My mother will cook for us—we'll keep it as painless as possible."

"Yeah, sure," Wilder said. "I'd be happy to help out."

Wollie smiled. "Thank you. I'd best get back to work."

Elias and Enoch might have cooled toward Wilder, but Wollie hadn't. He'd take some solace in that, because that meant that it was only a matter of time before things balanced out around here again.

And maybe helping out with a great big, Amish wedding was the way to get there.

CHAPTER SIX

SUE TOOK A BIG, jaw-cracking bite of a salami sandwich and heaved a sigh. She was so much hungrier than usual lately. She could eat and eat and never quite fill up these days, and she was willing to bet it had to do with being pregnant.

Wilder had gone out to work with the injured cow in the barn, and in the meantime, Sue was grabbing something to eat before she started picking the apples from the tree out in the yard. A few had started to drop to the ground already.

Besides, being with Wilder these days was sparking something inside her that she needed to keep firmly under control. He was handsome, sweet, protective… And she didn't have the luxury of exploring those feelings for him. She needed to figure out how she'd support herself and her child, not further complicate her life with romance.

She was going to be someone's mother... That thought was still weird. Would she be called Mama, Mommy, or would she be called *Mamm*, like she'd called her own Amish mother? What did it say about her that she didn't know?

She heard the screen door open, and she turned to see Jane come inside. Her eyes were wide, and she had that little suitcase in her hand again.

"Jane? What's going on?" Sue asked, putting down her sandwich.

"I jumped the fence again," Jane said. She marched inside and put her suitcase in the middle of the kitchen floor like she had last time.

"Again?" Sue smiled ruefully.

"Yah."

"Are you hungry?" Sue asked.

"Yah."

"I'll make you some lunch," Sue said.

She went to the counter and made a sandwich for her niece, deposited it on the table, then sat back down with her own food. She took another big bite and watched as her niece settled into a kitchen chair.

"So what's the problem?" Sue asked, swallowing.

"*Daet* says he's still going to marry Jerusha." Tears welled in Jane's eyes. "Even if I hate her."

"Is she really so terrible?" Sue asked softly.

"*Yah!*"

"What does she do?" Sue asked.

"*Daet* says she's going to be the *mamm* in the house," Jane said. "And *Mammi* is going to move out and go live with Uncle Samuel. And I'll have to do what Jerusha says. She'll give me chores, and she'll tuck me in at night, and she'll not be half so good as *Mammi*!"

"*Mammi* is moving out?" Sue asked with a frown. Her mother hadn't told her that.

"*Daet* says she's going before the wedding!"

"Oh…" Sue nodded. "I can see why you're upset, then."

"*Yah!* What will I do without her?" Jane asked tearfully.

"*Mammi* isn't going that far," Sue said softly. "Uncle Samuel only lives a short buggy ride away. She'll come visit you all the time, and you can go to see her."

"It's not enough," Jane said, her lip quivering. "Jerusha isn't nice at all if she won't let *Mammi* stay! Who kicks out a grandmother?"

"Oh, sweetie," Sue said. "It's not that Jerusha isn't nice. It's that when a man and a woman get married, they need some privacy to adjust to things. It's not easy learning how to be married and how to be a *mamm* all at once."

"Then she'll need *Mammi* more!" Jane said. "When people get married, they're supposed to live with family at first. I know that!"

"It's different when it's a second marriage, sweetie," Sue said. "Your *daet* was married before to your *mamm*. So it's not quite the same. I know it's hard for you, but I do think Jerusha will try very hard to be nice to you. She'll want you to love her."

And yet something new had occurred to Sue. Wollie needed his space with Jerusha to establish their home. If her mother was moving out to make room for this new wife, Sue couldn't expect to be welcomed in her time of need, either.

"Can I stay with you?" Jane asked.

"Here?" Sue chuckled. "I don't really live here, Jane. I'm just working here for a few weeks. It's not really my home."

"But I could stay with you, all the same," Jane said. "And then you could take me with you."

"I think your father would miss you very much," Sue said. "And so would *Mammi*."

"*Daet* will have a new family," Jane said, and her eyes welled up again.

"Oh, Jane." Sue circled the table and squatted next to her. "There is no replacing you. I know that for a fact. Your *daet* loves you with his whole heart, and a whole houseful of babies would never take your place."

"I want to wear blue jeans like you do," Jane said.

"Your *daet* won't let you," Sue said.

"And I want to ride horses like you do, too," Jane went on, undeterred. "And I want to wrestle down a calf, and I want to fix a roof, like you fixed a roof. I saw you doing it."

"Jane, a nice Amish girl works in the kitchen," Sue said.

"*You* don't!" Jane looked up at her pleadingly.

There was a tap on the door, and Sue looked up to see her mother poke her head inside.

"Jane?" Linda called.

"I'm here, *Mammi*," Jane said.

Linda came inside. She looked sad.

"Hi, *Mamm*," Sue said.

"I've had one girl run away," Linda said softly. "And I don't think I could survive two of you doing it."

Sue felt tears mist her eyes. "I know, *Mamm*."

"Do you really want to run away from your family, Jane?" Linda asked softly.

"I'm going to be like Aunt Sue," Jane said. "And I'll wear blue jeans and wrestle cows. It'll be great."

Linda's gaze slid up to meet Sue's, and she could see the reproach in her mother's eyes.

"Jane," Sue said, "I'm going to need help picking some apples today. Why don't you go find a bucket, and get some of those apples you can reach from the tree out there. I'll come help you in a minute."

Jane wiped her face, and for a moment Sue thought the girl might argue, but then she did as she was asked and headed out the side door, the screen bouncing shut behind her with a clatter.

"This isn't my fault," Sue said.

"I know…" Linda sighed. "She watches you from our property. And if you saw the look on her face when she spots you doing some chore or other... She's besotted with you."

"I'm a mystery," Sue said.

"What would you do if you had a child, and that child longed to run away to some far part of the world where you'd never see him again?" Linda asked softly. "Because that's what it's like for your brother. If Jane grows up to jump the fence, she might as well be in Timbuktu."

"I can sympathize with that, *Mamm*," Sue said. One day soon, Sue *would* have a child of her own. "I really can. I don't want to lure Jane away from the Amish world. None of this has been easy for me, and if Jane can stay happy living her life Amish, I think she should."

"What are you going to do, then?" Linda asked.

"I'm just a mystery," she repeated. "All Jane sees is an aunt from a distance who gets to do jobs that seem very exciting to a child. But she doesn't know me. She can imagine that I'm some perfect ideal. I think she should spend some time with me. I could tell her that living *English* isn't the easy way out. I could encourage her to get to know Jerusha."

Linda nodded. "That might be good."

"She's upset that you're moving out, you know," Sue added.

Linda pressed her lips together. "I know. But that can't be helped. I can't be in the middle of things. A mother-in-law has to step carefully."

"But she's feeling abandoned. Her father is getting married again, and you're leaving."

"What can I do?" Linda asked. "I've talked to her about it several times. So has Wollie. She's just… She doesn't like Jerusha."

"What if she saw *me* liking Jerusha?" Sue asked.

Linda's eyebrows went up. "That's not a bad idea."

"She wants to be like me," Sue said. "What if she saw me enthusiastic about Wollie's wedding and saying nice things about Jerusha? It might make a difference."

"It very well might," Linda agreed.

Sue looked out the window to where her niece had turned the bucket upside down to stand on so she could reach the lowest apples. The girl was smart—a definite problem solver. And that would come in very handy if she grew up wanting to work a ranch like Sue did. She couldn't help but feel proud of her.

"She's a lot like me, isn't she?" Sue asked.

"*Yah*, she is," Linda replied. "And that's what we're afraid of."

Linda bent and picked up Jane's little suitcase, and then she frowned for a moment, and put it back down.

"I'm going to leave this here," Linda said. "Sometimes it helps for a child to have something symbolic to do when she comes home, like carry her suitcase herself."

Linda went to the door and headed outside. Sue picked up the last of her sandwich and popped it into her mouth.

"Jane." Linda's voice was muffled through the glass. "I hope you'll be home for supper. I'll miss you very much if you aren't."

And Linda headed out across the grass.

How was a family supposed to keep their young people safe at home? With love, of course. You couldn't nail a child down. You couldn't order them to stay. But you could love them so well that it would break their hearts to leave. That was the Amish way.

And yet Sue had left, and watching her

mother tramp across that grass, her shoulders just a little bit stooped, Sue's eyes misted with tears.

Love hadn't been enough to keep Sue home, and that fact clung to her. If love hadn't been enough for her...what would make *her* love enough for anyone else?

As WILDER FORKED fresh hay into the cow's stall, he felt irritable, and he kept looking toward the barn door. There was something about Sue that tugged at him, and Wilder couldn't quite identify it. She was a legend around here—the Sue who outrode the boys and refused to obey when told to work in the house. There were stories about her burned pies because she'd sneak out to see the horses instead of watching her baking. She'd steal her brother's pants to wear, and lose her Amish *kapp* as she wrestled calves. Losing her *kapps* had been a big deal in these stories—something symbolic, he'd assumed. Apparently, she'd even caused another horse to rear up and a young man fell and broke his arm. The stories about Sue were plentiful and colorful...until she disappeared as a teenager, never to be seen again.

But even as a neighbor, Wilder had heard the stories about Runaway Sue. In his mind's eye, she'd been like Annie Oakley—spunky, brave and better than the boys around her. And now here she was on his land, working his cattle, eating in his kitchen. And that legendary Sue softened considerably as he got to know her.

There was one story that Wilder remembered quite clearly. Wollie had told him a very different kind of story about his sister...

I was in the barn doing chores when a big snowstorm blew in. It got cold fast, and I was scared. My daet was out tending to other chores, and I had to get back to the house by myself. I waited a bit to see if the snow would let up, but it didn't. So I decided to head back to the house. I pulled open the barn door, and there was my twelve-year-old sister, covered in snow and holding a flashlight. She'd come to get me, because she was worried. I was supposed to be taking care of her, not the other way around.

Of all the stories about Sue—the riding, the wrangling, the pants-wearing—that was the story that had stuck with Wilder, this fierce, fearless girl who wouldn't leave her brother out there by himself. That was the spirit he saw in Sue now—the intelligent, dedicated woman who carried WD-40 with her and knew ranching better than he did. And under all the competence was a heart that she protected, and that he longed to get to know.

Because a few years after that storm, Sue had left. Just walked away, and from what Wilder could tell, Wollie had never gotten over it. It was the kind of personal betrayal that clung to the man and left Wollie rather grumpy when it came to the subject of his sister.

Wilder finished up with the cattle, washed his hands, hung up the pitchfork and headed out of the barn.

He could understand unresolved sibling relationships. You couldn't choose your family, and you also couldn't choose the bedrock emotional issues you'd have because of them. So you might as well make peace with them.

Besides, Wilder was hoping that Sue would stick around—that by making peace with her brother, he'd see her more often, too.

Wilder heard Jane's laughter before he saw them, but as he headed toward the house, he spotted Sue and her niece by the apple tree.

Jane had a bucket, and they were picking apples. Sue's hair was loose around her shoulders, shining in the sunlight. She was on a stepladder, and she handed apples down to Jane, who stood there with her hands above her head, waiting for the next apple.

"I'm gonna make apple pie," Jane was saying, her words growing clearer as Wilder got closer, "and apple cobbler, and *Mammi* can show me how to make apple strudel. I think I could do it."

"Strudel is hard," Sue said, and she looked over her shoulder as if she'd sensed his approach, spotting Wilder. She shot him a smile and then turned back to the job. "And it would take you going back home again, wouldn't it?"

"No, you'll teach me," Jane amended.

"I never could make a good strudel," Sue said. "I'm not much of a baker, kiddo. But *Mammi* could show you."

"Then I'll make bad strudels, too," Jane retorted.

Sue came down the ladder, and Wilder hooked a thumb in his belt loop as he came through the gate.

"So you make bad strudel, do you?" Wilder joked as he walked up.

Sue laughed, and her eyes glittered with humor. "It's terrible. I mean, I can cook, but my strudel is lacking."

"So is mine," Jane said with an exaggerated sigh. "Some girls don't make good strudel."

"There's still hope for you, Jane," Sue said, and she turned to Wilder. "How are the cows?"

"The one with the belly issue seems to be eating well now," he said, and he looked over at the six-year-old with a bucket almost as big as she was in front of her. "I see Jane came to help."

"I actually came to stay," Jane said. "I'm going to live with my aunt, I think."

Wilder cast Sue a look of mild alarm, and she just shook her head.

"Can you carry these apples over to that bin over there?" Sue said, and Jane started off with the heavy bucket.

"She wants to live with you?" Wilder asked.

"She thinks so," Sue murmured. "Give me time. I think I can get her home without someone having to drag her there."

Linda's plump form appeared around the

Schmidt house and she went into the garden, picked something and turned back toward the house again.

"I wonder what *Mammi*'s picking out there," Sue said, loud enough for Jane to hear.

Jane put down the bucket a few yards short of the step, and she looked over her shoulder toward her house. The girl picked up the bucket again and struggled with it toward the step.

"Carrots," Jane replied.

Sue turned away and headed back to the apple tree. She moved the stepladder and climbed up to continue picking apples. Wilder followed her and fetched a bucket to collect what she picked. Jane's attention stayed fixed on her house.

"I wonder…" Sue said, and she lowered two large, red apples into the bucket. She leaned down far enough that her hair brushed his arm and he could smell the faint scent of hay that still clung to her clothes.

"What do you wonder?" Jane asked, turning back.

Sue straightened and reached up into the tree again, pulling another large, ripe apple free with a rustle of leaves.

"I wonder what *Mammi* is cooking," Sue said.

"I don't know." But Jane's gaze moved back toward the house again. "Maybe meat pie. She puts carrots in meat pies."

"I wonder if her feelings are hurt because you don't want to go home," Sue said.

"But it's not because of *Mammi*!" Jane said, tears glistening in her eyes. "It's because my *daet* is getting married, and that's why!"

"I wonder if *Mammi* misses you as much as you miss her," Sue said, and she reached back up into the leafy canopy again, turning her back.

Jane's eyes welled with tears, and her lower lip began to tremble. For a moment, she just stood there as if suspended between her choices, and then the first big tear slid down Jane's cheek.

"Mammi!" Jane wailed, and she started off at a run toward her home. "*Mammi!* I'm coming to help!"

Wilder couldn't help but smile. A good guilt trip went a long way with kids that age.

"Nicely done," he said, but when he looked up at Sue, he saw her holding those two, ripe apples in front of her, and tears shining in her eyes. "You okay, Sue?"

"I knew it would work," she said, her voice thick. "I cried for weeks when I left. And I was seventeen."

Sue put the apples into the bucket, and turned back to picking again.

"You gave up everything for your dreams," he said.

Sue looked down at him from the ladder, and for a couple of beats her gaze met his. He wished he could fix this for her, be her answer to whatever it was that was chipping away at her, but what could he offer? He was just a cowboy.

"I gave up more than you know," she said.

And now Sue was back, right next door to the family that had raised her, formed her and withheld her deepest desires to ride horses and work with the cattle.

Was Wollie right? Was Sue back for more than a job?

Wollie thought Sue was in trouble, but maybe it was simpler than that. Maybe she was just trying to find a way to go home.

CHAPTER SEVEN

SUE STOOD ON the stepladder, her gaze trained through the branches on the scene at her brother's house. Linda knelt at the edge of the garden and gathered Jane into her arms. She couldn't hear anything, just watched as Linda bent low, wiped Jane's face with the corner of her apron, and then gave her an extra squeeze. Jane seemed to be talking a mile a minute about something, and Linda looked up and met Sue's gaze.

The little runaway had come home...leaving her suitcase in the kitchen. Linda turned and led Jane toward the house.

Sue realized she was holding her breath and slowly exhaled. If only life were that simple again, but little girls grew into women, and solutions for adults weren't so easy. She came down the ladder.

"So, that's that," Wilder said.

"Yeah. It would seem."

"Sue—" His voice was low, insistent, and when she met Wilder's gaze, he didn't say anything else. He just stood there looking at her.

"It's okay, Wilder," she said. "Jane went home. Worries are over."

"Are they?" he asked. "You seem… I don't know… You seem like something is wrong."

"Life is complicated, Wilder," she said with a faint smile. "And I can't just go home like that. I'm not a child anymore."

He nodded. "Is that what you're trying to figure out—how to go back?"

"No." And for a split second she wished she could tell him. But she wouldn't. Instead, she said, "I talked to my friend Becky today, and she said that Chaney came by her workplace to ask where I was living now. She gave him the address here."

"Oh." Wilder nodded. "Oh! Okay. So he's going to come by?"

"I don't know." She shrugged. "Our relationship is over. I really have no desire to see him, but apparently, he wants to bring me my stuff. I didn't want her to give out this address. I'm really sorry if this is going to be uncomfortable."

"You deserve to get your things back," he replied.

She'd been perfectly willing to sacrifice them. Her peace of mind was worth more than some sheet sets and a few dishes from Target.

"So that's what's been worrying you," he said.

Part of it. A very small part of it. She shrugged.

"Do you want to talk to him?" he asked.

"Not particularly, but I will. I mean, it's the right thing to do. If he wants to give me my things and say a formal goodbye, I'm okay with that."

"Do you want me to stick close in case he gets weird?" Wilder asked.

He was close now. She was tempted to step into his arms, rest her head against the strong shoulder, but instead she swallowed and looked instinctively toward the drive.

"If you could, I'd appreciate it," she said. "Again, I'm sorry. I know this is wildly unprofessional."

"Meh," he said, and when she looked back, there was a smile tickling at his lips. "I think we sailed past professional a long time ago."

She couldn't help but laugh softly at that. "Again, sorry."

"Don't be. I'll stick close. You won't have to deal with him alone, if you don't want to."

His tone was so final that she felt a flood of relief in spite of it all. At least with this one worry, Wilder's solid, manly presence would make a difference. Chaney would have to back off with Wilder here.

"Thanks." She smiled up at him.

"I was going to ask you for an Amish explanation," Wilder said. "Your brother asked me if I'd help with something called an... *eck*?"

Sue blinked at him in surprise. That was the kind of thing a man asked his brother to do, or a best friend. In Wollie's case, it would be his nephews, or a good friend from the Amish community. Not the *Englisher* neighbor. "That's an honor."

"It only occurred to me now that it might be better if you did it," Wilder said. "I'm a neighbor. You're his sister."

"I'm a woman," Sue said. "There are blue jobs and pink jobs, and helping with the *eck* is very solidly in the blue category."

"Is there really no flexibility?" he asked. "I

knew a guy whose best man was his sister—she was the one closest to him. So she wore a tailored tux and stood in for him. It was really meaningful."

"They weren't Amish," she said with a small smile. "But it does sound like a lovely wedding."

"What if you showed up with some sandpaper and a hammer?" Wilder asked. "Would he turn you away?"

"Yes," she said simply.

"He's that stubborn?"

"He absolutely is." She laughed. "And so are the Amish traditions."

"You do realize that you need each other, right?" Wilder asked. "I mean, I know this isn't my business, but Wollie misses you something fierce. You miss him, and with him getting married soon, he's going to need his sister's support."

"It's complicated," she said. "Besides, he knows where to find me. But the elephant in the room is the fact that I'm no longer Amish. That isn't going to go away."

"I don't think that's the case," he said.

Sue shot him an incredulous look. Now he

was an expert on her relationship with her brother? "You don't."

He put his hands up, seeming to read her dry tone of voice. "Look, I know that was a bit cocky of me, but your brother came over and talked a bit. Guy to guy. He really does miss you, and I think the issue is that you left, period. He felt abandoned. I don't think it's about religion or culture so much as his sister left him behind."

Sue was silent. She could still remember the hollow feeling inside her as she'd headed down the moonlit gravel road that night. Her family had been asleep, and she'd been wondering if she'd regret this decision, or if she'd feel better about it in the light of day...

"I can't undo it now," she said.

"I know. It's just... He thinks you might be in trouble, and that's why you came back. Because you need help."

Sue took a few steps toward the house, her heart hammering hard. Was she that transparent? Or was it so unbelievable that she'd sort out a decent life for herself out there? She stopped short, then turned to face Wilder.

"And you?" she asked. "You think I'm in trouble?"

"I don't know," he said. "I know you're worried."

For one ridiculous, reckless moment, she wished she could just say it—but she pushed it back.

"My brother seems to be really opening up to you, Wilder," she said dryly. "You're the right one to help him with the *eck*."

Besides, her brother was right, and she hated that he'd spotted it so easily. She was pregnant, and she no longer knew the right path to take as a single mother needing non-judgmental support. But she did know that she wasn't going to get it from her brother.

Sue picked up the bucket of apples and headed toward the side door. Wilder beat her there and opened it for her so that she could head inside and deposit the bucket on the kitchen table. Jane's little pink suitcase was still sitting in the middle of the kitchen floor, and Sue set it on a kitchen chair with an irritated thunk.

"Jane packed again?" Wilder said.

"Afraid so." Sue opened the suitcase and peeked inside. There was a faceless cloth doll, a pair of socks, an apron and a coloring book with a few crayons rattling around in the bottom.

Sue opened the book and flipped through a couple of pages of coloring—purple bears, pink horses, a bright yellow barn. Jane was already pushing the limits, making her own rules.

"Should we bring that back to her?" Wilder asked.

Sue shook her head. "No, my mother wants her to bring her suitcase back herself. If we bring it, it isn't quite as powerful of a choice than if she comes to get it herself."

"She's six, though," Wilder said. "She's just a kid."

"And she was old enough to march over here and declare herself over the fence," Sue replied. "So she needs to learn how to make that right, how to walk it back."

"That's not easy for adults, either," Wilder said.

"You talking about me?" she asked raising an eyebrow. Sue picked up an apple, shined it on her shirt and took a bite. It was tangy and sweet, and she chewed thoughtfully.

"Why *did* you take this job?" Wilder asked quietly. "There must have been other people hiring somewhere. You're too talented to be limited to one option."

Sue pressed her lips together. "Maybe a small part of me missed home."

"Maybe Jane needs to see that," he said.

Sue met his gaze but he didn't back down.

"I hate when you have insight into my family that I don't have," she said. "But maybe you're right. Maybe she needs to see that I'm not a hundred percent okay without my family in my life. But I wasn't okay staying here, either. So... I don't want to lie to her."

"Can kids appreciate nuances like that?" he asked, and this time he looked less certain.

"I doubt it," she replied. "That's the problem. And I want to help Jane settle down, accept her new stepmother and find her place right here in her home community. Wollie thinks I'm some terrible influence—and in his defense, his daughter has been imitating me...but I don't want to turn her into a little replica of me. I want to spare her the pain I went through. And I want to spare Wollie that pain as a father, too."

"You're a good sister," Wilder said quietly.

"Yeah, I really am," she said, still irritated,

but she smiled to show no hard feelings. "I'm the best. Tell my brother that, would you?"

Wilder grinned and turned toward the fridge.

"Let's get some food on. I'm thinking of something quick—chicken alfredo, maybe?"

"That sounds good," she said.

But her stomach gave an unexpected little heave, and her head felt light. Sue loved alfredo, so why was her stomach reacting like this? She'd been hungry all day—feeling like she could eat and eat and never quite fill up.

It was the pregnancy, no doubt. She'd seen her older sisters pregnant when she was a young teen, and they'd been constantly hungry, too. Now she could appreciate what they'd been going through. She wished now that she could remember those bits of motherly advice Linda had given her pregnant daughters, but Sue hadn't been paying attention to those things back then.

There was some sort of Pennsylvania Dutch saying... Eat like a baby does? Something like that. Did it mean eating every two hours, or eating small quantities, or eating whenever she felt hungry?

"...and then there are the cattle to bring back from the far pasture," Wilder was saying.

"What?" she asked feebly, and she realized she felt a little weak all of a sudden.

"The herd out in the far pasture," Wilder said. "It's a full day's ride to get them if we ride pretty steadily. We stay the night at the pasture—there's a campsite we always use up there—a firepit, right by a stream for fresh water, and all that. There's some good shelter from the wind..." His voice seemed to fade as her stomach lurched again.

"Sounds good," she murmured, hoping she sounded invested in this conversation. Was this morning sickness? She knew that pregnancy stomach upset didn't only happen in the morning. One of her sisters was nauseated for the entire nine months of her first pregnancy.

Oh, don't let that happen to me...

"Yeah, but it's a nice ride. Really picturesque out there. You said before you liked riding herd, so the timing is great. Wollie and I do each other some favors when we're getting our cattle. He'll look in on the cows that are healing up in the barn for me."

"He's a good neighbor, too," she said, forcing a smile.

He turned to look at her. "So you're good to come with me? There's some rough sleeping for one night, but like I said, it's a great little campsite."

"Of course, I'm glad to do it," she said. "I love bringing the cattle in. I missed that when I was working with the large animal vet—riding herd, wrangling calves…you know, the fun stuff."

Wilder chuckled and turned back to the counter.

"It is the fun part, I agree," he said. "You know, there was this time my brother and I were out getting the cattle the first year we had this place, and…"

She tuned out of his story as she sucked in a shaky breath. She wasn't normally like this, but being pregnant, she'd have to expect a few changes. Her mouth felt dry, and she realized then she hadn't had anything to drink since that lemonade earlier in the day.

I'm dehydrated, she thought. *That's my problem.*

Wilder was still talking as he minced garlic with a large knife, but his voice was like a mumble in the background. A glass of water would fix this. Sue stood up, but as she rose, her head spun, her stomach seemed to be floating in the most uncomfortable way, and then everything went black.

WILDER HEARD THE THUMP and he looked over his shoulder, still telling his story about that first independent cattle drive with little to no experience, when they'd been forced to ford a stream that had billowed into a river...

For a moment, Wilder didn't register what he saw—a swirl of dark hair across the linoleum, her jean-clad legs sprawled over the floor and one arm flung out. It took his brain a beat to catch up, his heart thudding to a stop.

"Sue?"

Wilder planted the knife on the cutting board with a clunk and dropped to the ground next to her.

"Sue?" He smoothed her hair away from her face, and a tendril that had fallen over her lips moved with her breath, which was a wild relief. He felt her cheeks and her forehead—no fever. But she was incredibly pale.

Her eyes fluttered open, then. "Okay—don't move. Just lay there."

Something was wrong. She was hurt. Or sick? Women didn't just pass out like that for nothing. He should call for help—get an ambulance or something... He looked toward his cell phone, but it was across the room.

"What happened?" Sue murmured.

"You passed out."

She started to sit up, and he helped her scoot around so she could lean against the cupboard.

"I'm thirsty," she said.

That was something he could do, and Wilder felt some sense of control coming back to him. He stood up, went to the sink, got her a glass of water and grabbed his cell phone from the counter on his way past. Her hands shook as she took the glass, but as she drank, her grip seemed to firm and the color came back into her cheeks.

"Are you sick?" he asked. "What happened? I just need to know if I'm driving you to the hospital, or calling an ambulance."

"Neither." Sue handed the glass back to him. "I'm not sick. I'm fine."

"You're not fine." He barked out an incredulous laugh. "Fine people do not keel over in the middle of a conversation. Has this happened before? Do you get seizures, or—"

"I'm pregnant."

Her words didn't land for a moment. Wilder stood there with her empty drinking glass in his hand. He understood what she'd said, but he didn't feel anything at all, and then it hit like a bag of sand.

"You're *pregnant*?" he said.

"Yes." She ran her hands through her hair, pulling it away from her face.

"You're my ranch hand!" he blurted out. "You can't be pregnant!"

He heard how stupid it sounded the minute it came out of his mouth, but this was the very last thing he expected.

"I can be and I am." She held her hand out. "Help me up, would you?"

Wilder did as she told him, and boosted her to her feet, a protective hand behind her back, and he couldn't help but look down at the front of her shirt. She didn't look pregnant. Granted, her shirt was loose, but she looked pretty slim to him—no telltale bump.

"I'm fourteen weeks along," she said, then frowned. "Close to fifteen weeks now,

I guess. And I'm not showing yet. Apparently, that can happen pretty quickly once it starts, but it hasn't yet."

"Wollie thought you were in trouble," he said, his mind spinning to catch up. "And you are…aren't you?"

Wilder was still holding her elbow, and she looked up at him with a mildly amused smile. "I'm fine. You can let go of me now."

Wilder dropped his hands, suddenly feeling like he might have overstepped, touching her that way. "For the record, you were flat out on my kitchen floor. You were not fine."

"But I am now," she said, and she looked up, meeting his gaze. For a moment, it was like time stopped, and they just looked at each other. She was beautiful, but also vulnerable, and he felt a surge of protective instinct he couldn't tamp down again.

She'd passed out on his floor, and right now, every atom in his body wanted to pull her against him to feel the beat of her heart and the warmth of her breath—prove to that elemental part of his brain that she was truly fine.

"Do you need anything?" he asked. "Something sweet, maybe, or…orange juice?"

That was for diabetics, not necessarily for pregnant women, but it couldn't hurt, could it?

"I'd take some juice. I didn't drink enough water today," she said. "That's all. I saw my doctor before I took this job, and she said I'm fine to work as long as I stay hydrated. I guess that was why she said it."

"Okay, that's something we can fix." He headed for the fridge and got her a glass of orange juice. She sat at the table again, and he handed it to her. She took a sip and nodded.

"Much better," she said. "Thanks, Wilder."

"We should probably talk about this," he said.

"Is that legal?" She arched an eyebrow at him.

"Are you going to sue me for caring?" he demanded. "I'm not firing you, okay? I need to know how much you can safely do. I had no idea you were pregnant. If I'd known—"

"You'd never have given me the job," she interrupted.

He was silent. She was right. He'd have found an excuse and hired someone far less qualified. He would have been scared of her getting hurt, or...passing out on his floor?

"See?" Sue said. "I need the job, and I'm capable of working. This is how human beings come into the world. Women work while pregnant. In fact, women work all the way up until delivery."

"Not on cattle drives," he countered.

"You can't even tell I'm pregnant yet," she said. "And I covered all of this with my doctor. As long I don't do anything crazy, it's all perfectly safe."

If she had her doctor's approval, who was he to argue?

"You'll tell me if something is too much, though?" he said.

"Of course." Her tone betrayed her dwindling patience.

It would have to do. She had every legal right to work, and pregnancy was no reason to hold her back. If she could do the work safely, then that was what mattered, but he'd be watching closely to make sure he didn't miss any early signs that she was doing too much, that was for sure. He didn't want to have to peel her off the floor again...or worse, have to carry her out of a field and try to describe to a 911 operator exactly where they were.

He felt a shiver run down his back.

"Your brother wasn't wrong, then," Wilder said. "Did you come back because of the baby?"

"Yeah..." She shrugged slightly. "Well, yes and no. I came back because I think I'll need their help, but I don't know how much I want to accept. It's a nice little knot."

"Wollie does want to help, though," Wilder said. "He told me to let you know that if you need anything, you do have your family. He cares. You're his little sister."

"He's not anticipating *this*," she said.

"Neither were you, I'm guessing," he said. "This is life, Sue. It never goes as planned."

"Asking for my family's help is one thing," Sue said. "But it comes with strings. They won't be happy unless I'm back a hundred percent—Amish again. I'm still deciding what to do, and I haven't figured it out yet. Nothing here is simple."

"Okay..." He nodded. Obviously, he didn't know all the ins and outs of the culture, of her family dynamic.

"And Chaney..." He wasn't sure if he had a right to ask this, but he wanted to know where things stood with that guy.

"He's the father," she said. "Biologically speaking. And he knows about the pregnancy. That's complicated, too. But Wilder, I don't want my family to know yet. I'll tell them in my own time, *if* I tell them at all."

"You'd hide that?" he asked, squinting at her.

"I might!"

"This is a bigger deal than a wedding," he said.

She shot him an annoyed look, and he put his hands up. This was her business, and it was starting to look a whole lot more tangled and emotionally fraught than he'd even imagined.

"I won't say a word," he said. "I'm not about to get in the middle of your personal business with your family, but Sue, you've got people who love you. They are capable of adjusting."

"The Amish don't adjust," she said.

"But mothers and brothers might," he said. "And if you were next door, I could help you out, too. You could park your truck here, if you wanted. And you could come watch my TV, and enjoy some electricity whenever you wanted to." He smiled at her hopefully. "My cousins have had kids, and I've been told I'm just about a baby whisperer when it comes to settling down crying babies."

"You don't have to worry about me," she said woodenly.

"Who's worrying?" Wilder retorted, even though he was a little bit. "I'm just thinking that you're better company than my newly married brother who takes three times as long for any job that he takes his wife along for."

"Really?" Her defensiveness seemed to be slipping away now.

"Yeah, really. They've been married about a year now, but they still act like newlyweds. Totally wrapped up in each other. They're very much in love, and I can't wait for their new house to be built so I don't have it rubbed in my face every single day. You'd be doing me a favor by sharing my electricity for a few hours."

Sue chuckled then, the tension of a moment ago bleeding away. "That *would* be awkward."

"I just want to share the awkwardness." He cast her a teasing smile. "There is more than one way to do things, Sue. I'm just saying."

Sue stayed silent, and Wilder looked toward the food on the cutting board. "Let's forget cooking and just go into town for pizza or something."

"That would be nice." She licked her lips. "Wilder, I'm sorry if I've made things complicated for you with my brother, or the rest of the community. I know you've got to make things work here, and I'm not exactly an easy addition to that."

As complicated as she made things, she also made his days a little brighter, too, and she was very quickly filling up a place in his heart that had been empty for a long time. This was getting dangerous...

"Tell your family when you're ready," Wilder said. "But when you do, let them know that you threatened me with some unholy torture or something, okay? I need to get along with them."

"Deal." She smiled.

Wilder was getting attached. He knew it was a terrible idea, but he couldn't seem to help it, either. What was he supposed to do? He'd do his best to keep this as professional as he could. He'd deal with the rest when she was gone, go sort out his complicated feelings on horseback or something.

He grabbed his keys. "Let's go eat."

CHAPTER EIGHT

THE NEXT MORNING, Wilder made his pot of coffee, and he had a kettle steaming, too. It was a chilly morning with a touch of frost on the grass outside, and a dark, cloudy sky. The forecast didn't call for rain, but there would be a fair amount of wind, and the temperature was starting to drop.

The hot mug of coffee felt good in his hands, and when Sue came into the kitchen, pulling her hair back into her usual ponytail, he pulled a box of herbal teas from the cupboard, gave them a shake, and then put them on the counter.

"Thanks," she said, then selected a tea bag and grabbed a mug. When she'd doctored her tea to her liking with milk and sugar, she leaned against the counter next to him and they both sipped in silence for a couple of minutes.

"So what's the plan today?" Sue asked.

"We'll do the barn and stable before breakfast," he replied. "Then there's a fence post I noticed yesterday where someone went off the road and rammed into. I think we can fix it without having to replace the whole post."

"I can do the barn and stable myself," she replied. "You get started on the fence post. It makes more sense."

And that was exactly how he'd do it if it weren't for Sue passing out on the floor yesterday. But not now.

"It's okay," he said. "We can do it together."

She cast him an odd look but didn't argue.

"We'll get the work done a whole lot faster if two of us are working on it," he added defensively.

"Sure." She drank the last of her tea and put the mug into the sink. "Let's get going."

Wilder grabbed two water bottles and held one out to her. She smiled, took it and headed for the door.

Knowing she was pregnant definitely made things different for Wilder. He hadn't changed his mind about keeping her on, or about what she contributed around here. He truly appreciated her professionalism. But the fact that she was pregnant softened something inside him. She'd fainted yesterday, and that had shaken him more than he wanted to let on. She was strong, professional and a great asset, but she was also vulnerable.

Wollie had told him not to forget that she was a woman, and if nothing else, her pregnancy reminded him very clearly. She wasn't just another ranch hand, or another guy working the herd with him. While Wilder might not side with Wollie on his very strict ideas about gender roles, he did see the Amish man's point now that he knew Sue was pregnant.

He drained his cup of coffee, grabbed his hat and followed Sue out to the mudroom.

As they were outside, Wilder felt the north wind and was glad for his coat. He and Sue walked side by side toward the cattle barn. The wind blew stronger, and Sue hunched her shoulders against it. Some wisps of hair were ruffling free of her ponytail and blowing in front of her eyes. He caught her arm and moved around to the other side of her to shield her from the worst of the wind.

"Oh!" Sue said in surprise, and she looked up at him, now somewhat protected from the buffeting gale.

"Better?" he said.

"Yeah. Thanks."

Her coat sleeve brushed against his as they walked. Sue got to the barn door first. She pulled it open ,and he caught the door behind her. His thumb moved over her chilled hand—an accidental touch—and for a moment, they both froze, then pulled their hands away at the same time. Sue looked up at him, her clear blue gaze meeting his with some hesitation, then she stepped into the barn, and he followed her.

He hadn't meant to do that, and his thumb still tingled where it had moved over her soft, cool fingers. There was something about her that tugged at him, moved his hand toward hers as if magnetically drawn. It made his breath lock in his throat when she looked up at him like that. And standing here in the barn with her close enough that he could smell her soft scent, it was like his senses went as far as her and stopped there.

"I'll go get the calf's bottle," she said. "Actually, he looks ready for a bucket of milk to me. What do you think?"

Wilder gave himself a mental shake, and

he looked over to where the hopeful calf was waiting for them, his chin on top of the rail.

"Yeah, you could give it a try," he said. "No harm there."

She was probably right—the calf was maturing quickly, and the more independently it could eat, the less work for them. Sue headed for the calf formula, and Wilder turned toward the cow with the snakebite.

He sank onto his haunches and removed the bandage. The cow let him work without any fuss, and as he inspected the wound that was healing nicely, she chewed her cud. When he had the leg rebandaged, he looked over to the calf, who was drinking from a bucket. The calf lifted his head, milk dripping from his muzzle. But Sue wasn't there.

He looked around the barn and spotted her disappearing into the loft.

"Sue?" he called.

"Just getting hay!" she called back down.

"I can do that!"

"So can I!"

He sighed and headed in the direction of the loft. He stopped at the ladder and had to jump back as a bale came down, bouncing in a puff of dust off the concrete floor.

"Sue, I said I could do it."

Her face appeared in the opening, and she shot him an irritated look that mirrored his own. "I did this yesterday morning."

"You passed out yesterday afternoon," he retorted.

"I was dehydrated!"

"Sue, just let me do it," he said. "I hired you to help out, not do everything yourself."

"You hired me to do a job, Wilder."

"I think I'm the one who says what your job is!" As soon as it came out of his mouth, he knew it sounded petulant.

"Yeah?" She raised her eyebrows. "I've been polite up until now, but I know more about running a ranch than you do. And you know it, too. So let me work."

Her face disappeared from the opening, and he let out a frustrated huff.

"You're pregnant!" he called up.

"I know!" Her voice filtered down to him from above. "Heads-up."

Another bale came down, bouncing off the first. Wilder snagged it by the twine and moved it aside. Sue's boots appeared on the ladder.

"Could you just take it easy a little bit?" he said.

"Why?" She climbed down the rungs, reached the bottom and turned to face him.

"Why?" He shook his head incredulously. "I'm really glad you're here—probably happier about it than is even remotely appropriate. And I do need your help. I trust your instincts. But you *can't* work as hard as I do."

"Can't? I told you I'd tell you if something was too much," she said. "I get that me being pregnant is a shock, and I'm sorry about the fainting, but I'm just as pregnant right now as I was yesterday when I did this same job. And the day before. The only difference is that you know it now."

"The difference is that you passed out!" he retorted.

"Again…" She shot him an impish smile that reminded him of Jane. "Sorry about that."

"You are one frustrating woman, Sue," he said.

"I've been told," she replied. "But I'll keep you posted on what I can handle, and I'll drink water."

As if to prove the point, she picked up one

of the water bottles, unscrewed the cap and took a swig.

"What if you misjudge what you can handle?" he asked.

"If I'm not doing the job, then what am I doing here?" she demanded.

"You *are* doing the job. You have nothing to prove to me, though. I know you're good, okay? You're better than two subpar men put together, which is who I'd have to hire to replace you. But this is still my ranch. I still call the shots. And if I tell you to lay off, then you need to lay off."

Sue put the bottle down and met his gaze. "This is my pregnancy."

He blinked at her. "What?"

"This baby inside of me is mine," she said, pulling off her work gloves. "This body that is housing this child—also mine. I'm not your woman to protect. I can take care of that myself."

He felt the verbal slap. He was overstepping. Who was he but the guy who'd hired her for a few weeks? He had no right to ask anything of her, regardless of how he'd started to feel for her. She wasn't his to protect.

"Okay," Wilder said. "You're right."

"Thank you."

It wasn't professional…but then neither was her ex coming to drop off her stuff, or her family asking him to look out for her, or any of this! The most important things in life weren't professional.

"But is it so terrible to have me want to take care of you?" he asked. "I'm sure it's some testosterone-driven instinct inside of me, but I want to make sure you're safe, fed and happy while you're under my roof. And I want to make sure you aren't overdoing it. So it's not the way it's supposed to be. I get it."

"Under your roof." Her tone was dry.

"Poor choice of words. I'm sorry." He stepped closer. "But here's the way I see it. You're here to help me out, and if I'm stressed out thinking you're going to overdo it, then it's not as much help as you think. Because whether or not I *should* care, I do. All right? Forget the roof. So I'm not going to treat you like one of the guys. You're not one of the guys. You're very different!"

"I'm female," she said.

"You're a woman." He caught her gaze and held it. "That's different. And more than that…you're Sue. You're my neighbor's little sister. You're the heroine of a hundred stories told while leaning against a fence. You're not just some worker. I'm sorry. I can't help it. And I'm not going to turn my back and let you hurt yourself on my watch, either. I'm not apologizing for that."

Sue lifted her chin, but something in her snapping gaze had softened.

"Wilder, I have to be able to do this on my own," she said, and her voice trembled. "If I'm the heroine of a hundred stories already, I'll be at the center of a hundred more soon. I don't have the luxury of leaning on anyone."

"Sure you do. With me around, at least."

"For what, a few more weeks?" she asked, shaking her head. "I'm a single woman. I think I know the workload ahead of me. I don't have this baby's father in the picture. I certainly don't have an Amish man to take care of everything for me. I'm on my own. I'm not going to pretend otherwise and get soft."

"You might not have an Amish man," Wilder said earnestly. "But for the next few weeks, you've got me, and I think you'll find that I'm not so bad. But Amish or *English*, we've all got the same testosterone running through our veins, and when we have a pregnant woman on the job, we take that seriously. You're not going to talk me out of it."

"You need to let me work, though," she said. "I've got to earn my wage, and I need the money."

"All I'm asking is that we work side by side," Wilder replied. "And that you let me do the heavy lifting. I'm counting on your intelligence in the work around here anyway. Like you said, you're more experienced than me. So relax. Let me be the brawn. You be the brain. I think we'll do just fine."

She was silent for a moment, and she put her hand on the rail next to him. All he could think about was how easy it would be to put his hand over hers…that was it. Just touching her hand. But it was all-consuming. He tore his gaze away.

"Okay." Sue nodded to the bales of hay next to them. "I wasn't really planning on carrying those around the barn, anyway."

Good. This was what he needed, too—something to pour his strength into so he'd stop thinking about holding Sue's hand, or bringing her fingers up to his lips… He pushed the thought back.

"I'll take care of that. You get the pitch-fork." Wilder hoisted a bale and headed over toward the cattle stalls. Taking care of the heavy lifting around here was as much for him as it was for her. She'd stay safe, and he'd have that outlet.

Because having a beautiful, interesting, complicated woman in his house and on his land was turning out to be harder to balance in his own emotions than he'd expected.

And not just any woman... Sue.

He wouldn't explain it to her, but she *was* different. Because no woman in his life so far had tugged him in like this in such a short amount of time.

Sue was more than special. She was trouble.

SUE FORKED HAY into one of the stalls, shaking it loose with her pitchfork to spread it over the concrete floor. It smelled light, fresh and clean. She'd always loved the smell of hay, and she liked the process of cleaning out a stall, turning a mess into something healthy again for the animals in her care.

The fact that her pregnancy was slowing her down sparked a little panic, and even this familiar, satisfying work wasn't calming her like it normally did. She'd relied on her abilities—which matched or surpassed the men she worked with—ever since she started her *English* life. She'd felt strong, capable, and it reassured her that she didn't need a whole community behind her to take of herself. That was important, because when she'd left, she'd lost more than her family, she'd lost an entire support network that would have held her up, told her she was a good person and helped her organize her life. She'd walked away from absolutely everything, and all she'd had left were her own abilities and nerve. Now? Now, she was pregnant, and her body was making new demands on her, and being skilled and strong wasn't going to be enough. She'd need help…and that fact scared her.

And Wilder wasn't playing along with letting her pretend nothing had changed.

The baby moved, and she paused, memorizing the feeling inside her. Yes, everything was changing, and it was both wonderful and terrifying. And she knew that Wilder was right. She couldn't keep going like she used to, and maybe that was scariest of all.

Sue and Wilder finished with the barn and

stable, and after a breakfast of sausage and eggs, they headed out to the field to check on the cattle. Wilder didn't bring up how hard she was working again, but as she cantered around the field, scanning the cattle, she found his dark gaze on her from time to time. Just…taking note, perhaps. Then he gave her a nod, flicked his hat and rode off to the other end of the pasture, doing the same inspection that she was doing with the other half of the herd.

She watched him go—tall, strong, lanky in that country boy kind of way that she'd always had a softness for.

"Cut it out," she murmured to herself. She was fresh out of a serious relationship with the wrong man, and the last thing she needed was to be parking her emotions with this cowboy.

When they headed back toward the barn, Wilder fell in beside her. The hills rolled off into the distance, the late morning sun warming the grass and clover gone to seed. It smelled fragrant, and hinted at cooler weather around the corner.

Wilder rode close enough to her that she

could have reached out and slapped his knee if she wanted to, and she cast him a smile.

"You've shown great restraint in not asking me how I was feeling or anything like that," she said.

"Thanks for noticing." He grinned. "I was rather impressed with myself, too." He was silent for a moment. "Do you know what you're going to do—with a baby coming, I mean. Do you know how you'll balance it?"

"I'm going to need my family's help," she said. "But I'm going to wait until after my brother's wedding before I tell anyone. I don't want to take any attention away from his big day."

"That's decent of you," he said.

"I'm also dreading telling them, so there's that," she said.

"What about the father?" he asked. "You mentioned him before, but you didn't really explain."

Right. Chaney. He was an embarrassment, too.

"He asked me to get an abortion when I told him I was pregnant," she said. "And he's got a job out in Utah he's going to. He doesn't want to be inconvenienced. I'm happy to just let him go."

"He owes you child support," Wilder said seriously.

"I don't care to chase him down once he's gone," she replied with a shrug. A lump rose in her throat. She had believed Chaney was a better man than that. She'd figured he was misunderstood, not given a proper chance. How naive had she been? "I'll figure it out. Lots of single mothers before me have."

"And he doesn't want to know his child?" Wilder asked. "He wants to see you again. Maybe he's changed his mind."

"When I left, he was pretty clear about not wanting to be a father," she replied. "I wouldn't ever stop him from knowing this child, but I'm not foolish enough to try to rely on him, either. I need my own solutions."

Wilder nodded. "If it were me, I'd want to know my child, but more than that, I'd also want to take care of my kid's mother. Just saying."

His voice was low, earnest, and he didn't look at her. Just rode on, his jaw tensed. Was this upsetting him?

"Yeah, but you're a good man," she said.

He glanced at her then, his dark gaze catching hers and holding it. "If you need anything, I can help you out."

Her heart skipped a beat.

"You said that before," she said, hoping to shake him loose from this earnest mood of his.

"I meant it before," he replied. "And I mean it now. You don't deserve to be treated that way."

He didn't look away, and she could see the sincerity in his expression.

"We agree on that," she said quietly.

"How come you put up with his garbage?" he asked.

No one had asked her that yet, and Sue looked over at the tall cowboy in mild surprise.

"I mean, you're strong," he went on. "You're smart. You know what you want. You're drop-dead gorgeous...why would you put up with any of his games?"

She thought back to when she'd met Chaney. They'd both been doing some part-time work on the same ranch. He'd been flirtatious, and she'd been flattered.

"I guess I didn't know they were games,"

she admitted. "I was more naive than I thought."

"No one warned you about guys like that?" he asked.

"Oh, in the broader sense when I was growing up," she replied. "But it was normally couched in the idea that if I stayed Amish, I'd be safe from that kind of thing."

"So in other words, no one spelled it all out for you," he said.

"I guess I've learned the hard way," she replied.

But Sue had learned the lesson. Chaney's insecurities hadn't gotten better with some tender loving care. His bursts of anger hadn't been the worst of him. In fact, he'd been hiding a whole lot more. And when he said he had no intention of being a father, he'd meant it. Chaney had said in so many words exactly who he was. She was the fool who hadn't believed him.

"Look, I'm divorced, so I'm not exactly a relationship expert, but I do know how guys think, and some of us are a real piece of work," he said.

"So what are the warning signs from your perspective?" she asked.

"Being mean, raising his voice, saying nasty things, playing with your emotions, baiting you with promises he never fulfills…" Wilder shrugged, then he looked over at her. "Not telling you that he's the luckiest man on the planet to even have a chance with you."

"Oh…" she breathed. "Yeah, Chaney never did that…"

"Well, there you go," he said as if that settled it.

"That's it?" she said.

"An insecure man never wants you to know what you mean to him," Wilder said. "He doesn't want you to know that you could do better. He figures if you knew that, you'd be gone. A secure man, on the other hand, wants you to know exactly what you mean to him, because that the best he's got to offer."

"Huh." It made sense from her own lived experience, but it was the first time she'd had a man state so bluntly how it all worked.

"Sue, you're talented," he said. "And you're whip smart. You're also sweet, and kind, and truly decent. That's a rare combination these days. Don't sell yourself short. You could have any man you wanted."

Did that include him? He caught her gaze and held it.

"I'll try to remember that," she said, and she felt shy suddenly. Any man... There was only one man who seemed worth her attention these days, and he was her boss. It would be a very bad idea. She'd met a lot of men working on ranches and farms, and a really decent man was pretty rare, too.

When they got to the stable, they swung down to the ground. Sue's legs were a little sore from the long ride. They led the horses inside to take off the tack. She started to undo the saddle's girth strap, and Wilder put a hand on her shoulder.

"Leave that. I'll take care of it," he said.

"I can do it—" she started, but his warm gaze stopped her.

"Sue, let me treat you well," he said softly. "Okay?"

Her breath caught. What could she say? She felt the blood come to her face, and she stepped back.

"Thanks," she said.

"No problem." He cast her a warm smile and turned back to the horses.

Funny—this was the sort of thing that she'd

hated in the Amish world—men's work, and women's work. But somehow, having this cowboy be gallant felt different. She couldn't help the smile that came to her lips as she turned toward the door.

"I'll meet you in the house," she said. "I'll start on lunch."

She looked back once, and the horse stamped her hoof in clean straw as Wilder went about unsaddling his own mount first. He didn't turn back, just kept doing the job in front of him. There were good men out there, but she'd stumbled across this one too late.

SUE STOOD IN the kitchen warming up some chili in the microwave. There were some crusty buns in the cupboard, and she rooted through the fridge for the butter.

She heard the screen door open, and without looking up, she said, "Lunch is just about ready."

"Sue?"

That wasn't Wilder, and Sue stood up to see a familiar woman standing in the doorway of the mudroom.

"Jerusha?" Sue said, and she smiled. "It's nice to see you."

"You look…almost the same," Jerusha said, a blush coming to her cheeks. "Jane here has been telling us all about Aunt Sue."

Jane emerged from behind Jerusha, and she gave Sue a mischievous smile.

Sue came forward and gave Jerusha a hug. "Congratulations on the wedding. I'm really happy for you."

"Thank you." Jerusha looked down at Jane with a tentative smile. "We'll have a happy home, won't we, Jane?"

Jane gave Jerusha a look out of the corner of her eye, but she didn't answer.

"I think you'll all be really happy," Sue said. "And whatever makes my brother happy makes me happy."

Jane shot Sue an annoyed look, and Sue couldn't help but chuckle. "Come in and tell me everything."

"Is there time?" Jerusha asked.

"Wilder and I are about to have lunch before heading back out. So maybe you can't tell me everything, but you could tell something, at least. Like, how excited are you? You're about to be a married woman."

"I'm really thrilled," Jerusha said, and the pink bloomed in her cheeks again. "I honestly thought my chance at marriage was over. I mean, I've been single a long time." She suddenly paled. "I didn't mean—" She cleared her throat. "There's always hope. I had just given up on it for myself."

"Don't worry about me being sensitive," Sue said. "I'm really happy for you. You'll make a great addition to the family."

"Will I see you much?" Jerusha asked. "I've been wondering if you're moving back."

"I don't know," Sue said honestly.

"You must miss your family," Jerusha said.

"So much! It's so nice to get to know my niece for the first time—" she cast Jane a smile "—and to see my mother... She's getting older. I noticed that right away. Time goes by too quickly."

"What have you been doing all these years?" Jerusha asked.

"Working ranches, mostly," Sue replied. "But my last job before this one was with a large animal vet. I really liked that—I got to see how a lot of different farms ran, and working directly with the animals was fulfilling."

"Where did you live?" Jerusha asked.

"Wooster—so not too far away."

"Alone?" Jerusha's expression looked pained. The thought of a woman living by herself was a terrible one for the Amish. No one to care for her, to provide for her...but the truth, that Sue had been living most recently with her boyfriend, wouldn't be acceptable either.

"Can I get you something to drink?" Sue asked to change the subject.

"I actually didn't mean to stay too long," Jerusha said. "I've got to go back and help your *mamm* with some canning, but... I actually came by to ask you something. Something important."

"Oh?" Sue hoped her hesitation wasn't showing.

"I wanted to see if you'd be one of my *newehochers*," Jerusha said, her cheeks blushing pink again.

A bridesmaid. Jerusha was inviting Sue to be part of the wedding party... Sue's mouth went dry, and she looked down at Jane who was staring at her with a look of open curiosity. What Sue said right now would sink deep into that little mind.

But two-and-a-half weeks from now when this wedding happened, Sue would still be pregnant—about seventeen weeks along at that point, and very likely she'd start looking pregnant, too. And there she'd be, standing in front of everyone with her pregnancy on display when the attention was supposed to be on the new couple.

No, it would be crass, and she wouldn't do it. But she also couldn't explain it.

"Jerusha, I'm truly happy for you," Sue said slowly. "And I think you and Wollie will take very good care of each other. I one hundred percent support your wedding, and I wish I could say yes to standing with you, but I... can't."

Jerusha's face fell. "What? Why not?"

"Because..." Sue floundered, looking for a reason—any reason...

"I just can't," she said feebly. "I'm so sorry."

"Oh..." Jerusha nodded a couple of times. "Okay. Well, I'll let Wollie know. I just wanted to include you, since you're family and all."

Jerusha was embarrassed, and Sue felt the insulting blow she'd just delivered. But when they found out about this pregnancy—either because Sue told them after their wedding, or because it became unhideable—they'd see why. And probably be grateful that Sue had kept herself back.

"But I'll be one the guests," Sue said, hoping it would make some difference.

"*Yah*. Thank you." Jerusha turned toward the door, and the happy pink in her cheeks had turned to an embarrassed blazing red. "I'd best get back. Come along, Jane."

"Jerusha, I'm really sorry. I really am happy for you," Sue said.

Sue looked down at Jane, and the girl was biting her bottom lip. She followed Jerusha obediently enough, but Sue saw a sparkle in Jane's eye that worried her. Sue had just set a very dangerous precedent, and it hadn't been lost on her niece.

CHAPTER NINE

WILDER CAME INTO the house and dropped his hat on a peg. He could smell some chili in the kitchen, and his stomach rumbled. Chores were done for the time being, and his mind was already moving ahead to the cattle drive they'd start on the next day. Wollie had agreed to take the bottle calf over to his own barn until they returned, a favor that Wilder appreciated. This was what neighbors were for. And Wollie had taken one more opportunity to remind him that his sister was indeed a woman, and shouldn't be worked as hard as a man would be. This time Wilder had to agree. He couldn't tell Wollie about Sue's pregnancy, but he did tell him in all sincerity that he'd be doing the lion's share of the physical work, with Sue there as a second cowhand.

Wilder looked over his shoulder before shutting the door. He could make out the back of a woman's yellow dress and Jane trailing behind her. He let the screen door bounce shut.

"Did I see Jane leaving?" Wilder asked as he came into the kitchen.

"Yes, you did." Sue put two bowls onto the table. "That was Jerusha, my brother's fiancée, you saw leaving with her."

"Oh, yeah?" He looked out the kitchen window, but they were out of sight now. Sue's expression was grim. "Why do you look like someone died?"

Sue raised her eyebrows, and then quickly smoothed her expression. "Because I just did something terrible. She asked me to be a bridesmaid. I said no."

"Wow." Wilder let out a slow breath. "For non-Amish people that would be a pretty big deal."

"For Amish people, it's even bigger," she replied.

"Why'd you say no?" he asked. "It might go a long way in smoothing over some family relationships to participate in the wedding. And to turn her down…"

"Trust me," she said with a sigh. "I know how awful it was, and I tried to reassure her that I was very much in support of her marrying my brother, but I'm not sure she believes me."

"So why not just do it?" he asked. "I'm going to be sanding down an...*eck*, I think he called it."

"Yes, an *eck*," she said with a wan smile. "And good for you. But I can't. I'm pregnant, and while I'm not showing yet, I will be very soon. If I'm a bridesmaid, that will put me on display with a pregnant belly in front of everyone. It would be a massive scandal, and it would definitely take the attention off the bride and groom. I can't tell them why yet, but there is no way I can stand up and be her bridesmaid in good conscience."

"And you can't explain?" he asked.

"Not yet..." She rubbed a hand over her eyes. "I have to figure out what I'm going to do, because they're going to have all sorts of questions. If I tell them now, all of the attention will be on solving my problem, encouraging me to come home properly and settle into Amish life... That isn't fair. Jerusha deserves a few weeks of wedding preparation where the focus is on her. So does Wollie, for that matter."

"You're trying to do the right thing," Wilder said.

"I really am." She smiled ruefully. "Even

if it doesn't look like it right now. Besides, they're used to me being the bad one. This doesn't change anything. Now they can carry on, have a lovely wedding and forgive me later."

He knew what being the black sheep felt like. That was his role for far too long, and he felt some sympathy for her position. A person could get used to being the "bad one," but it was a heavy burden to carry.

"So maybe it's not so bad that we're going to be riding herd for the next couple of days?" he asked.

"The timing is perfect." She smiled, but there was sadness in her eyes. "See? It all works out."

THE NEXT MORNING, Wilder checked the saddlebags for the third time to make sure he had packed everything. With a full day's ride out to the herd and then back again, forgetting something like matches or a can opener could mean a lot of inconvenience.

They'd gotten the chores done early and left the injured animals in the barn with extra feed and water for while they were gone. Wollie would check in on them. The morning was cool, but the sun was over the horizon and the sky was clear.

Wilder refastened the bag and looked over at Sue who was doing the same. Her hair was tied back in her usual ponytail. Her blue eyes were fixed on the job in front of her as she checked buckles and straps. She was beautiful like this, he realized—focused on a job she cared about.

"Are we good to go?" he asked.

"Yeah..." Sue tightened the strap on a sleeping roll that lay just behind her saddle. "I think I've got everything."

Wilder led his horse, Samson, out the stable door, and Sue followed leading Mona, a mare who was good for a long ride, but also fast on her feet and experienced with herding cattle. Once outside, Wilder closed the stable door and then they hoisted themselves up and into the saddles. The horses stamped in anticipation.

"Let's go," Wilder said, and he caught Sue's gaze. She shot him a brilliant smile.

"Let's go," she echoed.

The cross-country ride was beautiful this time of year. The leaves had started to turn on the trees, while the grass was still green, and would stay that way until a good, hard frost prompted it to turn brown. The air had a definite bite that made Wilder glad for his coat and gloves. The horses were eager to stretch their legs and run, and they galloped across the first field, went through the far gate and exited onto open country. Sue settled her horse into a canter next to him, and he couldn't help but notice the way it made her blue eyes light up.

"Isn't this the best?" she asked with a grin. "This is why I work ranches. There's no life like it."

"I couldn't agree more." Her smile was infectious.

"When I have a baby at home, this sort of thing won't be so easy to do, though," she said.

"They don't stay tiny forever," Wilder said. "Pretty soon, they're big enough to learn how to ride."

"That's true." She guided her horse around a little outcrop, and when she came back to his side, she glanced over at him. "There is a very easy solution for me, you know."

"Go home?" he said.

"Yeah." She sighed. "I could go back—be

the Amish woman who left and returned. I could raise my child Amish, have the support of my family and my community…"

"It doesn't sound so bad," Wilder said.

"…and never ride herd again," she said.

He nodded. There it was—the problem.

"So there really aren't any Amish cowgirls?" Wilder asked.

"Nope."

"You couldn't just be the first one?" he asked, only halfway joking. "Blaze a trail for the girls coming after you?"

"I wish…" she said.

But even Wilder knew that the Amish didn't maintain their distinctive community by blazing trails and trying new things. They stayed to their own path, did things their own way and absolutely refused to change unless it was completely inescapable.

"The way I see it, I have two options," Sue said. "I can come home, live an Amish life. I don't have to join the church, but I would have to respect the Amish ways and not make waves."

"Or?" Wilder said.

"Or… I could get a job in town, get some kind of childcare arranged for my baby and live a regular life as a single mom in Wooster."

"Not so terrible," he said.

"But harder in a lot of ways." She cast him a guarded look.

"You'd have more time with your baby if you moved home," he said.

"Exactly…" She sighed again. "I know lots of women work, drop their children off at day care… But I don't have anything more than a high school diploma, which is four years more than other Amish girls get, so I'm grateful for it. But the career I want is in ranching, and that's not really possible with a baby in tow. So I'd have to figure something else out."

"Either way, you don't get to work with cattle," he said.

"Exactly."

Even he couldn't hire her on full time. When Conrad and Annabelle got back from their travels, they'd have no more need for another ranch hand around here, and they couldn't afford it full time anyway.

"I'm sorry about that," he said after a few beats of silence between them.

"Don't be," she said. "I'm going to enjoy this time working with cattle while I've got it, and then I'll make the best decision I can for myself and my baby."

"What direction are you leaning?" he asked.

"Honestly?" She glanced over at him. "I have no idea. I'm really torn. But I do have right now—and I'm going to make the best of it."

They rode all morning, and the rolling hills melted into some rocky terrain. A brisk wind whisked over the land, chilling Wilder's face and hands. Overhead, a V of geese trailed across the sky. One goose peeled away from the flock and headed down to the ground. A second goose followed it, while the rest of the flock carried on, honking as they flew.

"Did you see that?" Sue asked. "Those two geese coming down?"

"Yeah," Wilder said.

"If one is tired or sick, another will always go with it," she said. "My father taught me that. A flock never lets a goose suffer alone." She smiled faintly. "He would tell me to go back home—to accept help from my community."

Wilder wasn't going to argue with her take-away from the scene, but if he was going to draw a lesson from it, he noticed something different. The flock kept flying—only one goose followed the first in the descent. One stayed loyal, not the entire flock.

And right now, he was the one riding at her side.

Wilder shook the thought free, though, because it made him a little nervous. Was he wanting to be her solution, here? He was just a cowboy keeping his ranch running. He wasn't a man in a position to solve anyone's problems.

"Well, for what it's worth," Wilder said. "For as long as you're here, I'm glad to have you around. You're a pretty unique blend of talent, interesting ideas and good looks."

She looked over at him, her gaze unreadable.

"Sorry if I overstepped with the good looks part," he added, suddenly feeling uncomfortable. He didn't have to say every single thing that popped into his head.

"You can call me pretty anytime, Wilder." A smile tickled her lips. "This is part of the experience that I'm just going to enjoy. Because once I'm hugely pregnant, or the exhausted mother of a newborn, I don't think I'll be hearing much of that."

"If you're around the right guy, you will," he said.

She cast him a smile, but didn't answer.

For what it was worth, if she were around him, he'd be telling her what he thought of her, and some tiredness or a baby in her arms, or even a large pregnancy wasn't going to change facts. Sue Schmidt was gorgeous, and she deserved a guy who saw that.

SUE FOLLOWED WILDER'S lead as they headed across the rolling farmland. There were no roads as far as she could see, and the large, cumulous clouds left patches of chilly shade across the landscape. As they rode, she looked over at Wilder who seemed to be almost one with the horse he was riding. His hips moved with the animal, the rest of him staying straight and tall.

He thought she deserved better, and she knew he was right. But she hadn't been prepared for the outside world, either.

"Being raised Amish, I was taught to read the world in a certain way," she said. "To look out for Amish boys who would be all talk and no commitment, for example. I was taught about how fast a rumor could travel around a small community like ours, that sort of thing. But I was also taught that *Englishers* were completely different from us. They played by different rules. They had different expectations."

"Are we so different?" Wilder asked.

"Maybe not," she said with a low laugh. "I honestly thought that *Englisher* men would laugh at me for wanting to settle down and raise kids. The men I got to know made me feel like my Amish upbringing was like saying you came from outer space, you know? I had to relearn so many things."

"Like what?" he asked.

"Like the day I realized that driving in a car isn't more dangerous than being in a buggy. My *daet* had told me all my life that going that fast was like inviting death. In fact, a buggy is probably more dangerous! There's less to protect you in an accident."

"Yeah, definitely," Wilder said. "We have seat belts, car seats for kids, airbags…"

"Right?" she said. "But when you're told one thing from babyhood on up, you don't tend to question it. So I found myself questioning absolutely everything. I didn't know anymore what was true and what wasn't. I didn't know what applied to the outside world, and what didn't."

"Including what made for a good man, and what made for a guy to avoid," Wilder said.

"Exactly."

He nodded. "I had a similar experience when I stopped drinking. I had to relearn how to deal with stress, and how to look at friendships. Sometimes you have to tear up your foundation and start over."

"Yes." She nodded, and she felt a little thrill of excitement. "You actually understand this!"

"Sure, I do," Wilder replied.

"If I'd had an *Englisher* family, I could have asked my brother, or my cousins about these guys. I could have brought them home to meet my family and have their input," Sue said. "But I didn't have any of that, and I feel so silly now for falling for Chaney's lines, but I was just glad that an *Englisher* man found me attractive. I felt so dowdy and plain."

Wilder shot her an incredulous look. "Sue, you're neither of those things. You're a knock-out."

"You seem to think so," she said.

"Anyone with eyes would think so!" he retorted. "But I get it. You were out of your element, and Chaney took advantage of that."

"He wasn't always a jerk," she said. "He could be kind and fun. But he had me convinced that marriage and kids, being Mr. and Mrs., that was all pretty antiquated. I guess I believed him."

"Not everything you were raised with is useless in the outside world," Wilder said. "A good man *will* commit. In fact, he'll be really glad to call you his, and to be yours. Lots of people want monogamy, marriage and kids, too. In fact, a guy who loves you will be thrilled to know you're pregnant with his baby. And he'll step up."

"Like I said, I feel pretty silly now," she said, and she looked away.

"Don't," he said. "You were tearing up your foundation and rebuilding from scratch. Something caught you by surprise. That's it. Live and learn, right? You'll know better going forward, and you'll choose a better guy."

She looked over at him, and there was no

judgment from this lanky cowboy. He just shrugged.

"You're still a catch, Sue," he said. "Don't lower your standards one inch."

"How did you learn all this?" she asked.

"The hard way," he said.

She shot him a smile. "Really?"

"Most of it, yeah," he replied. "But I'm not going to beat myself up for mistakes that are in the past. I can now appreciate how lucky I am to have everything I do. Sometimes people stumble across something really great, and they don't appreciate it until it's gone. Like marriages, or family...or a nice big ranch. I'm not one of those guys—not anymore at least. I know how hard it to come across something truly great in life, and I'm holding on with both hands."

"Good for you," she said softly. Maybe she could learn from Wilder's hard-won wisdom and stop beating herself up, too. This baby was a new start. Whatever she ended up doing to support this child, she wasn't going to miss a minute of gratefulness for the chance to be a mother.

She'd always wanted children, and maybe she hadn't envisioned it happening quite this way, but she was deeply happy about this baby. Chaney was going to miss out on the miracle of parenthood, but what could she do about that? He was definitely a mistake, but this child was not.

As she breathed in the fresh air and felt the comforting rhythm of the horse's canter beneath her, she had a feeling that her life was going to become a series of moments like this one—beautiful opportunities she didn't want to miss, and couldn't count on ever having again. Wasn't that motherhood in a nutshell?

When the sun was high in the sky, they stopped for lunch. For Sue, the salami sandwiches and granola bars were the best lunch she'd ever eaten—she was that hungry. They'd stopped at a rocky creek that had a pool of calm water for the horses to drink from. There was a well-used firepit already dug there—a sure sign that this was the regular resting spot for fetching the herd.

Sue sat on a fallen log next to Wilder as they both chewed in silence. She was hungry, but she was also getting cold. She'd taken her gloves off to eat, and her fingers were chilled, as well as her cheeks and the tip of her nose.

The horses grazed farther away, heads

down in the plentiful grass and clover that had gone to seed already.

"Do you normally start a fire here?" Sue asked.

"When it's cold," he said. "Sometimes we need the chance to warm up." He reached over and took the hand that wasn't full of sandwich, running his thumb over her fingers. "You're pretty cold. I could kindle a fire if you want."

His hand moved over hers for a moment longer, his fingers strong, warm and surprisingly gentle. Then he pulled back. Her skin felt warm where he'd touched her, and she slipped that hand between her knees.

"It's okay," she said. "We want to get to the herd before dark, so we'd better not waste too much time."

"You sure?" His gaze held hers, and for a split second, it almost felt like he was asking something else, like the question in his warm brown eyes was something deeper. She broke off eye contact.

"Yeah," Sue said. "We'll build a big, roaring blaze when we get there."

"Deal." He smiled, then scooted closer to her on the log so that his leg pressed up against hers and she could benefit from the warmth from his body. He passed her a steaming cup of coffee from his thermos.

"I'm not drinking coffee these days," she reminded him.

"That's why this is decaf." He shot her a grin. "I dug some out of the back of the cupboard. I forgot we had it. Is that acceptable?"

"Yeah, it is." She accepted the cup with a smile and took a sip. It was warming, and had both cream and sugar already mixed in. "Thanks, Wilder."

"My pleasure." His voice was low, deep, and when she glanced over at him, his attention was on his own cup, steaming in the cold air, but he still leaned toward her almost imperceptibly. "Is this better?"

"It is. I'm warming up," she said.

He lifted his arm, reached through to grab her free hand and pulled it through. Having her arms twined with his put her even closer against his body, his shoulder close to her cheek. He caught her fingers in his warm palm, and she tentatively leaned her cheek against his muscled shoulder. He was warm, solid and he smelled faintly of musk.

"This is wildly unprofessional," she murmured.

"You want me to move?" he asked softly.

"No," she said.

"It doesn't count out here," he said. "This is survival—keeping warm in a cold wind, and working together to get the cattle back. We can return to a nice professional distance when we get back."

She looked up at him, and when he glanced down, she saw a twinkle in his eye.

"You promise?" she asked.

"Scout's honor."

She could hear the mild joking in his tone, but this did feel nice—a strong man, a gentle touch. With any other man, she'd never felt quite like this.

"This is the kind of thing I told myself not to expect with *Englisher* men," she said.

"What kind of thing?" he asked.

"I don't know…" Suddenly she felt a little shy saying it out loud. "Being taken care of."

"Amish men know how to take care of their women, do they?" he said, and she sensed a shade of competition in his voice.

"Well…yeah."

"A cowboy can do the same," he said. "You just need the right kind of cowboy."

"And to let slip that you're pregnant," she said, attempting to joke.

Wilder looked down at her, then his attention moved to the grazing horses. "Even if you weren't pregnant I'd want to do this." He still didn't look at her, but his grip on her hand tightened a little bit. "You needing some support—that's not just for while you're pregnant. Your brother was right—you're a woman. And maybe I'm old-fashioned, but I think a man should make a woman's life easier. And while he's going about making her life a little easier for being near him, he has the challenge of trying not to feel more for her than he should."

"That's how it works?" she said softly.

"Yep. That's how it works."

"And holding my hand is making my life easier?" she asked with a little teasing nudge of her elbow.

"Well, it's sure making mine easier," he said. "Because I've been thinking about holding your hand for a long time now. If that's totally over the line, you can feel free to berate me for it once we're back at the house again."

"Nah," she said, and she rested her cheek against his shoulder again.

Wilder felt so familiar, somehow—a fellow lost soul.

Mona came wandering in their direction, and Wilder straightened.

"Are you warm enough to keep moving?" he asked. For a second, she was tempted to say no, to enjoy this a little bit longer, but there was a job to do, and he wasn't the only one who needed to hold himself back from feeling too much.

Sue nodded. "Sure. Let's get going."

She couldn't sit there, tucked into his side forever. There were cattle waiting.

THEY REACHED THE cattle as the sun was setting, and Sue kindled a fire while Wilder did a quick patrol and herded in some of the cattle that had wandered too far. Squatting next to the crackling new blaze, she could feel that her body's dimensions had changed. It was harder to squat, for one, and her jeans were tighter around her middle. How long before other people noticed?

From out in the field, she could hear Wilder's whistles and hollers as he brought the straggling cattle in closer to the rest of the animals. The thunder of hooves as the animals came in a few at a time was a comfortable rhythm. She rooted through a saddlebag for cooking utensils, and she got to work. Simple bratwursts would taste like a feast tonight.

That evening, Wilder pulled out a harmonica and played a few tunes. Cattle liked music—that was a ranching secret. If they wanted to keep the cattle near, give them a little music to keep them interested.

After cleaning up their food, hanging the remains in the tree to avoid attracting any wild animals, they stoked the fire a little higher with some dead wood from the nearby trees, and unrolled their bedding for the night. They lined up the sleeping bags so that their heads were together and their bodies were pointed away from each other. Both stretched out alongside the fire for maximum warmth.

Sue got as comfortable as she could on the foam roll by lying on her back, and she looked up at the starry sky. A few clouds darkened the west, but overhead, all was clear and bright, with a nearly full moon spilling silvery light over them.

She heard Wilder exhale a long sigh, and

she thought he was about to fall asleep. It was just as well—he'd need to be rested by daybreak. No one had the option of sleeping in under the open sky. They'd get up with the sun.

A glowing log popped, and sparks floated up into the night. She sat up.

"You okay?" His voice was quiet.

"I was thinking I might need to put more wood on the fire before I fall asleep," she admitted.

"I'll do it." But he didn't move.

"Now, or…?"

He chuckled. "I won't fall asleep before I add more wood, trust me. This isn't my first cattle drive."

"Sorry." She lay back down. Sometimes it was better to just let a man take care of the things he said he'd do. Especially if he was her boss. "I thought you were asleep."

"Nope. Just thinking."

"What about?" She looked in his direction, and all she could make out was the top of his head. He reached toward her and she reached back, his warm fingers folding over hers.

"I was thinking about how I'll probably

always remember this drive," he said. "It'll be special."

She smiled faintly. "You're going to have worked harder on this one than on any other."

"Don't count on that," he said. He released her fingers, and she rolled over onto her side toward the fire. He did the same, and when she looked up, she could see the length of him stretched out kitty corner to her under his sleeping bag.

"I'm complicating your life, aren't I?" she said quietly.

"A bit," he said.

"I'm sorry about that," she said.

"Don't be," he said, and he looked at her, then, his dark brown gaze meeting hers. "I'm here with you because I want to be. And I'm taking care of you because I want to, too. I'm not the kind of guy who gets trapped too easily."

"Okay." She wasn't sure what else to say to that, because Chaney had blamed her for exactly that when she told him she was pregnant—trapping him. While she knew it took two to make a child and his accusations came from selfishness and immaturity, they'd still stung.

"Now go to sleep," he said. "I'll watch the fire. You need rest."

"So do you."

"You need it more." His voice was low, and there was a hint of command to it. "I'll take care of things tonight. Just trust me, okay?"

She was too tired to bother with untangling her feelings surrounding that, so she let her eyes drift shut, and her body felt like it was melting into her bedroll. The flutter of her baby inside her settled into quiet.

Trust him… Tonight, that was easy. Funny—it took being out in the wilderness with a man she hardly knew to feel truly and deeply safe. This was a sensation she'd have to try hard to forget when they got back, because she couldn't lean on him. Not beyond this cattle drive.

Wilder Westhouse would make some woman very happy, but he wasn't her man.

CHAPTER TEN

WILDER WOKE UP with the rising sun and stretched his tight muscles. He looked over toward Sue's sleeping form and smiled to himself. She was curled up on her side, her head tucked down into her sleeping bag.

Even with her face burrowed in her sleeping bag, she was gorgeous. Her hair was tangled, and he watched her for a moment, then unzipped his bag. When he started to rustle around, Sue stirred and woke up, too.

"Good morning," she murmured.

"Sleep well?" he asked.

"Better than I expected to," she said.

That was gratifying to hear. Let her at least rest well without worry when he was with her. They rolled their sleeping bags and bedrolls, then made breakfast, which consisted of some muffins, instant oatmeal, apples and a couple of protein bars. It wasn't fancy, but it did hit the spot. They ate together next to a dying fire

as clouds moved in overhead. It didn't look
like rain—just high cloud cover that chilled
the air. It was the perfect weather for a cattle
drive, because when they worked up a sweat,
they wouldn't be sweltering in the sun.

When they had both brushed their teeth and
washed their faces in the icy stream water,
Sue zipped her toiletry bag and tucked it into
the saddlebag she'd draped over a stump.

"Why don't you clean up and pack while I
go get the straggling cattle?" Sue said.

"You sure?" he queried. She was asking
for the harder of the tasks.

"Yes, I'm sure." She pulled her hair back
into a ponytail again, wrapping the tie around
her hair a couple of times while she eyed him,
waiting for his answer. "Let me ride, Wilder.
I don't have much time left where I can do
this."

"All right," he agreed. "You have a good
point."

"You have to admit, the cattle drive is the
best part of the job," she said.

He grinned in response, and Sue swung up
into her saddle. She heeled the horse into motion and galloped off around the edge of herd.
He watched her go—her ponytail streaming

out behind her. She was beautiful—more than beautiful. The woman was intoxicating. And he was crossing lines here by holding her hand, warming her up and acting more like a boyfriend than a boss. In the moment, he just couldn't help himself.

"I'm an idiot..." he muttered aloud to himself.

She'd suggested the day before that he wouldn't be acting like this if it weren't for her pregnancy, and she was partly right about that. He wouldn't have been acting on it, but he'd still be longing to. And falling for Wollie's estranged sister was definitely going to complicate matters.

He looked over his shoulder as Sue got behind a heifer and urged the animal toward the rest of the herd. She was incredible... and watching her on horseback, her skill on display, he felt a rush of emotions—pride in her, and a tenderness that went deeper than he was comfortable with. He was most certainly starting to feel things he shouldn't feel for this woman.

Wilder set to work cleaning up the campsite. He doused the fire and gathered up the garbage, compressing it into a bag. Then he reloaded the saddlebags and hoisted himself into his saddle. It was time to get to work. She was right that the cattle drive was the best part of the job. But Sue was quickly becoming the best part of this cattle drive.

The first leg of a cattle drive was always the hardest, before a lead cow took her place at the head of the herd and the rest followed in the right direction. As herd animals, cattle were happy to follow, but it took a little bit to get that momentum going.

For the first couple of hours, Wilder and Sue kept to the back of the herd, urging them forward. Wilder took one side and Sue took the other so that the cattle were squeezed in the right direction. Some of the older cows would remember this process and know what was expected of them, but the younger ones were skittish and more prone to react spontaneously.

As they worked, he admired Sue's skill in herding cattle. She knew when to back off and let the cattle just go at their own pace and when to move in and give them that little extra pressure. She cut off a young steer that was making a run for it, and diverted him back to the herd.

Wilder and Sue weren't close enough to talk to each other since they had to be on opposite sides of the herd to keep them moving, and Wilder's thoughts moved to some advice he'd gotten from an old cowboy.

Marry a woman who doesn't mind opening and shutting gates all her life.

It was meant as a joke—ranching wives worked hard, but a cowboy also needed someone who'd jump in and out of a truck or tractor to take care of the gates, be that his wife or one of his kids. Life was so much easier with that second person as a supportive part of the team.

But that old cowboy had obviously never met a woman like Sue, because relegating her to gate patrol would be a wild waste of her abilities. While even the memory of Sue plastered against his arm as he drove the tractor to move the hay bales warmed his blood, he'd never be the man to hold her back in order to keep her close. She was far too impressive for that.

But this pregnancy would hold her back in her ranching career…as would motherhood for the first little while, at least. And dare he say it—so would her Amish family. Sue didn't belong in a kitchen, or out collecting eggs. She belonged on the range, in the barn and wherever the cattle were. And there was a small piece of his heart that had started to whisper that she belonged with him.

A cold wind had started to blow, chilling Wilder's hands and feet when he spotted a half-grown calf over in the bushes. It was a young steer, and he seemed to be stumbling. Injured, perhaps? Sick? Wilder wheeled his horse around and headed over in that direction, hoping to urge the animal up out of the brush and back into the herd, but when he got behind him, Wilder saw the problem. There was a tangle of blue baling twine wrapped around one back and one front leg, hobbling him. This was why Wilder was a stickler for collecting any bits of twine or plastic and carrying them back out of the hills with him—they could be fatal to wildlife.

Wilder dismounted, keeping a calming hand on his horse's flank while he assessed the situation. The herd was still moving forward, although a little more slowly. He pulled a knife from his belt and approached the calf slowly.

"Hey, buddy…" he murmured. "I'm going to help you."

It was best with cattle and horses not to talk too much, and when he got close enough to the calf that he was able to grab the twine, the animal let out a frightened bawl and launched himself backward.

Shoot. Wilder tried again, but the same thing happened. He couldn't just leave him here, and if the gentle approach wasn't going to work, he'd have to rope the animal and cut the twine free. But he'd try once more…

Wilder grabbed a handful of twine and this time he didn't let go, no matter how much the calf kicked. He got his knife in there and started to saw at the twine, popping it one string at a time.

Suddenly, he felt a blow to his shoulder, and he went sprawling several feet forward, his knife knocked out of his hand. He rolled over as a large cow came thundering toward him, her head lowered menacingly.

This was obviously the mama cow come to defend her baby, and he rolled out of her way just as her powerful hooves hit the ground next to his head. He got up and spread his arms wide.

"Hey!" Wilder bellowed at her. "Cut it out!"

He scanned for his horse, but the stallion had cantered off about fifty yards, getting away from all the excitement, and Wilder looked from his horse to the hobbled calf, and back to the angry cow.

"Wilder?" Sue rode up, and she seemed to assess the situation in an instant. She wheeled her horse around and came between Wilder and the cow. He ran over to where he'd dropped the knife, spotting the hilt among some weeds. He scooped it up and headed back for the frightened calf. No time to calm him now, he'd have to go for it.

He grabbed the twine and started cutting at it again, snapping each string and pulling it free from the tangle.

"Behind you!" Sue called, and he turned to see the cow coming at him again. He used the thrashing calf as a barrier between himself and the angry mama until Sue was able to wedge her horse between them once more, pushing the cow back. His hackles went up—it was more than his own safety at risk here, and putting herself between a cow and calf wasn't a safe thing to do, but there wasn't any other choice. At least she was on horseback.

He grabbed the last handful of tangled twine and threw himself bodily on top of the young animal to hold him down while he finished cutting through it, finally releasing the calf's legs. He grabbed handfuls of twine and pulled it away from the kicking legs, and when Sue hollered, "Behind you!" again, he jumped away from the young steer and let it run toward the angry mama cow.

Wilder stood in the brush, breathing hard, his shoulder aching from the initial blow. He tucked his knife back in his belt and gathered up the bits of twine around him in the brush and grass, watching the pair to make sure they didn't come back in his direction.

"Hya!" Sue hollered and heeled her horse into motion in the direction the cow and calf, and they both ran up the incline toward the rest of the herd.

Wilder followed at a safe distance, and he whistled for his horse. The stallion came cantering back in his direction now.

"Thanks," Wilder called out to Sue, who'd reined in a few yards off.

"No problem." Sue scanned the herd that had almost come to a stop again, then swung down from her horse and walked over to him.

She put a firm hand on his shoulder and he winced.

"I'm fine," he said, but he didn't have the heart to move away from her touch. "As for you, that wasn't the safest solution back there."

"Says the man who nearly got trampled by a mama cow," she retorted. "You should stop at the thank you."

"Fine." He smiled faintly and rubbed at his shoulder. "Thank you. But if anything happened to you—"

She shot him a flat look and he chuckled, letting it go. Sue wasn't a newbie.

"You okay?" she asked, softening her tone. "You literally flew through the air before you landed. That cow meant business."

"If I'm not, what do you intend to do?" he asked with a wry smile. "Call for help and give directions to…"

She rolled her eyes. "Fine, fine."

"If we keep moving, we'll get them all back by sunset," Wilder said, and he rotated his shoulder under her touch. "I'm glad you're here, Sue."

She smiled then. "I bet you are."

Wilder chuckled and shook his head. Was

she flirting with him? He couldn't be sure, but she swung back up into her saddle and waited until he'd done the same.

"You were just rescued by a woman," she said teasingly. "Can you handle that?"

"Me?" Wilder barked out a laugh. "I have no problem with competent women. I'm even okay with a woman who's better than me. I hired you for a reason, Sue Schmidt. You're the best."

He urged his horse forward, past Sue and to the other side of the herd. When he looked back at her, he found her gaze locked on him, and a peculiar look on her face. Gone was the teasing, and in its place he saw a hint of... sadness.

Then Sue seemed to shake herself free of it, and she let out a shrill whistle, starting a steer back into the herd, and they all moved forward again. She might be the better cowpoke between the two of them, but he was still a man, and let her be better than him at his own job, but his instinct was to crush whatever it was that was breaking her heart like that.

SUE AND WILDER stopped for lunch in the same spot as the day before, next to the babbling stream. The cattle grazed, and Wilder set up a picket line for the horses. They were having noodle soup cups, cheese sandwiches and protein bars for lunch, and she was munching on a power bar already as she positioned the pot over the flames to heat up the water.

The baby wriggled inside her, and in her crouched position, she felt it more strongly than she'd felt the movements yet, and she froze. Another wriggle—definitely more than a flutter now.

Wilder shot her a smile. "You holding up okay?"

"Yep." She nodded, and couldn't help but smile. "I can feel the baby move."

"Are you serious?" He leaned forward from his seat on the log, his elbows on his knees.

"I've been feeling it for a couple of weeks now," she said. "It's neat. It makes it feel more real."

The water in the pot was close to a boil, and she rose to her feet. Wilder stood up, too, and hooked a thumb in his belt loop as his gaze swung over the grazing herd. Sue watched him for a moment.

"Do you want me to talk to Chaney for

you?" he asked suddenly, turning back toward her.

"And say what?" she asked.

"I don't know—let him know what a fool he is for walking away from his own baby, for one," he said. "Maybe he needs someone to point out that he should man up."

"If he needs it pointed out, even a good rattle won't make any lasting changes in him," she said. "Don't bother."

Sue bent down to check the pot, and it had started to boil now. She used a folded towel to pull the pot off the fire, squatting next to the opened noodle cups. Her waist was thicker, and squatting wasn't as easy as it used to be, but she carefully poured the hot water and pressed the paper lids on the cups shut to let the noodles soften. She looked up to find Wilder's gentle gaze still on her.

"I'm not heartbroken over losing him," she said when he hadn't spoken. "Chaney was a mistake, and I don't know... I'm not terribly sad that it's over. I don't know if that's heartless..."

"Nah, it's fine," Wilder replied. "He doesn't deserve your grief."

His words were unexpectedly sweet, and

she looked away, afraid of betraying how tenderly those words had landed. Maybe it was more than the great outdoors, the rolling hills and the work she loved so much... It was all a little bit sweeter with Wilder here. And he made her feel like she was doing something right at long last.

Sue sat back on the log and felt moisture wicking up through the back of her pants.

"That's wet," she said, making a face.

"Here—" Wilder laughed and reached for her hand. He pulled her up. As she rose to her feet, she found herself within inches of the tall cowboy, and he didn't move back. He stayed here, her hand in his, feeling the warmth of his body in the chilly afternoon. His grip on her hand loosened, but he didn't let go. His gaze caught hers, and she felt a shiver work up her spine.

"It's like everything in my life has spun out of control," she said softly. "It's hard to prove to my family I didn't make a mistake when I'm coming back for help."

"Hey..." He reached up and touched her cheek with the back of a finger. "I, for one, am glad that your life brought you here. You've brightened up my world considerably."

Suddenly everything they'd said, the banter, the conversation, all seemed to drift away. What was left was the musky scent of this strong man in front of her, and his gentle, calloused touch. His hand slipped around her waist, and she looked up at him, his dark gaze moving down to her lips.

Standing here in the frigid wind, she had a strange sense that they were both alike in some fundamental way. Maybe it was their love of the work, or this strange magnetic pull that kept tugging them together, but this was the first *Englisher* she'd met who felt like he was made of the same stuff she was.

And she'd been lonely for a long time...

"Sue, I—" He licked his lips. "I want to kiss you."

"You do?" she breathed. She wasn't sure why this surprised her, but it did.

Wilder touched her face again, but this time, he ran his thumb along her jawline, stopping at her chin. He lowered his lips just a whisper away from hers, and she could feel the tickle of his breath. She tipped her face upward just a little, and her lips brushed his.

Wilder's strong arms came down around her, and it was like she'd unlocked him, somehow, because he took over the kiss, his lips searing hers. He gathered her close against his chest, the chill of the day disappearing. His stubble brushed her face, and when he finally pulled back, she was left breathless.

"I've been thinking about that for a while now..." Wilder murmured.

"Me, too," she admitted.

He bent and touched her lips again with his. This time his kiss was less urgent, more tender, and when he pulled back, her heart-beat pattered in her chest.

"My life is upside down right now..." she whispered.

"I know, I know." He cleared his throat and released her. "And I'm not trying to complicate things. I'm sorry if I overstepped there—"

"It was nice." She smiled, feeling some-what bashful suddenly.

"It was, wasn't it?" He smiled, too.

"Look, we obviously have some pretty natural attraction between us," she said.

"Yeah, that's the truth," he said. "Maybe we just needed to get that out of our systems."

But the way his eyes softened when he looked at her, this wasn't out of his system any more than it was out of hers. And if she waited another minute, she'd find herself right back in his arms again where she fit so perfectly. Behind them the cattle lowed to each other contentedly, reminding her of the reason they were here. They were almost back to the ranch, almost back to the place where she'd be forced to think things through a little more realistically, and that would be a good thing.

"We should get moving," Sue said.

"Yep." He sucked in a slow breath and then nodded again. "Back to work."

Work was her refuge—the one place she felt entirely in control. She'd think it all through once she was in the saddle again. Because that kiss had been too wonderful to dismiss, and a little too dangerous to let happen again.

CHAPTER ELEVEN

THE REST OF the ride back to the ranch went faster. Sue settled into the rhythm, but she was tired. It had been a long two days, and she didn't have as much energy as usual. Her doctor had told her to expect it and not push too hard. She hadn't mentioned that to Wilder, but he seemed to be keeping an eye on her, because when she started to flag, he'd have them stop for a few minutes, dismount, drink some water, have a snack, and she'd get her strength back before they continued on. Ordinarily, she'd be annoyed at the coddling, but he meant well. And she probably needed it.

The lead cow and the other more senior cows could tell they were close to the home pasture, where they knew they'd have a feeder full of hay. Their pace picked up considerably, and by the time Sue could see the barn like a red postage stamp in the distance, the sun was low in the sky.

"You go on straight to the stable," Wilder said. "I'll take care of everything else out here."

"I can pitch in," she said.

"I'm not saying this as your brother's friend, or as...a guy who obviously cares about you," he said. For a moment, his voice softened, then he cleared his throat. "I'm saying it as your boss. I want you to go into the house and put your feet up."

It was tempting, and while she thought about it, he added, "Plus I need you to order us pizza. The number is on the fridge. There's some cash in the drawer under the microwave. Whatever pizza you want, just order it. It takes a bit for delivery drivers to get out to us from town."

"All right," she conceded. "I won't argue with that."

Wilder fell in beside her, their knees a few inches apart as they rode together. He reached out and took her hand, giving it a quick squeeze. "And since I think you'll worry about the work, if I end up needing help, I'll get your brother to give me a hand."

"I was going to overthink it," she said with a low laugh.

"Thought so." He pulled keys out of his pocket and handed them over. His fingers didn't touch hers, though, as she accepted the key ring.

He was close, yet those few inches felt like a gulf between them. That kiss hadn't faded in her mind. It was supposed to... She was supposed to get her balance back and remember exactly why this was a bad idea, but riding next to this cowboy filled her head with memories of those strong arms around her, and the tickle of his day-old stubble against her face.

He was sweet, gruff, protective...

And her very temporary boss. She had to stop this. She had a baby on the way, and plans of her own to make. Plus, as a rancher Wilder needed to court her family's good opinion. And if they thought he was holding her back from being Amish again, he'd never get it!

When they got to the nearest pasture, they drove the cattle through the gate. The cows had spotted the nice, full feeders and headed directly for them. Then Wilder shut the gate and they parted ways.

Sue rode down to the stable and when she

dismounted, her legs stiff, she couldn't help but smile. Wilder was a good man...and she would have valued him as a friend, if she hadn't gone and kissed him. Would it be awkward now? Would he avoid her?

Her smile faded. He'd sent her back to make sure she didn't overdo it because of her pregnancy...right? Her fear now was that he'd sent her back because he was uncomfortable around her now. And that was exactly why a woman shouldn't get romantically involved with her boss. She rubbed her hands over her face.

"I'm such a fool," she murmured.

If Wilder was going to be awkward and distant, maybe it was for the best, she told herself. She didn't need any distractions from her own problems right now. She needed to make plans, and they couldn't be complicated by this handsome rancher.

Sue unsaddled the horse, brushed her down and set her up with some new feed as a reward for her hard work the last couple of days. There was still hay in the feeder out in the horse pasture, so the animals would be fine for now. Then she headed toward the house.

She was thinking about pizza when she

heard her mother's voice behind. She turned, and Linda bustled up to her.

"Hi," Sue said tiredly. "We just got back."

"*Yah, yah,* Jane spotted you coming over the hills," Linda said. "Your brother doesn't like you traveling with a man. It's not appropriate."

Sue sighed. "It wasn't travel. It was a cattle drive."

"Still…you're a beautiful woman. You might not appreciate how men will see you," her mother said.

No, Wilder had made it very clear how he saw her on that drive, and she felt a shiver run up her arms at the thought of it.

"I'm grown, *Mamm,*" she said softly. "I'm sorry if I upset Wollie, but this is my job. I'm just doing what I'm paid for."

Her mother didn't answer, and Sue unlocked the side door and she led the way inside. Her mother followed her in, and as she plugged her cell phone in the charger at the counter, she felt her mother's gaze on her. Was it the cell phone that was offensive? Or something else?

"*Mamm,* I need to order dinner. I'll just be a minute, okay?"

"*Yah*. Sure."

Sue grabbed the number off the fridge and dialed. She ordered a large pepperoni pizza, gave the address and hung up the phone. She was already hungry, and she grabbed an apple from the fruit bowl. Her mother stood by the counter, her eyes downcast.

"*Mamm?*" Sue said. "Is it so awful to see me working? I'm good at what I do. I saved Wilder's hide out there, you know."

"I don't mind you working, Sue." Linda raised her eyes to look Sue in the face. "I've always loved to see you doing what you love. You know that."

"Then why do you seem upset?" Sue asked. "Because a cattle drive is part of the job. It takes at least two cowhands at the very least to keep a herd moving. Wilder couldn't do that on his own—"

"It's not the cattle drive, either," her mother said. "It's—" Linda licked her lips. "Sue, why can't you just be part of the wedding?"

"Oh…" Sue smiled faintly. "*Mamm*, it's best this way. Let Wollie and Jerusha enjoy their day without me in the middle."

"You wouldn't be in the middle," her

mother countered. "You'd be a part of things. Jerusha is really hurt that you told her no."

"I tried to explain," Sue said. "I can talk to her again, but maybe you could tell her that I mean well, but—"

"Jane is refusing to be part of the wedding now, too!" Linda burst out, cutting her off. "She told her father that if Aunt Sue could say no, then so could she!"

"She didn't!" Sue gasped.

"She did! And if you saw how hurt your brother was, you'd feel terrible," Linda said. "It's already complicated. This is a second marriage, and Jane isn't warming up to Jerusha as well as we'd all hoped she would. It would be very helpful if you could be an example to Jane about how family puts personal feelings aside and celebrates a wedding."

"This isn't about a grudge, *Mamm*," Sue said, shaking her head. "Is that what you think? Do you think I'm so petty that I'd offend my brother and his fiancée over some old injustice? I don't want to draw attention away from them! I'm *Englisher* now, and you know that everyone will be talking when they see me."

"You'll be dressed Amish—" Her mother

blanched. "You will be dressed Amish, won't you, Sue?"

"It's not about the dress!" Sue was tired, and she had no arguments left to give.

"People will talk if they see you part of the wedding, and they'll talk if they know you refused to be part of it!" her mother said. "Why won't you just be a *newehocker* for Jerusha? People will talk anyway!"

"Because I'll be out to here by the time they get married!" Sue held a hand a few inches in front of her stomach. "That's why!"

Her mother stared at her. "What?"

"I'm pregnant," Sue said, tears misting her eyes. "I'm fifteen weeks along. I'm still not showing, but I'm pregnant."

"Oh, Sue…" Linda reached out and took her hand, her gaze moving down to Sue's middle. Then she pulled her into a hug. "I didn't know…"

"You weren't supposed to know," Sue said, squeezing her mother back, and then straightening. "No one was. I'm still trying to figure this out."

"Who is the father?" Linda asked.

"His name is Chaney, and he doesn't want anything to do with this baby," Sue said. "So there will be no wedding for me, and I will be an unmarried mother. I'm just telling you that outright in case you were hoping for something there."

"No, no..." Linda's eyes welled with tears. "But I wish you'd told me earlier."

"I needed to have more answers before I told you," Sue replied.

"About what?" Linda asked.

"About how I'm going to support this child," Sue said. "Because it isn't so easy when you're a single *mamm*."

"I know," Linda said. "But we'll sort it out. We're a family. This is what families do."

They sorted it out. They sat down around a table and they found solutions. And the one who had the problem would very likely be buried under all those good intentions. They wouldn't see staying *English* as a reasonable solution. They'd see this as proof that her rebellion hadn't worked out, and that it was time to come home where she belonged. It would be intense, and lengthy...

"But this is not what families do in the middle of a wedding," Sue said earnestly. "So you see why we need to keep this secret, don't you? Just until the wedding is over. Then we can talk about it as a family, but Wollie and Jerusha deserve to have their special day. And I don't want their memories of it to be about me! I didn't come back to do that to them!"

"But you came back for help?" her mother asked hopefully.

"I came back for a job!" Sue shook her head. "Maybe a little bit for help… *Mamm*, I'm not coming back ashamed of myself. I'm not going to admit I'm wrong about living my life *English*. I didn't want to start a family quite this way, but I'm so happy to be having a baby."

"Have I judged you?" Linda asked, hurt.

"You will, though!" Sue rubbed her hands over her face. "I didn't come back for help the way you're thinking."

"Then why are you here?" her mother demanded. "To work a job for a few weeks with Wilder Westhouse? That's all?"

No, it wasn't all. But she could see now how impossible it all was.

"I just missed you," Sue said, and her chin trembled. "And I might need your help, but I'm not coming back contrite and ready to be Amish."

"I miss you, too, my dear," Linda said earnestly. "But look around you. You're pregnant, and you can't rely on the father. Your brother is getting married, and you've offended both him and his fiancée. Your niece is trying to be exactly like you, and you're still dead set against coming back to the life we raised you for. That might be fine for you—you made your choice, which is everyone's right— but what about Jane? Do you want her to do things your way? And because the father of this child isn't being a man, you're working a physical job in your condition, and your life doesn't have to be this hard. I'm not asking you to be ashamed of anything, but I am asking you to see reason. This is not a life that has worked out!"

Sue's breath caught in her chest. If it were some sort of moral judgment, she might be able to summon up some indignation to shield herself from it. It was her mother's plain-spoken observation that hit hardest because she knew it to be true. Sue's life had not worked out the way she hoped.

But somehow, out there in the fields with Wilder, she hadn't felt like a failure...

"Whether it's worked out or not," Sue said, blinking back tears, "it's still the life I've chosen. This is why I didn't want to tell anyone yet. I don't know what I'm going to do, but I won't be pushed into anything."

"I'm not pushing you," Linda said. "I'm just—"

"Mamm!" Sue didn't have the strength. "I'm really tired. I'm hungry. And I don't have any good answers for you right now. Let me figure this out. Okay?"

Her mother pressed her lips together, but her eyes were filled with all her unsaid arguments. She didn't need to say them, because Sue knew everything her mother would say.

"I don't think you can keep this secret any longer, Sue," Linda said. "It's better to at least tell the family what is going on, or they'll be more upset. Besides, we need to find a solution… maybe bring you home."

But coming home wasn't as simple as her mother might think.

IT FELT GOOD to have the cattle home again, and when Wilder was finished with the herd and the injured animals in the barn, he brought his mount back to the stable where he had a bit more work to finish up. It had been a long day, and his muscles ached in that satisfied way that told him he'd given his best. It had been a good cattle drive, and now he could start looking forward to the winter work.

Wilder's gaze kept moving toward the house, and he tried to pull his attention back to the work at hand. He was tempted to check in on Sue, just to make sure she was okay, but he could see a bobbing Amish *kapp* on the back of Linda Schmidt's head through the window, so if there were any problem, Linda would let him know right quick.

Besides, Sue had family issues to sort out that didn't involve him. They *shouldn't* involve him…even if something deep inside kept tugging him toward this woman anyway.

"Stop it," he muttered to himself.

Sue might be the amazing woman he was incredibly attracted to, but she was also complicated…and she was his employee. A good man didn't just see where it went with a woman who had as many responsibilities as Sue did. That was selfish, even if she had started to touch a vulnerable place in his own heart.

He checked his cell phone, and now that he was in range, he saw that he'd missed some texts from Conrad. He was asking about the cattle drive.

It went well, Wilder texted back. Sue is really something.

Oh? Conrad replied.

She's good with the herd, Wilder typed, and he pocketed his phone again.

If hiring Sue was bad for their standing in the community around here, dating her would be even worse. He'd overstepped with that kiss. He knew it.

Wilder unsaddled his horse and put him into the stall next to Mona. As he expected, Mona was already brushed down. He headed back out of the stable to go fetch another bale of hay from outside, when he spotted Jane standing next to the corral fence. She beamed at him.

"Hi, Wilder."

"Hi, Jane," he said. "How are you doing?"

"I'm good. I came to look at the horses. Do you think you'll have another baby horse soon?"

"No, not in the near future, kiddo," Wilder said.

"Hmm. That's too bad." She sighed. "Did you have fun on your trip?"

"It wasn't a trip," he said. "We went on a cattle drive to bring the cows back for winter."

"Oh."

"Your father does that, too."

"*Yah*, and he brings my uncle Jethro with him, and my uncle Zeke, and my uncle Vern. They all go."

Wollie had a smaller ranch, but a whole lot more support from his family. Wilder envied him that.

"Stay on this side of the fence," Wilder said. "I don't want you to get hurt."

"I know," Jane said. "I'm not little anymore."

Not little. She was six, not forty! Wilder chuckled. "Good. I'm glad."

Wilder headed around the side of the stable, and Jane trailed along after him.

"I really love my aunt Sue," Jane said, leaning against the side of the stable while Wilder grabbed a bale of hay by the twine and tugged it forward, off the pile. "I'm going to be like her when I grow up. I'm going to be a cowgirl."

"Yeah?" Wilder smiled. "I think your aunt Sue is pretty special, too."

"Did you know Aunt Sue won't be in my *daet*'s wedding?" Jane asked. "I'm not going to be, either. You can say no! I didn't know that."

"Oh…" Wilder grimaced. "Jane, your dad will be so sad, though."

"Then he shouldn't get married," Jane retorted.

"But he really wants to get married." He looked down at her. "Don't you want a new mom?"

"No."

Wilder shrugged. "Okay." How was he supposed to argue with that? "Did you tell your dad that you don't want to be in the wedding yet?"

"*Yah*," she said. "And he said that Aunt Sue is selfish and that she's always been selfish, and that's why she left. And then *Mammi* said that wasn't true, and my *daet* said it was, and my *mammi* said that Aunt Sue had to find her own path, and my *daet* said that she could have any path she wanted but she could also cooperate with family functions, and *Mammi* said that Aunt Sue might have other reasons we don't know about, and *daet* said her reasons would be dumb."

It all seemed to come out in a rush, and Jane was breathless by the end of her recitation.

"And then *Daet* and *Mammi* noticed I was there, and they said that family is very important and that I should never break their hearts like Aunt Sue did."

Wow—now that was a glimpse into an Amish family squabble.

"Don't you think not being in your father's wedding will break his heart?" Wilder asked.

Jane considered this for a moment. "It's better than running away. I'm going to bring my suitcase back."

Wilder shouldn't get involved in this. It wasn't his business, but somehow this one little girl had wormed her way into life here on the Westhouse ranch.

"So your dad is really mad at Aunt Sue, huh?" Wilder asked. Whatever. She was already chattering. He was just…guiding the flow a bit.

"*Yah*, he is," Jane said. "I've never seen him this mad before. He says me and Aunt Sue need to apologize to Jerusha, but I'm not going to."

"You won't?" Wilder gave her a look of

mock surprise. "But it would be the nice thing to do. Poor Jerusha."

"Me and Aunt Sue aren't wrong," Jane replied. "We think my *daet* doesn't need a wife."

"Is that really what Aunt Sue thinks?" Wilder asked. "I don't think she thinks that."

"It's what I think," Jane replied.

Wilder had a new appreciation for Sue's desire to keep her secret. Sue would sort something out with her niece, he was sure, but Jane looked bound and determined to skip this wedding if she could find a way out of it.

The side door opened and Linda stepped out. She had Jane's suitcase in one hand, and she held it out to the little girl. Jane went over and accepted the suitcase mutely. Linda had wanted Jane to fetch the suitcase herself, but it looked like she'd changed her mind.

"Hi, Linda," Wilder said. "How are things?"

The older woman looked at him, her face wan, and she seemed to be trying to decide on something. "Well, life stays interesting, doesn't it?" Then she turned to Jane and said something in Pennsylvania Dutch.

"I have to go home now," Jane said to Wilder.

"I'm glad you're taking your suitcase home," Wilder said.

"Yah," Jane said. "I have a better plan. Bye."

"Bye, Jane."

Jane caught her grandmother's hand, and they started off across the yard when Linda called over her shoulder, "Wilder?"

"Yes?" He squinted at her in the sunlight.

"She needs at least eight hours sleep a night, regular meals and she should not be lifting anything heavy. Anything!"

Ah. So Linda now knew. He met her gaze, and he saw the worry in her lined face. He didn't blame her. She was doing what any good mother would do—she was looking out for her daughter when she needed support the most, and it was reassuring to see it.

"I fully agree, Linda," he replied. "I'm not letting her overdo it. I promise."

She nodded curtly and then started walking in the direction of the neighboring farm, Jane carrying her suitcase solemnly next to her. Linda didn't turn back again, and Wilder headed inside.

Sue stood with her back to him, facing a row of cupboards, and when he closed to door, she didn't turn, but she did hitch her shoulders and seemed to be wiping her face.

"Sue?" he said softly.

"I'm fine," she said, her voice tight, and when she turned, he saw her eyes were red.

"You don't look fine to me," he said. "What happened?"

"So much for me keeping my pregnancy a secret," she said with a sigh. "I told my mother. It was easier than making up some other phenomenal reason for not being a part of the wedding."

"Okay…" He wasn't sure what to say, so he crossed the kitchen to stand near her. He moved a strand of hair off her cheek with one finger, and she looked up at him with fresh tears misting her eyes.

"And she's upset about it?" he asked hesitantly.

"No, not about the baby," she said. "More about my life choices."

"Hey, you're a good person," he said with a frown. "I don't know what she said to you, but—you're good. Okay?"

"I know." She wiped at her cheeks again, and a fresh tear rolled down. He wanted to help somehow, to fix this, to make her feel better, but he didn't have any words to do it. He couldn't bad-mouth her family, even though he was right ticked off at Linda for making Sue feel like this. He wasn't a man of many words normally. He had a hard time putting his feelings into coherent sentences when it mattered most, but he could do something.

"Come here," he said gruffly, pulling her into his arms. She dropped her head onto his shoulder as he held her close, and he could feel the hot stain of tears soaking into his shirt. She let out a shuddering sigh. "This baby is going to have a wonderful mother. I know that for a fact."

She sniffled. "Thanks."

"I mean it."

He didn't loosen his hold on her, either, and she settled against him. This felt right—being able to wrap his arms around her and attempt to hold her together. Miles over the line of professional or appropriate behavior, but whatever. Even if her family was letting her down, Wilder wouldn't.

Sue wrapped her arms around his waist, and Wilder rested his chin on the top of her hair.

"They aren't used to people having babies before a wedding, are they?" he murmured.

"Not so much," she said. "My mother is disappointed. Not in the pregnancy, exactly, but in not being prepared for it, I guess. She expected better planning from me."

"Well, I've done stuff that has left my family pretty upset, too," he said. "Trust me, they get over it. Life goes on. This will pass."

"I know…" She sighed. "But Jane is saying she won't be part of the wedding either, and apparently that's on me."

"You're her excuse," he said. "I talked to her outside. She's using you as her scapegoat here. She doesn't want her father to get married, and she's using everything in her arsenal to stop it."

"You talked to her?" Sue pulled back and looked up at him. "What's she saying?"

Wilder shrugged. "She doesn't want her father to get married, and she's claiming that you're on her side."

"I want Wollie to get married!" she said.

"I don't know what to say," Wilder said. "She's fibbing. Just a tiny bit. This is not shocking behavior in a six-year-old."

"Right…" She smiled shakily. "Thank you, Wilder. You make this all feel…less insane."

"Good." He smiled in satisfaction. "I'm glad. That's what I was going for."

She wiped her cheeks again, and then brushed the top of his shoulder where her tears had soaked into his shirt.

"Sorry," she murmured.

"Don't worry about it," he said, and he caught her hand and twined his fingers through hers. "I'm strong enough for this. I mean it. You can stop apologizing. You don't need to."

Whatever she was going through, she didn't have to do it alone. He'd be here for her anytime she needed him. And it wouldn't even be a choice on his part, because there was something about her that just kept tugging him back. If the whole world let Sue down, he'd be the man who stood firm for her.

CHAPTER TWELVE

THAT NIGHT, Wilder slept deeply, and it took a full five minutes of a blaring alarm to wake him up at 4:45 a.m. for chores. He'd even allowed himself an extra half hour to sleep in after the cattle drive, and when he swung his legs over the edge of his bed, he heard the sound of movement in the kitchen.

Sue was up… Somehow he hated having slept in longer than she had.

Wilder went to the bathroom to clean himself up and shave, and when he ambled into the kitchen, he spotted Sue leaning against the counter, a mug between her hands. The kitchen smelled like coffee.

"Morning," she murmured. Sue's figure was a little fuller this morning. It was hard to put his finger on it. If he didn't know about her pregnancy, he wouldn't jump to that conclusion, exactly, but she was rounder. And her belly was softer. He liked it.

"Morning," he said. "Is that decaf in the pot?"

"Nope," she said. "Just in my mug. I made more for you."

"You're the best," he said, and he shot her a smile. She smiled back.

"I know," she said jokingly. "But I figured I owed you after yesterday. I was a bit of a wreck."

"No, you weren't," he said, and he ran a finger down her arm before he pulled a mug from the cupboard. "You're human. There's no shame in that."

"I was a weepy human," she said. "I normally try to hold myself together better."

"Meh." He filled his mug with steaming coffee. "That's forgivable."

She nudged his arm with her elbow. "You're just being nice."

"Why shouldn't I be nice?" he asked. "Learn to expect that from men, Sue. This is your due."

Her cheeks pinkened, and he wondered if he'd gone too far in his advice giving. But he meant it—she could expect a whole lot and get it. At least from him.

"Sleeping on a mattress was heavenly," Sue

said. "Being on a cattle drive always makes me feel so pampered once I get back to civilization."

"Yeah, me, too," he said.

"I wonder if that was my last one." She took another sip from her mug.

"It doesn't have to be," he said. "What if you came with me next year as my guest?"

"How would that be different?" she asked, her gaze flickering toward him.

"I'd feel less guilty about kissing you," he said.

She laughed softly. "Don't tempt me, Wilder."

She lowered her mug, and he couldn't help but look at those pink lips. It was taking all of his willpower to hold himself back from kissing her again.

"Why not?" he asked. "This doesn't have to be over, Sue. If you were comfortable leaving the baby with your mom for a night, you could come along. Ride herd with me."

"We'll see." But there was a smile on her lips now, and he liked that.

He drained his coffee and removed his phone from his pocket to check the time. They'd better get out there and get the first round of chores done before they came back for breakfast.

"I think after chores this morning I'll go face things," Sue said, putting her mug into the sink. "The secret is obviously out, so it'll be better to just sit down with my family and talk."

"It's easier than dreading it for weeks," he told her.

"I agree," she said. "It's time to take control of my life."

Wilder drained his own cup and put it into the sink next to hers. Good for Sue—she deserved to call the shots. And here was hoping she'd sort this all out with her family. If there was one thing he knew about his neighbors, it was that they loved Sue. They'd help her any way they could.

So would he. Even if he had no further claim to her than being her brother's neighbor. Sue deserved better than she'd gotten so far. In that, he and the Schmidts were entirely united.

AFTER CHORES AND BREAKFAST, Wilder did a few dishes while Sue crossed the scrub grass to the Schmidt farm. He cleaned up the kitchen, washed the counters and added a few items to the weekly grocery list. After about half an hour of setting his own home in order, there was the rumble of a truck's engine outside.

Wilder went to the side door. A battered gray pickup pulled up next to his vehicle and a man hopped out. He wore jeans and a grubby-looking trucker's cap, and he stopped and looked at Sue's Chevy. He walked toward it, shaded his eyes and looked in the vehicle's window.

This would be Chaney. The man was shorter than he'd imagined.

"Can I help you?" Wilder said.

The man slapped the side of Sue's vehicle and then ambled in Wilder's direction—a little too laid-back for manners. He was being cocky.

"Yeah, I'm looking for my girlfriend," the man said.

"Who's your girlfriend?" Wilder asked, just to be difficult.

"Sue Schmidt. She here?"

"Not right now," Wilder replied.

"Maybe I'll come inside and wait for her,

then. Her truck's here. She can't be far. The name's Chaney."

"Wilder." He ignored the proffered hand. "Are you here to bring back her things?"

Chaney tucked his hand into his pocket, and for a moment, they eyed each other. "Is she here or not?"

"She's not here, as I just said," Wilder repeated.

"Look, man," Chaney said. "I don't know what she said about me, but I'm not some monster. We've been living together for six months, and we had a fight. It happens to the best of us. She overreacted, as she can do sometimes. It's forgivable. But I'm doing the right thing, and I'm here to bring her home. I'm being decent here."

"Apparently, you didn't let her take her things," Wilder said.

"I'm trying to make up with her," Chaney said. "She can have her stuff if she wants to come pick it up. I'm not going to steal her things, but I'm going to talk to her. This is a private matter."

Wilder didn't answer. Sue had been clear about where she stood with this guy, but sometimes people changed their minds. Who was he to get in the middle—even if every atom of his being screamed to do so?

"Just tell her I came by," Chaney said. "Tell her… I don't know… Tell her that I'm sorry if I mouthed off too much, and that I've got to take that job in Utah. She'll know what I'm talking about. I want her to come with me, but I don't have a lot of time."

"I'll let her know when she gets back," Wilder said.

"She's not taking my calls," Chaney added. "She probably blocked my number. So get her to call me. It's important. I can't just leave without talking to her."

"Sure," Wilder said. This was Sue's life and her choice to make. But this was also the man who'd told her he wanted nothing to do with the child he'd fathered. "I can promise you that I'll pass along the message. But if she doesn't want to talk to you, she won't. And I don't want to see you on my property again unless she asks you to come."

Chaney scowled at him, then his annoyed gaze slid back toward Sue's vehicle. "I paid for her new brakes on that old piece of junk. She owes me for that, too."

There it was—the man's true nature.

Wilder had known it would surface here eventually.

"I'll mention it." Wilder crossed his arms and leaned in exaggerated nonchalance against the door frame. "Take care now."

Chaney got back into his pickup and rolled down the window. He tapped his hands on the top of the steering wheel in a drumming rhythm, then shook his head.

"I'm going to wait for her," Chaney said. "I don't believe you'll tell her I was here."

Wilder eyed the man for a moment. Whatever. Let him sit there for a few hours if he wanted to. Wilder went back inside and slammed the door shut behind him. The message would get passed along if Chaney ended up leaving before Sue returned. He was a man of his word, even if the message would come with Wilder's two cents about how much this Chaney guy was worth.

SUE LEANED AGAINST the fence next to Wollie. They were facing the house, and she could see Linda passing by the kitchen window from time to time, bustling about doing some baking. Linda already knew the state of things, and they were trying to keep the secret from

Jane still, so she and her brother had come outside.

The morning sun was low, and frost sparkled on the grass in the shade where it hadn't been burned off yet. Sue rubbed her hands together to warm them, and Wollie stood there, motionless.

"So that was why you told Jerusha you wouldn't be part of the wedding?" Wollie said.

"That was why," she replied. "I'm really happy for you two. I think it's great that you're getting married again, Wollie. I really do."

Her brother nodded a couple of times. "And you won't get married to the father?" His voice was low.

"I don't expect you to agree with me, Wollie, but no. I'm not marrying the father. He's not a good guy."

"Then why were you living with him?" Wollie asked, shaking his head.

"Because I didn't know that at first!"

"If you were living Amish, you wouldn't have made such a mistake," he said.

"I might have made a worse one," she said. "I might be married to the wrong man with no way out! Look, we can argue all day about which mistake would be worse, but I'm not here for that. I'm having a baby, and the father has chosen not to be in the picture."

"Okay," her brother said, and he cast her an agonized look. "It's just that...you're my little sister."

"I'm all grown up," she said quietly. "I can take care of myself."

They were silent for a moment, and the sound of clucking hens from the chicken coop surfed the cold air toward them.

"I'm not sure this solves the problem with Jane refusing to be part of the wedding, though," Wollie said.

"Probably not," Sue agreed.

"I want to be the one who explains this to Jane," he said somberly. "It's...very delicate. I'll have to tell her carefully."

"Although she'll figure out the truth eventually. I mean, I'll have a baby, after all."

Wollie didn't smile at her humor. "She wants to be just like you, Sue."

"I can talk to her about it," Sue suggested. "Wollie, I do want to help. I'm not here to cause trouble for you. Not on purpose, at least."

"I'll explain it to her tonight," Wollie replied. "But I will explain it with our Amish morals. If you want to talk to Jane about being part of the wedding, maybe come by tomorrow and do it then."

"Okay," she said. "I'll do that."

Wollie sighed. "But what about you? What will you do now that there's a baby coming? Long term, I mean."

She met her brother's gaze, then shook her head. "I don't know."

"Really?" He rubbed his hands over his face. "Even now, you won't come home?"

"Come home to where?" she demanded.

"You could stay with us," he said.

"You're getting married, and you and Jerusha will need space to yourselves. I'm not a teenager, I'm a grown woman. So forgive me for not wanting to stay with the newlyweds, Wollie," she said with a sigh.

"Then there's Uncle Samuel's family," he said. "I'm sure they'd make room for you. You could share a room with *Mamm*. Or there's Ben and Lydia Schafer. Their daughter is disabled and needs a companion. They've been paying an *Englisher* to come help her with her exercises, but I'm sure they'd be glad to have someone Amish."

But Sue wasn't Amish, and she met her brother's gaze, pressing her lips together. He seemed to come to the same conclusion because he sighed.

"*Yah*, you'd have to come back to living Amish," Wollie said. "Then we could figure something out. Maybe you could help take care of someone's *kinner* while taking care of your own baby. There are solutions, but they would involve living Amish again."

"I'm not Amish," she said softly. "You know that."

"You were *born* Amish," he retorted. "There's no undoing where you came from. You might not be so convinced that our way of life is the best way to live, but you're Amish, Sue. As cute as it is that you think you're not."

Her anger spiked, but she shut her mouth. She and her brother had always butted heads over these things, and her pregnancy wasn't going to broaden his views at all.

"Wollie—"

"What other options do you have?" he

asked. "What do *Englisher* women do if they have a child on their own?"

"They have families, too," she said. "And they work jobs, and they might get a family member to take care of their child while they work, or they might get some government financial help. But they find ways."

"Here's the way I see it," her brother said, softening his voice. "You could get a job and do it the *English* way. It would be hard. You wouldn't be passing your child into our own *mamm*'s arms, and that would make it harder. Or you could come home and do it our way. You'd be able to raise your own baby. You could find a job where your child could be with you, or you could let your family take care of you. But it would be easier, and you wouldn't be separated from your baby."

Heaven help her, but it did sound tempting. There was a certain comfort in the Amish ways that prioritized a mother being with her children no matter what. She dropped her gaze, and her brother seemed to sense she was caving in, because he put a hand on her shoulder and added, "I know we've had our disagreements about our way of life, but practically speaking, this makes sense. You must see that."

And she could. That was part of the problem. Coming home made sense, and working as a ranch hand, which was the job she loved most in the world, wasn't going to be possible with a baby in her arms. Nor did it pay enough to cover childcare. It was either go back to town and get a job, pay for day care, and do her best…or come home.

Riding the range wasn't going to be a possibility in either case. She could come do a cattle drive with Wilder, like he'd suggested, but the day in, day out ranch hand work? That would be a thing of the past. It now came down to what was the best situation in which to raise her child—Amish or *English*? Could she swallow her pride and the last fifteen years, and return to a *kapp* and apron? *Could* she?

"I'm still thinking things through," she said. "But thank you for understanding my predicament here. Please explain to Jerusha for me. I'm sorry I hurt her feelings. I didn't mean to. I just didn't want to be the shocking sister-in-law who stole the attention."

"I'll explain," Wollie said. "And we'll talk again, *yah*? We'll find a solution."

"Don't worry about my solutions until you're finished with your wedding," Sue said. "I've got a paying job, and my doctor assures me I can work it."

"I'll talk to Wilder about making sure he doesn't ask too much of you," Wollie said. "I mentioned it before, but I didn't know about the baby then."

"I've already taken care of it," she said. "He knows about the baby, and he's being obnoxiously accommodating about the whole thing. You'd approve, I promise."

"Hmm." Wollie sighed. "Then he'll be careful. I'm sure of that. But you be careful, too, Sue. None of us are quite as tough as we think we are."

"I'll be careful," she said seriously. "I mean it. I want this baby to be as healthy as possible. Okay?"

"Yah." Wollie cast her a wry smile. "It's the best I'll get from you, isn't it?"

"It really is." She shot her brother a grin. "I'd better get back and help out with chores. It's what he's paying me for."

She saw her brother's expression darken

at the mention of her job, but he didn't say anything more. Sue gave her brother a nod in farewell, and headed back across the yard in the direction of the Westhouse ranch.

"Aunt Sue!" Jane called from the side door of the house. "Aunt Sue?"

Sue turned to see Jane standing in her little pink dress, her hair ruffling in the chilly wind.

"*Yah*, Jane?" Sue called.

"Are you going to do more work now?" Jane asked.

"*Yah*, that's where I'm going," she replied.

"Can I come, too?" Jane pleaded. "I'll be good! I'll help!"

Sue glanced over her shoulder in her brother's direction and saw him chewing the inside of his cheek irritably.

"No, Jane," Sue said. "Not this time. You'd better help your *daet*."

Sue turned back toward the Westhouse property. No, nothing about going home again would be simple, not even her relationship with her young niece. And while Sue could admit that her choice in boyfriend had been a mistake, her child was not. This baby was her miracle, and she'd never apologize for it.

She thought over her options. If only there was one solution that could stand out among the rest, but there wasn't. Life wasn't that simple. As she approached the ranch house, she spotted Chaney's truck, and her stomach lurched.

So Chaney had come, after all. She'd better face him now and keep this as civilized as possible. Sue angled her steps around the stable and toward the drive where his vehicle was parked. Chaney must have spotted her, because he got out of the truck and slammed the door, waiting for her to get to him.

"Hello," she said, stopping a couple of yards from him. "Becky said you might come by. Did you bring my things?"

"No…" He shrugged. "I'm here to take you home. Are you still mad at me?"

"No," she said. "I'm not mad. But we are over. I don't think we can salvage this."

Chaney sighed. "Look, I'm sorry, okay? I was probably a little harsh. I probably shouldn't have yelled at you when you told me you were pregnant."

"I'm not going to Utah," she said. "And I'm going to have the baby."

"Look… You don't have to," Chaney said.

"I know in Amish-land here, there aren't too many options, but for the rest of us there are choices. What about *me*? I don't want to be a father. Doesn't my choice factor in at all?"

Sue eyed the man for a moment, waiting for some sort of emotion to rise inside of her, but she felt nothing. What about him, indeed...

"You don't have to be a father, Chaney," Sue said finally. "I don't need you."

Chaney shook his head. "You've got a choice—have the baby and figure it out by yourself, because I'm not contributing to a kid I didn't choose to have. Or, get an abortion and come with me. There's no reason anything has to change between us. We were happy."

"*You* were happy," she retorted. "I'm not going anywhere with you. I meant it when I broke up with you. It's over. Done. If you don't want to be in your child's life, I won't chase you down."

Chaney brightened slightly at that. The sound of the screen door drew Sue's attention, and she looked back to see Wilder come outside.

"You okay?" Wilder asked.

"I'm fine," she said.

"This your new boyfriend?" Chaney asked irritably.

"No, this is my boss," she replied curtly. "And I'd better get back to work."

"You're being really immature," Chaney said.

She turned back and looked at him. How many times had he said something like that to her? How many times had she stood up for herself only for him to call her the problem?

"Go to Utah," she said.

"Are you going to take my calls?" Chaney's voice took on a more petulant tone.

"Are you going to pay child support?" she snapped back.

Chaney muttered something under his breath and hauled open his truck door.

"There's a whole wide world out there, Sue," he said as he got back into his vehicle and started the engine. "You don't have to live like this."

She looked around herself at the trees starting to turn yellow, the frosted grass in the shade, the melted frost that shone in large drops in the sunlight, the golden glow of a fall day just beginning. She had no idea what Chaney saw, but she knew what she longed for. And his old way of riling her up seemed to be working again, because her chest felt tight, and her pulse raced. But she wouldn't argue with him.

Not this time.

"I will call you when the baby is born," she said, trying to keep her voice even. "If you want to know your child, I welcome it."

Chaney didn't answer, and he pulled around and headed up the drive, his tires spinning gravel.

Sue's heart was pounding hard, but she felt good. She wasn't taking that man's garbage for a second longer. She turned, and she saw Wilder standing there with his thumbs in his belt loops and a grin on his face.

"Nice!" Wilder said.

"Yeah?" She felt the adrenaline start to fade then.

"You were fantastic," Wilder said, and he held out his hand. She gratefully took it—something to ground her pounding heart.

"Are you going to take my calls?" He was mimicking Chaney now with a whiny voice. "And you were all, are you going to pay child support?" Wilder barked out a laugh, and she found the tears that had been welling up inside her start to abate.

"I don't know what I saw in him," Sue said.

"At least you see the real guy now," Wilder said, and then his pace slowed, and he looked down at Sue. "Are you okay?"

She nodded, and he came to a stop. "Are you sure? That was probably pretty intense."

Sue thought for a moment, feeling around inside herself, wondering if she wanted to have a good, cathartic cry, or maybe go scream into a field somewhere…but no. With her hand in his strong grip, she didn't need any of that.

"It was pretty intense," she said. "But I said what I wanted to say. I'm good."

Wilder bent down and pressed a soft kiss against her forehead. He did it so casually, as if they always kissed each other, and it felt good.

"You're impressive, Sue," he said, his voice low and deep. "Remember that."

If only she could live her life seeing herself through Wilder's eyes. Because when she was with him, she felt like the superhero he seemed to see.

CHAPTER THIRTEEN

THE NEXT MORNING, Wilder squatted next to the cow with the snakebite to examine her leg. He looked over at Sue who was mixing up formula for the calf, and when she turned, he saw something he hadn't noticed yet—her stomach had grown.

It was like it had happened overnight. Where her belly had been mostly flat, it now protruded a little bit. She looked at him and he quickly dropped his gaze. That would be rude to mention…but he'd noticed, and he felt a strange rush of protectiveness for her. He put his attention back on the cow in front of him, and as he took off the last of the bandage, he inspected the healing leg.

Sue came over and bent down to look, too. She smelled good—something fruity and floral. He liked it.

"It looks good," Sue said. He glanced back at her.

"I think she can go back to the herd now," he said. "There's no more swelling, and the wound is healed over...well, except for that scabbed part."

"Yeah, I agree. You could send her out and keep an eye on it. If she knocks it and it starts to bleed again, you could bring her back, but I think it's healed well, myself."

He appreciated her input—she'd spent a good amount of time working with a vet, after all. Wilder tossed the bandage to the side, then stood up. Sue's hand fluttered over her stomach. He smiled hesitantly.

"Is the baby moving?" he asked.

She nodded, and looked down at her stomach. "*Yah*, a little bit. Kind of like a tickle."

She was pretty in a different way this morning, too. Her cheeks were a little pinker, and there was a sparkle in her eye that he hadn't seen before. Was it just the relief of having dealt with her ex yesterday, or something more?

"I guess I'd better get this cow out to the herd," he said, heading over to the big sliding door.

"I'll finish up the last stall," Sue called over

her shoulder as she headed in the opposite direction.

For the next few minutes, Wilder drove the cow out of the warm building, across the barnyard, and over to the field where the rest of the herd was grazing. He gave her some fresh hay to reward her once they were outside, and lured her with more hay over by the gate that led into the pasture. He tossed the last of the hay over the fence, and the cow plodded happily after it. He shut the gate and leaned on it, his mind moving back to the woman in the barn.

She was vulnerable. That was what stood out to him the most. She was smart, impressive, talented, gorgeous...and she needed support. He remembered his divorce. There hadn't been children to complicate things, but even when he and Misty both knew they were better off apart, that final goodbye had been incredibly hard. So he could sympathize here...

Was Sue really okay with her breakup, or was she just keeping up appearances for the sake of her pride?

Wilder headed back into the barn and heaved the sliding door shut after him. The calf was drinking formula from a bucket, and he could hear the rustle of hay over by the bales.

"Sue?" he called.

"Over here." Her voice was muffled.

The hay bales were piled high where he'd left them yesterday morning, and he stopped short, watching as Sue attempted to squeeze sideways between two piles. She inhaled deeply, straightened her spine and tried to squeeze through, but she wasn't going to make it. He could see that from here.

"What are you doing?" he asked.

She looked back at him. "I left my pitch-fork back here." She frowned. "I fit through here yesterday. And today, I can't get past."

She sucked in her breath, tried again, and her cheeks flushed a darker pink. He couldn't help but chuckle.

Sue looked down at her stomach. "Is it just me, or...have I gotten...bigger?"

"This is the only time I'll admit to this with a woman, but yeah," he said with a low laugh. "You look a lot more pregnant today."

"I thought so, but I wasn't sure if I was just imagining it." She stepped away from the bales. "Can you grab me my pitchfork, please?"

"Sure." He eased through the bales and grabbed the handle, then came back out.

She accepted it with a rueful smile. "This is going to be hard to get used to. In my head, I look a certain way, but apparently, that's changing."

"You look beautiful," he said.

"Thanks… I feel…lumpy." She laughed. "For lack of a better word."

"Pregnancy looks good on you."

"Oh…thank you." She ran her hand down her stomach again. "Wow…it feels more real. This is going to be harder to hide now, isn't it? I guess it's a good thing I told my family."

"That would have been a surprise, all right," he agreed.

She plucked at her shirt and stood up straighter. "Can I hide it still?"

Her softened belly still poked out and he chuckled. "Nope. No more hiding."

She picked up her pitchfork and headed toward the newly vacated stall. She had a wheelbarrow waiting. Wilder grabbed a fresh bale by the twine and followed her.

"Things are going to be different now," she said.

"You mean with family?" he asked.

"Oh, yeah, with them, too," she said, then she laughed. "No, I mean with work. What I can do without my stomach getting in the way...how much I can ride, risks I can take. I'm well and truly pregnant now, aren't I?"

"You were well and truly pregnant before," he said, "but I get what you mean. I guess you'll have to slow down a bit."

"My doctor says I'll tire out more easily, and I shouldn't push past that when it happens," she said.

Sue started to muck out the stall, and a couple of yards away, the calf knocked over his empty bucket. Wilder grabbed the bucket before it could leak the last little bit of formula onto the concrete floor and rinsed it in the sink.

"I think that's smart," he called back to Sue.

"This is the life I love, though," she said, voice raised so he could hear her as she mucked. "The ranch work, the cattle, the riding... This is what I left the Amish world for, you know."

"And the other freedoms...right?" he said.

"*This* was the freedom I wanted," she said. "To be a cattlewoman."

Wilder paused, surprised. "Driving cars, watching TV, flicking on a light?"

"Don't get me wrong. I don't want to give those up, either," she said. "But I don't want to just go back to town, get a job in a grocery store, and…live my life. I got a taste of the work I really love, but having a baby in the mix isn't going to be easy."

"I wish I could keep you on after my brother gets back," he said. "We don't make enough profit yet to pay a full-time salary, though."

She smiled faintly. "You don't have to worry about me. I'll be fine. I shouldn't be feeling sorry for myself. The fact is, when I'm a mother, everything will be different. It won't be all about what I want anymore—it will be about my child. And that's the way it's supposed to be."

"What if you stayed here with me?" he asked.

Sue straightened. "A baby taking over your home, waking you up when it cried at night? No, Wilder. You're sweet, but you have no idea what you're offering. Besides, you've got a brother and sister-in-law living here, too. I'm sure they'd have opinions about your offer."

Wilder nodded. "True."

"Besides, you don't want to get in the middle of this with my brother and the Amish community."

"Your brother is a friend," he said. "And the men around here respect me."

"I'm one of their own," she said seriously. "And the *right way*—" she used air quotes "—is for me to go back. I'm still deciding how I'm going to sort all this out, but they have a very clear view of what I should be doing. Do you know about shunning?"

"I thought you weren't baptized so they couldn't shun you," he said, his heartbeat speeding up. "I thought—"

"Listen…" She cast him a gentle smile. "The concept of shunning isn't supposed to be cruel. I know that it sounds awful, but the idea is that when someone goes wrong and starts doing something really self-destructive, they use some tough love to bring them back to safe territory. If you won't listen to reason, they'll simply stop talking to you. The person who's gone down that dangerous path is supposed to get a wake-up call and come back again. I'm trying to think of an *English* equivalent…"

"Interventions for an addict?" he asked.

"Yeah, something like that," she said. "The addict is going to ruin their life, and the friends and family step in and say if you don't get help, we won't be helping you. You can't come over, because you steal from us. You can't come visit the kids because you leave them too upset. That kind of thing."

"But you aren't hurting anyone. You're working a job," he said.

"The Amish community thinks that by pulling away to live an *English* life, I'm on a path to self-destruction," she said. "You can argue otherwise and I will probably agree with you, but it won't change their minds. Leaving the faith is serious enough that if I had been baptized, I'd be shunned. My family wouldn't be speaking to me. My niece wouldn't be allowed to get to know me. I'd be like a stranger to them unless I was in miserable need of help, at which time they could provide me with food and shelter, but not conversation and relationships. Just the basics."

"Wow…" he murmured.

"Exactly. The point is, these nice Amish men who respect you now will not respect you if they think you're getting in the way of my family bringing me home. There is only one right end to this for them. Don't fool yourself. My brother is anticipating bringing me back to the Amish life. So is my *mamm*."

Even Wilder knew that was the Schmidt family hope, but he hadn't realized how far this would spread. The community would turn against him, too? Was he really meddling in Amish business by wanting to help Sue? That hardly seemed fair. She was her own woman, and he could help whoever he wanted to help.

"And when they realize you won't go back?" he asked.

Sue let out a slow breath, and ran her hand tenderly over her belly. "I'm still thinking about it."

"So you might go back—all the way." His heart hammered to a stop. He hadn't seriously considered that. This Sue—free, happy, impressive—might not have the luxury of continuing on this way.

"It might be the best choice for my child. I don't know."

"Right," he said. "I understand. You have to think it through and be sure of what you want."

"Yeah." She looked up and met his gaze hopefully. "You get it, don't you?"

"Of course." But he couldn't say he liked it.

What would it be like to see Sue in her Amish dress and *kapp* over the fence on her brother's property? Would their time together still mean anything? Or would it be like another lifetime?

"Will you tell me what you're planning to do when you decide?" he asked.

"Of course."

"If you go back—all the way, I mean—will I still be… I mean, will we still—" He let out a huff of breath. Whatever this was between them didn't even have a name. "Will we be the same?"

She shook her head. "No, we wouldn't be."

If Sue went home to her family, the door would be firmly closed to him, and that realization was like a kick in the gut.

It shouldn't hurt so much. Sure, he was feeling things for her, and there was a mutual attraction here, but this wasn't supposed to be a long-term solution for either of them.

Maybe he'd be wise to get his own feelings under control now, before someone seriously got hurt.

THAT EVENING AFTER THE supper dishes were washed, Sue hung her dish towel over the stove handle while Wilder wrung out the cloth and hung it over the tap. Dinner had been quiet, and she'd noticed a change in Wilder since their talk that morning. He hadn't tried to hold her hand again, and the brush of his hand against her back had stopped completely.

She missed it, she realized. There had been casual endearments that she'd started to take for granted, and with them gone, she felt the loss more than she should. They stood with a few feet between them, and she smiled faintly.

"You seem tired," she said.

"Nah, I'm fine," he replied.

"Oh, well…" She knew what had caused this awkwardness. She'd finally told him out loud what it would be like if she went home again. He'd been imagining something different, and maybe she had too. She wished she could have it all—the Amish family, the handsome rancher, a little bit of everything. But that wasn't how this worked.

"I'm going to go talk to my niece," Sue said. "I promised my brother that I'd try and fix this with her."

"Yeah, of course," Wilder said. "That's important."

"Thanks."

She felt a tickle in her belly, and she touched her stomach in response. Sue tugged at her jeans, which were feeling just a little too snug now, and headed for the door.

The evening was cool, and Sue noticed that more leaves were turning gold at the edges of branches as she walked briskly toward her brother's house. An extra buggy was parked in the drive, the horse out of sight—probably in the corral. She felt a wave of misgiving. Who was visiting her brother? She slowed her pace. Was this going to be an ambush with some well-meaning neighbors?

She almost turned back, but then thought better of it. She'd promised to talk to her niece tonight, and she didn't want to let her brother down. For all she knew, someone had come to help her brother with ranching duties. Besides, she'd have to get used to coming across members of the community sooner or later.

When Sue knocked on the side door at her brother's home, there was a scurry of little bare feet, and the door was flung open. Jane stood in the doorway already dressed in a nightgown and her hair wet and combed after a bath. She beamed up at Sue.

"We saw you coming across the field," she announced. "And *Daet* says we can visit with each other like grown-up ladies do!"

Sue looked over her niece's head into the sitting room. No one was there.

"Do you have guests, Jane?" she asked.

"No." Jane deflated a little bit. "Just Jerusha. And *Daet* and Jerusha won't let me hear what they're talking about."

As Sue stepped inside, her mother poked her head around the corner.

"Hello, Sue, dear," Linda said with a smile. "Jane has been bouncing for a solid two hours now, waiting for you to visit."

"I haven't!" Jane said.

"No?" Linda raised an eyebrow.

"Maybe..." Jane smiled sheepishly. "I'm just happy to see you, Aunt Sue."

Sue couldn't help but smile back. "I'm happy to see you, too, sweetie."

As Sue stepped past her niece, Linda's gaze moved down to Sue's abdomen, and her eyes widened.

"Well, well," Linda said, coming into the room. "You've popped."

"I have." Sue felt her cheeks warm, and she smoothed a hand down her stomach. Jane looked at Sue's stomach for the first time now.

"So it's true, then?" Jane breathed. "You're having a baby, Aunt Sue?"

"*Yah*, I'm having a baby," Sue replied. "And we should probably talk about it."

"Am I allowed to talk about it?" Jane whispered, looking back at Linda.

"*Yah*, you are," Linda said. "Your *daet* said it would be okay. Now will be a good time for you to ask all your questions in the privacy of our own home."

"Do you want to sit down as a family?" Sue asked her mother softly. "What does Wollie have in mind?"

"He wants you to talk with her alone," Linda said.

"*Yah?* You sure?" Sue asked hesitantly. "He doesn't want to hear what I say?"

"Sue, he trusts you." Linda patted her arm. "You two sit down and talk. Wollie and Jerusha are out with the horses. I'll let them know you're here. But Wollie wanted you two to have some time alone."

Sue could feel the honor of her brother's trust in a sensitive situation like this one, but she could see the logic behind it, too. Jane needed to hear from her aunt that the Amish life was the best one, and if the girl thought it was a pressured response from the family, it wouldn't mean quite so much. Wollie was betting on Sue's solidarity here.

"Let's have a seat, Jane," Sue said.

For the next few minutes, Sue gently explained that she'd wanted to get married very badly, but the man she was with convinced her that it wasn't an *English* thing to do. And she'd believed him. She explained how if she had it all to do over again, she would do it differently, and how little girls could learn from other people, see the struggles they went through, and avoid the choices that caused pain.

"So your boyfriend lied to you?" Jane asked soberly.

"*Yah*, he did."

"Are they allowed to do that?" Jane shook her head. "Are grown-ups allowed to lie?"

"Well," Sue said thoughtfully, "they aren't supposed to. Not every man behaves the way he should. That's why it's a very cautious decision who a girl courts. I wasn't careful enough."

"Will you get married now?" Jane asked.

"No, sweetie," Sue replied. "There won't be a *daet* for this baby. Just me."

"Like Missy Heuther?" Jane asked. "Her *daet* died, and now it's just her and her sisters and their *mamm*. And they don't have a *daet* in the house. Is it like that?"

"Almost like that," Sue agreed. "Except it won't be as sad. No one died, you see. And Chaney—that's the father's name—will simply go away. We won't be sad about it. If this little one ever wants to meet his father, we might be able to find him and make it happen. Perhaps they'll write letters to each other, or talk on the phone... We'll see how it goes. But I'll be a single mother, like Missy's *mamm* is. I'll take care of my baby alone. And you'll have a little cousin to play with sometimes."

"So it won't be sad?" Jane said.

"No, not sad at all. It'll be happy. We'll

be a little family, and we'll love each other. Not every family looks the same. Like you don't have a *mamm*, but you have a *mammi* and your *daet*, and even me, who love you very much."

"That's true," Jane agreed soberly.

"The thing that makes a happy family is the love between everyone, right?" Sue said.

"*Yah*, we love each other very much," Jane agreed.

"So, you see?"

Jane nodded a couple of times. "Okay, then."

"Okay, then." Sue smiled. "Do you have any other questions?"

"Can I touch your tummy?"

"Sure. I don't think you'll feel much, though."

Jane put her hand on Sue's stomach. "It's squishy."

Sue chuckled. "Mummy tummies start like that."

"Do I feel a baby moving around?"

"No, you feel my stomach digesting food," Sue said with a laugh.

"Oh…"

There was a movement at the doorway that

led to the kitchen, and Sue saw the edge of a violet dress just visible. Jerusha? Linda was wearing pink. It was time to get to the crux of this conversation.

"Jane, speaking of families..." Sue said.

Jane straightened, her eyes narrowing slightly.

"... Jerusha wants to join this one," Sue said. "And I feel so bad for her, because it's not easy to join a new family. She has to rely on us being kind to her. It would be so hard to come to a new family you want to love and discover they don't like you. Wouldn't that be hard?"

Jane dropped her gaze. "But I don't need a new *mamm*."

"Just for a minute, let's look at the other side of it," Sue said. "What if Jerusha's family wasn't nice to your *daet*?"

"That would be terrible!" Jane's eyes filled with tears. "My *daet* is the strongest, kindest, smartest, bestest *daet* ever! And they should be nice to him!"

"I wonder how Jerusha's family feels knowing that their sweet Jerusha isn't welcome here..." Sue said.

"But I don't need a *mamm*!" Jane pleaded. "I have a *mammi*!"

"You'll still have a *mammi*," Sue said. "And you'll have your *daet*. One day, I'd like to get married and my baby will have a new *daet*, too. Sometimes families have to shift around a bit to make room for more love. But that won't mean less love for you. You'd have someone else to cook for you and show you how to do things. You'll have a *mamm* to do your hair and tell you stories. I know that Jerusha would be so proud to have you as her little girl. So very, very proud. She'd love you with all her heart."

Jane pressed her lips together. "I should be nicer, Aunt Sue?"

"I think it would be the right thing to do," Sue said. "I think it would be very nice of you to be part of the wedding."

"But you aren't!" Jane protested.

"I'm having a baby, Jane," Sue said quietly. "And that's not…expected…around here. I'm trying to let the wedding be about your *daet* and Jerusha, not about my squishy tummy. If it weren't for this baby coming, I'd be very happy to be part of the wedding."

Jane sighed. "So I should be part of the wedding anyway?"

"Yes, sweetie," Sue said. "That's what I think."

Jane was silent for a moment, her little lips pressed tightly together.

"Okay," she said at last. "I'll do it."

"And you'll be nice to Jerusha?" Sue asked.

"Do you really think she'd be proud of me?" Jane asked uncertainly.

Jerusha appeared around the doorway, her cheeks flushed and her eyes shining with unshed tears. She smoothed her trembling hands down her apron, and Jane looked up in surprise.

"I'm sorry to have overheard you talking," Jerusha said. "But yes, Jane! I'd be such a proud *mamm* to have you as my oldest girl. I'd tell all the other ladies how my daughter was the kindest, smartest, best girl ever. If you'd let me be your new *mamm*."

"Yah?" Jane said hopefully.

"Yah." Jerusha came into the sitting room and sank onto the couch next to Jane. "You know that the oldest is always the favorite, don't you? Because she's her *mamm*'s helper."

"I could be your favorite?" Jane whispered.

"You already are," Jerusha said earnestly.

For a moment, Jane just stared at the woman, her eyes wide and brimming with tears, and then she tipped toward Jerusha ever so slightly, and Jerusha took the initiative and wrapped her arms around the girl. Jerusha looked up at Sue and mouthed *thank you*.

Sue stood up. It looked like it was time to let Jerusha and Jane talk now, but Jerusha stopped her.

"Sue, I want you to be in my wedding party," Jerusha said. "Even pregnant. I don't mind a bit. You'll be my family, too, and I'd be so honored if you'd stand with me as a *newehocker*."

This wasn't what Sue had expected, and her mind spun, grasping for an excuse. She was *pregnant*! Wasn't that enough?

"You don't have to—" Sue started.

"I know, but I want you there," Jerusha said. "You spoke so beautifully about being a family, Sue. And this family includes you. Please?"

Jane looked up at Sue then, her big blue eyes fixed on her. It was time for Sue to practice what she preached. Was family important enough to put aside her own misgivings about presenting her pregnant self in front of the entire Amish community she'd been raised in? Hiding wasn't going to be possible anymore, and if she wanted a family, then she'd best start acting like she did. Because as much as she wanted to do this entirely on her own, that wasn't going to be possible.

Sue nodded. "Then how can I say no? I'd be happy to, Jerusha. Thank you."

She and Jane would both be a part of this wedding. Family was family after all.

CHAPTER FOURTEEN

THE NEXT MORNING, Wilder hopped onto the back of the wagon as Sue stepped on the gas. The tractor growled as it crawled toward the pasture. They were topping up feeders with some fresh silage and replacing salt licks. It was easier to do it all at once, and faster still with two of them working together.

"So you're going to be a bridesmaid?" Wilder said, picking up their conversation where it left off.

"A *newehocker*, but yes," she said, glancing over her shoulder and raising her voice to be heard. "Jerusha assured me that my pregnancy made no difference to her and she wanted me there."

"They weren't as scandalized as you thought," he said.

"She was grateful that I got through to Jane," Sue replied.

"That's nice, though, isn't it?" Wilder said. "That's family."

Sue nodded, and she slowed the tractor, and then hit the brakes as they reached the gate. Wilder hopped down and swung open the gate so she could drive through. When he closed it again, he jogged up to the wagon and hopped back up.

"I'll still be a scandal," she said, speaking over her shoulder again so he could hear her. "I'll have to be explained to the children and teens—why I'm pregnant out of wedlock, and all that. It's a very big deal for the Amish. When I was a young teen, there was a woman in her early twenties who got pregnant. Like, obviously pregnant. The whole community leaned on her boyfriend to marry her."

"And once they were married…" he said.

"All was well then," she replied.

"That's a good thing," Wilder said. "It kind of surprises me."

"They're human, too," she said. "But I won't have an easily tied-up story for them. I'm dreading the wedding, honestly, because they'll see me as a problem to fix."

"Just trying to be helpful?" he asked with a chuckle.

"Stubbornly helpful," she replied, and shook her head. "But it won't be that easy. There will be a lot of opinions—I'll put it that way."

He watched as Sue bounced on the seat as she went over a bump, and he braced himself for the same bump a moment later.

"Sorry!" she called over her shoulder, then she stopped at the first feeder.

Wilder jumped down and grabbed a tub of fresh, chopped veggies and corn silage to dump into the long feeder trough they'd set up next to the hay bale feeder. The cattle would need to fatten up for winter when the cold weather came. He shook the feed into the trough, and the cattle perked up, lumbering over to check it out.

Once the second bin had been added to the trough, he tossed the empty containers onto the wagon bed and jumped back up.

"They're happy you're back, aren't they?" Wilder said when he settled behind her once more.

"*Yah*, they are," she said, and he noticed the Amish pronunciation slipping into her speech. "They have their hopes up that I'll come home properly. I know that. Part of me feels bad because I'm not the same person anymore and I don't want the same life they want, but they are my family."

"And what if a nice, well-meaning guy gets in the way of your homecoming?" he asked.

Sue looked over her shoulder at him again, and her eyes were filled with conflicting emotion. "You mean if I had someone special in my life—say a sweet cowboy—who made it easier for me to stay *English*?"

"That's what I'm asking," he said.

She smiled, her eyes crinkling up at the corners, then she turned to face forward again.

"There would be some hard feelings there," she said, her voice nearly lost in the rumble of the engine. "I can't lie."

They circled around to the second feeder and Wilder performed the same task again, filling the trough with silage and setting up a fresh salt lick for the cattle. As he tossed the last plastic container back onto the wagon bed, he spotted one of his neighbors, Enoch Lapp, on the road that led past the pasture. The Amish man reined in and waved.

"Is he here for me, or you?" Wilder asked.

"You, I'm sure," she said. "Besides, I'm not

in the mood to chat with the neighbors right now. If you don't mind, I'll just take the tractor back to the barn, and I'll feed the calf."

He met her gaze for a moment, and he felt a surge of protectiveness. She didn't have to make nice with anyone she didn't want to while she was with him. Enoch was a neighbor—not her family. Wilder could shelter her from this much.

"No problem," he said. "I'll take care of it."

"Thank you…" Her shoulders relaxed. "I'll see you at the barn later."

He shot her a smile, and she took the tractor in a slow circle to head back. Even as Sue sat on the tractor seat, he could make out the faint bulge of her pregnancy, and he wondered if Enoch would notice. How long until word spread? Were the Schmidts keeping the secret, or was word out already?

Wilder strode over to the fence, pushed down the middle barbed wire and pulled up the top one to make space to ease through the fence. His hat took a tumble as he got through, and he scooped it up from the ground.

"Good morning," Enoch said.

"Hi," Wilder said. "How's it going?"

"Oh…not too badly," Enoch said with a

slow nod. "Just getting ready for the cold weather. You know how it is."

"Sure do," Wilder agreed. "I got my herd back from the summer pasture a couple of days ago. Have you gotten yours back yet?"

"We're going tomorrow," Enoch said.

"Do you get family to help you out with fetching the herd?" Wilder asked.

"*Yah.* I have my brother, of course, and a couple of nephews who come with me. It's good experience for them."

"I could see that," Wilder said. "That's great."

Enoch nodded a couple of times, then pressed his lips together. He wasn't here to chat about the cattle, it would seem, and Wilder crossed his arms over his chest, waiting for the other man to come to the point.

"I talked to the other farmers about your plan for a community watch," Enoch said.

"Oh, good," Wilder said. "Are they interested?"

"Well…maybe so, maybe not," Enoch replied, his tone cautiously noncommittal. "The thing is, we've got other things to concern the community right now, and it's a whole lot closer to home than some potential thefts."

Enoch glanced toward Wilder's field, and Wilder followed his gaze. Sue had hopped down from the tractor and was opening the gate to drive through.

"Can I tell you a story?" Enoch asked.

"Sure." Wilder looked at the other man curiously.

"Thirty years ago, a teenage boy ran away from home. He was my brother, and he left a note on his bed, and never came back. I never did see him again. He just…vanished. And if you think that the family would be angry, you're wrong. We were bereft. It was like a death. One day, we had him with us—my older brother who'd joke around with me and talk with me late at night in our shared room about the deeper things. The next day, he was gone. My mother cried every day. She could be standing there doing dishes, and you'd see her shoulders start to shake… My father mentioned him in every prayer. Every single one—blessing the food, before going to bed, before starting work for the day…he'd always put my brother in that prayer, because my brother was always foremost in his thoughts. And to this day, my elderly mother, who is now suffering from dementia, asks about my brother. Sometimes she thinks he's just gone to do the milking, but you can tell by the worried sound in her voice that she knows better deep down."

Wilder swallowed. His neighbor had never opened up like this to him before. He was baring his soul here on the side of the road, and even the wind seemed to stop out of respect.

"Every few years there's a teenager who leaves," Enoch went on. "It's not so rare. But every time it happens, the hole leaves a family reeling, like it did to mine. Fifteen years ago, it was the Schmidts' turn. When Sue left, they went through all the grief that we did. And we couldn't make it better—couldn't bring her back. They thought about her every day, too, and talked about her around their table. They worried about her and tried to pretend that the hole was healed, but it never does heal. Not really. The thing is, she's back now. Almost… And I can see the hope and yearning in my friends' eyes when they talk about her, because it might undo some of that pain. Sue Schmidt is one of us. She's one of *them*. They raised her. They loved her. Wollie grew up with her. And you can agree with our way of life or not, but families need each other. I don't care what culture you come from. They *need* each other."

Enoch fell silent, and his steel-gray eyes misted. He blinked a couple of times and cleared his throat.

"I'm so sorry for your loss," Wilder said, his own throat thick with emotion.

"Are you sorry for the Schmidts' loss?" Enoch asked pointedly.

"Yeah, of course…"

Enoch held his gaze for a moment. "Seeing as you're *English*, I might need to spell it out a bit. We can see that there's a special closeness between you and Sue. For our people, that might lead to an engagement announcement. I don't know what it means for you, of course. And we like you a whole lot, Wilder, but you're not Amish. Sue needs to come home…not almost home, not close to the fence, but all the way home. If you were really a part of our community—an honorary member, so to speak—you'd help us with that."

"You want me to…try to convince her to go back?" Wilder asked with a frown.

"We want you to stop standing in her way."

"Sue is a grown woman," Wilder said, surprised. "If you think I have any control over her, you're mistaken. We don't do things that way. She'll make her own choices. I wouldn't dream of trying to manipulate her or hold her back from anything she wanted. Talk to Wollie. He knows."

Enoch didn't look convinced. "Just know that as a community, we work together for everyone's good. And right now, we're working together for the Schmidts."

"Okay," Wilder said hesitantly.

"And the other farmers are still uncertain about you. They're wanting to see if you've got our best interests at heart, or just your own *English* way of doing things. They aren't sure."

And how Wilder handled this situation would tell them what they needed to know about the community watch plan, as well as their relationship with him going forward. He didn't need the rest of it to be spelled out for him.

"I'm trying to be a good neighbor," Wilder said. "I really am."

"Yah, yah…" Enoch nodded. "I do think you're doing your best, and you have been

a good friend, Wilder. I'm not saying otherwise. But the Amish ways are different. I just thought I'd explain. So you know."

So he'd understand the swift consequences if they befell him. It was only fair.

"Thank you, Enoch," Wilder said. "I do appreciate your frankness on this matter."

"Oh, and one more thing. Wollie asked me to pass along a message if I saw you," Enoch said.

"What message?"

"He was hoping you'd help him with his *eck* tonight," he replied.

That was a swift change of topic, and Wilder cleared his throat and nodded. "Right. Of course, I will."

"It's an honor to be asked," Enoch said. "A real honor."

Not to be squandered. Yes, Wilder understood.

"Well... I'd best keep moving. Have a good day, then," Enoch said, and he flicked the reins. He gave Wilder one final nod as the wagon started forward.

The message was clear. His future as a trusted member of this rural community— Conrad's future, too, for that matter—was at stake. Wilder was supposed to be turning a new leaf, making up for years of selfishness. If he was smart, he'd take the warning and make it clear he wasn't meddling in Schmidt family affairs.

But what about Sue? Who'd support *her* if she didn't want to go "all the way home"? Who'd be the shoulder for her to lean on, the one to listen to her worries? Who'd be the one to truly understand her? Because Sue deserved to have everything that she wanted... even if it went against her well-meaning family.

THAT EVENING, Sue and Wilder headed over to her brother's place next door. Her brother would be working with Wilder on the *eck*, and she would have some time with her mother and niece. The wedding was fast approaching, and Linda would take a trunk of her personal items and go to her brother's farm where she'd live in his newly vacated *dawdie hus*.

So tonight would be special—a time to enjoy the family on familiar ground before it all changed again.

Sue had brought a pair of maternity jeans

with her, knowing she'd need them eventually, and this evening she rooted through her drawer and pulled them out. It was time. Her current jeans were pressing into her stomach, and she'd had to undo the top button on them. When she pulled the soft panel of her maternity jeans up over her stomach, she breathed a sigh of relief. They were so much more comfortable!

But when she caught a glimpse of herself in the mirror on the back of her door, her breath caught.

She looked so…pregnant!

She had a long way to go, of course. But this wasn't a figure that she recognized anymore. A soft wiggle from within drew her attention away from her reflection.

"Hey, in there…" she said softly, running a hand over her belly.

When she headed out of her bedroom and into the kitchen, Wilder looked up. He startled, blinked, then shot her a smile.

"Hi," he said.

"I saw that," she said. "I'm half tempted to squeeze back into my old jeans, just to feel more like myself."

"You look beautiful, Sue," he said.

"You keep saying that."

"I keep meaning it."

She felt her cheeks heat. "I feel very round."

"Hardly," he said. "You'll be way rounder than this soon enough."

She swatted his arm and he laughed.

"Really, you look great." His warm gaze softened, and he bent down and pressed a kiss against her forehead. The distance that he'd been keeping between them lately suddenly closed again. He froze.

"You didn't mean to do that," she whispered.

Wilder's breath was warm against her forehead. "No… I told myself I'd cut that out…"

A lump rose in Sue's throat. She wasn't sure why, but the thought of him never kissing her forehead again made her want to cry.

"Because it's too complicated," she said, swallowing hard.

"It is…" He took a step back. "I'm sorry, it's harder than I thought it would be to stop this."

"What did Enoch want?" she asked.

"Oh…" Wilder hesitated. "I wasn't going to tell you, but…he basically came by to warn me off."

"Of what?" she asked.

"Of you."

Her heart skipped a beat. "What?"

"Apparently, I've made it pretty obvious how I feel about you. I should have been more discreet, I guess."

Irritation was rising to cover her initial surprise. "So he decided to stop by and tell you to do...what?"

"To keep in mind that if I get in the way of your ability to reunite with your family, then they'll take that personally," he replied.

"You aren't in the way," she said. "What's his problem?"

"I don't know. That was the message, though."

"And what if there were something between us?" she demanded. "What then?"

"Well, there is something between us... isn't there?" Wilder said. "We've gotten close. Probably far too close."

"And that's anyone else's business?" she said, shaking her head. "Yeah, we've gotten close. I don't know what this is, but... I know for sure it isn't Enoch Lapp's business."

Wilder smiled ruefully. "I agree."

But there was still some worry in his gaze,

and she sighed. This was the problem with a tightly knit community. They were there to help, whether you wanted it or not.

"Do you care what Enoch Lapp thinks?" she asked.

"Well, I do need to work with him," Wilder said. "And I need his cooperation if I'm going to succeed out here. And he's...been a friend."

"What did you tell him?"

"Uh—" Wilder shrugged. "Not much. He said his piece and moved on."

Right. So Wilder hadn't put the man in his place. And maybe she didn't blame him, either. She knew his desire to make this ranch a success and to gain his neighbors' trust. She was the one making waves.

"I'll get Wollie to set him straight," she said with a sigh.

"No," he said. "Don't do that."

"What?" She looked up at him in surprise. "Look, Wilder, this is Amish business. They can get like that. If my brother—"

"This is between men," he replied, cutting her off. "This is between me and Enoch, and a few other farmers who need to know they can count on me. I'm taking care of it, but don't say anything to Wollie."

316 A COWBOY IN AMISH COUNTRY

"Fine." But her own anxiety had just gone up a notch.

"I don't mean to snap at you," he said, softening his tone.

"You don't have to live by Amish codes, Wilder," she said.

"I don't have to go against them, either," he replied. "I like a lot of it. A handshake means something. A man is as good as his word out here. Relationships matter, and so do families. I'm not opposed to any of that."

"And when some neighbor decides you shouldn't feel—" She swallowed.

"Sue…" He caught her hand and tugged her closer. He bent down and caught her lips with his. His kiss was short, sweet, soft. Then he pulled back. "No one can dictate what I feel, okay?"

She nodded. "Okay."

She didn't know why, but that was comforting. This Amish community had loved her well when she was a girl, but it had become stifling as she grew into a woman who wanted more. And they'd stifle her again with all of their best intentions. How was it anyone's business what she was feeling for this man?

Her heart squeezed as she looked at the rugged cowboy. Yes, she was falling for him head over heels, and it might be entirely stupid for her to do so, but it was her heart on the line, no one else's.

Sue and Wilder headed across the scrub grass to her brother's farm, and when they got to the house, Wollie had his *eck*—a wooden frame with a shallow shelf attached, ready to hold meaningful items for the couple—leaning up against the side of the stable. Wilder's hand touched hers, lingered for a moment, and then he stepped away.

Wilder didn't look back, and Sue sucked in a shaky breath.

"My, my, Sue," Linda said, bustling up. She put a tender hand on Sue's stomach. "You know, our dresses are so much more comfortable during a pregnancy. I can get you one. You'll hardly even notice how quickly you grow in a cape dress."

"No, but thank you, *Mamm*," Sue said.

"They're just practical, dear," Linda said.

"*Mamm*…come on. I know how comfortable they are. I don't want one."

"But you don't know how comfortable when pregnant. I do," Linda said. Then she shrugged. "But you'll find out. Jerusha's sister dropped off your dress for the wedding earlier today. She said she stopped by Wilder's place for you but no one was there, and she didn't want to leave it outside."

"Oh, that's nice," Sue said.

"And after you wear it for the wedding, the dress is yours," Linda said hopefully. "Maybe you'll want to wear it around the house. Really, Sue. I'm not trying to make you Amish so much as I'm trying to make you comfortable."

"I'm comfortable," Sue said. "Trust me."

Jane danced up then, and she caught Sue's hand. "Aunt Sue, I made peanut butter cookies!"

"Are you hungry?" Linda asked.

"I could eat," Sue replied. If her mother wanted to dote on her, Sue wasn't going to turn it down. But maybe it could be in the form of food instead of changing the way she dressed.

"And we got our dresses today!" Jane said. "My dress and your dress match, Aunt Sue. They're the same color! They're teal."

"Really?" Sue smiled down at her. "It'll be fun to match with you."

"And we can try them on while *Daet* and Wilder work on the *eck*," Jane said.

"Can I have cookies first?" Sue asked.

"*Yah*, of course!" Jane said with a grin. "And *Mammi* made strudel, too. She said I couldn't have any until she cuts it for the men."

"Hardly fair," Sue said, casting her mother a teasing smile.

"Siding with our Jane, are you?" Linda laughed. "I wanted it to look nice for when the men come to eat."

"Wilder will hardly notice," Sue said.

"All right, then…let's go on inside…"

Sue looked over to where Wilder and Wollie stood, both with arms folded in front of their chests as they looked at the wood-work in front of them. She could hear the low murmur of their voices, but she couldn't make out what they were saying. And as if Wilder could feel her eyes on him, his gaze suddenly flicked in her direction. A smile turned up his lips, and he touched the rim of his hat.

Wollie glanced over at her with a surprised expression. Then he looked back at Wilder, and by the expression on his face, a sudden realization seemed to have to hit Wollie all at once. Wilder had just tipped his hand.

But Sue followed her mother into the house and inhaled the familiar scent of her childhood home. She would just have to get her heart under control, because as much as Wilder might promise that no one could affect his feelings for her, she knew this community a little better than he did.

CHAPTER FIFTEEN

THE REST OF the evening was quiet. Sue tried on the dress to make sure it fit. Amish dresses adjusted and were fastened with pins at the waist so that if someone gained weight, or even during the first four or five months of a pregnancy, they could be altered.

Jane loved that they matched, and Linda brought out cookies and blackberry cobbler, and even made some sandwiches that everyone could munch on. Sue enjoyed this feeling of being cared for for an evening, and her mother's gentle insistence that she "eat for the baby's sake, my dear. You need nutrition." Sue didn't need much encouragement.

"*Mamm*, why did Wollie choose Wilder to help with the *eck*?" Sue asked.

"They're friends," Linda replied.

"He's got future brothers-in-law, cousins, nephews, friends he grew up with…" Sue eyed her mother. "And Wilder's *English*."

Her mother pressed her lips together. "So are you, dear."

"He did it for me?"

"I think it was part of it," Linda replied. "You're over there, and Wilder and Conrad have been incredibly helpful to all of us the last few years. I think it's possible that your brother is changing."

"Loosening up?" Sue asked.

"Well...he'd have to if he wants to make room for you and the baby, wouldn't he?"

"*Mamm*, like you just said, I'm not Amish anymore," Sue said softly.

"My dear girl, you were born Amish, I raised you Amish, and while you didn't choose our path in life, Amish swims through your veins." Linda slid another scoop of blackberry cobbler in front of her. "And we're your family. When times get hard, and you have nowhere else to turn, people come back to family for help. Others—friends, acquaintances, bosses, even—have no reason to sacrifice for you or to care about you on the deepest of levels. But your family does. This is why *Gott* gives us family. You can choose your friends, but you can't choose your family. And we are yours. Like it or not."

"*Mamm*, you know I love you!" Sue said.

"I do know it." Linda poured a glass of milk and placed it next to the plate of cobbler. "But you also can't choose your background. We're what you have. And we love you, too."

"I never did fit into the Amish life, though," Sue said softly.

"That isn't true," Linda replied. "What about you, Sarah and Rachel? You were best friends, and you used to sew together in your own little sewing circle. And you'd gossip and talk and laugh, and... You were all very happy then."

"*Yah*," Sue said softly. Sarah's family moved away shortly before her *Rumspringa*, and later on, Rachel had gotten married to an Amish man in Florida and moved there.

"And as for you butting heads with your brother, well, many sisters and brothers do that. It's how young people learn about the opposite gender. Boys learn how to be nice to girls, and the things that infuriate them. Girls learn that boys are not quite so tough as they pretend to be. It's part of growing up, Sue. It's not a sign that anything went wrong. It's just...family!"

Sue looked at her mother across the table, surprised. "You didn't see me not fitting in?"

"I saw a girl finding herself," Linda said. "Every teenager feels misunderstood. Every girl that age thinks that no one could possibly fathom the complicated emotions coursing through her. It's part of the age. I felt the same way. So did your sisters, although they were older than you so they'd gone through it all much earlier. And I can only assume your friends felt the same way."

Was it possible that her memories of the Amish life were more normal than she thought?

"My dear, memories are personal," Linda went on. "And I will never say that your memory of an event is wrong. Because it isn't. It's how you saw it, how you experienced it. But memory is clearest and most precise in community. You might remember being miserable at a birthday party. I might remember a twelve-year-old girl who was going through a stage that all girls go through. Your brother might remember that you hurt his feelings. You might remember that he had it coming... You see, one event has many people attached to it, and you can't always know what was happening in their heads. You belonged, Sue. You always belonged. I know you didn't feel like the Amish life fit you, but the Amish *people* loved you. If that makes any difference at all."

"It might…" she murmured.

"So, as you make your decisions about how you will raise your child, keep that in mind," Linda said softly. "You can come home. I've been praying for you to come home ever since you left. We could help you raise your child with love and belonging. I just know it."

No one else in her life owed her that kind of stability… She had friends, but her life shouldn't impose on theirs. They loved her, but not enough to support her to the level that her family would. That was life…

And she'd have to make a very serious choice soon—come home, or determine to keep her freedom. There would be consequences either way.

The men worked hard that evening to finish. Then Sue and Wilder walked back to the house. Wilder caught her hand as they came around the stable and out of sight of any of her family who might look out a window, and she leaned into his warm strength.

"Do you want to watch a movie tonight?" Wilder asked.

"So you've given up on keeping your distance?" she asked. She said it jokingly, but she meant to remind him of his previous intentions.

"Yeah," he said, tugging her a little closer against him.

And she was tempted to cuddle up next to this comforting man and lose herself in a fictional world where everything had a reason, and everything worked out in the end. But she couldn't afford to waste any more time.

"No, I'd better get to bed," she said, and she gently pulled her hand free.

"Right," he said, and she could see the hurt in his eyes. "Of course. Have a good rest."

Sue didn't want to hurt Wilder, but she didn't want to lead him on, either. Cozying up with Wilder wasn't going to help her think things through clearly.

THE NEXT COUPLE of days were busy. Sue and Wilder worked to get the bucket-fed calf back to the herd, and Wilder started mowing, raking and baling a pasture that he'd left to rest for the season.

Sue did the chores, mucked out the stable, brushed horses…and all the while, her mind was spinning. Would she go back to Wooster and get a job in a store or a restaurant and put her child into day care? Would she work long hours to provide for her baby, and keep this freedom she'd grown to love so much?

Or would she sacrifice her freedom in order to be there with her child all day long, raising her little one with a loving extended family around them? There would be no TV, no movies, no internet, or light switches. There would be hard work of a different sort—laundry, cleaning, cooking, serving—but with her child right at her side.

She couldn't have both the freedom she loved and the security she craved. It was one or the other. So it came down to this: What would be better for her child?

The day of Wollie and Jerusha's wedding dawned crisp and clear. The sun sparkled off the frost-tipped grass, and Sue watched through the kitchen window as buggies began to arrive next door, started to fill the scrub grass between the two farms. Horses were brought to another field to graze. Weddings were long events, and people were settling in for the entire day.

Sue went into her bedroom and slipped into in the teal *newehocker* dress Jerusha had supplied. When she was a girl wearing a cape dress, her waist was neat and small. But now, she had to wrap the dress above her doming belly for it to fit comfortably, and she nimbly pinned it into place with the little container of straight pins her mother had sent along. The bride would wear blue, and her white wedding apron, but Sue and the other *newehockers* would go without their aprons to set them apart. Her mother had also sent a crisp, brand-new *kapp* to cover her hair.

Sue's hair didn't twist up into a bun as easily as it used to do, and it took her a couple of tries to get a nice, low bun pinned into place with some bobby pins. She regarded herself in the mirror for a moment, then pulled the *kapp* into place over her hair.

Her reflection stared back at her—an Amish woman, visibly pregnant. Her breath caught in her throat. This wasn't like trying the dress on yesterday with her mother and niece tugging at it and chattering away. This felt more serious—and she could feel her old

Amish self slipping back into place—Sue Schmidt, Zeke and Linda's youngest daughter, Wollie's sister…a friend to so many others.

Sue used to wear dresses like this one and dream of blue jeans. She used to stand in the kitchen doing dishes like a good Amish girl and dream of working with the cows instead. It was never the life she wanted, even if she'd been dearly loved.

And here she was again…

The baby moved inside her—a stronger flutter than before, and she ran her hand over her belly. She wasn't a girl anymore. She was a grown woman with difficult decisions ahead of her.

Sue tore her eyes away from her own reflection and pulled open the bedroom door. She headed down the hallway to the kitchen, and when she arrived, she found Wilder dressed in his own Amish garb—drop flap pants, a white shirt, black suspenders. He was eyeing a formal black felt hat that lay on the counter.

"You look the part," she said with a smile.

"So do you." He shot her a grin. "I actually think the clothes are pretty comfortable."

"Oh, yes," she said. "So is the dress. My mother has been telling me how cape dresses are the ultimate maternity wear, and I'll never admit it to her, but she's right. Comfort was never the problem for me."

Sue went to the kitchen window and looked outside at the buggies. A field full of buggies used to be the sign of an exciting day ahead. She used to love seeing the community's buggies all together in one place, but now it brought a knot to her stomach.

She'd see *everyone*...and they'd see her. She wasn't ashamed. But she didn't like that much attention, either, or the unwarranted judgment that would be coming from a few people, at least.

Wilder came up behind her and looked out. "So it begins, huh?"

"So it begins..." She leaned back against his chest, and he slid a hand around her waist. It was a natural movement, and instead of pulling away, she stayed motionless, enjoying his touch.

"We keep trying to stop doing this," he said quietly, his voice rumbling behind her.

"I know..." she whispered. For the last couple of days, she'd been working long hours, staying out of reach of those strong, tempting hands, and she'd been going to bed early to avoid cozy evenings together. It wasn't that she didn't enjoy every tender moment of Wilder's attention lavished on her, but she couldn't get used to it. She had to be strong, and she was very quickly becoming reliant on this man.

"Are you okay now?" he asked. "Have you figured out what you'll do?"

She slowly shook her head. "I think I have to go back, Wilder. I need to go home."

WILDER FELT LIKE his heart was about to hammer out of his chest, and he took a step back from her, letting his hands drop from her soft waist. She looked so different in her Amish dress, her hair pulled back and covered with a *kapp* just like the ones he saw on all the women in these parts. The dress fit her so differently than jeans did—it some ways it softened her, but it also put an unspoken barrier between them.

But she was talking about going home, and he suddenly had an image in his head of that smarmy cowboy who'd been trying to convince her to go with him to Utah. Where was home for Sue now? He realized in a rush that he didn't know.

"Like, back to Wooster?" he asked. "Back to Chaney?"

"No." Sue shook he head and smiled wanly. "I'm very much done with Chaney. I'm talking about going back to the Amish."

He blinked at her, her words taking their time to land. "Like…all the way back? Going home in earnest?"

"I have to be rational here," she said. "I'm having a baby in a matter of months, and when I do, I'm not going to be able to just jump back onto a horse. I'm going to have to heal, and I'm going to have a newborn. Whatever I do, working someone else's ranch isn't going to be a feasible possibility for a few years with a little one in tow."

"You need support," he said softly.

"I do." She licked her lips. "I've been giving it a lot of thought. I don't want to drop my baby off at a day care if I don't have to. That would be too hard for me. I know a lot of excellent moms do it, but maybe they're stronger than I am. Or maybe they don't have a family offering what mine is offering…"

"What *are* they offering?" he asked.

"To let me raise my child. They'd let me be a woman in a kitchen, taking care of her little one. I hated that—for years I absolutely loathed it—but right now I can see the gift that it is," she said, her eyes filled with pleading. "You can see how I'd need that, right?"

"Yeah, of course."

"They're offering to let me live the life of an Amish woman, where I'd take care of my baby, raise my child myself, cook, clean, sew and *be here* twenty-four hours a day for my little one."

And for a woman getting ready to have a baby, he couldn't blame her one bit for her choice. She had a family who loved her, and they couldn't be discounted, either.

"I can see why you'd choose that," he said, a smile touching his lips. "You'll be close by, though. You can come over and watch TV with me, or go riding, or... I'll let you wrangle a few calves this spring. What do you say?"

"I'll be Amish."

Wilder swallowed. Right. He knew how it would be.

"But you could come see me, right?" he

said. "I'd keep your secrets, Sue. You know that."

"If I go back, I'll have to back properly," she said, her blue gaze meeting his with agonizing directness. "No secrets. Besides, maybe it's time I realize that my adventure out here with you *Englishers* was a failure. When the chips are down, where do I have to go?"

"You *Englishers*?" Those words stung.

"You know what I mean."

"Am I really so different from you? I'm a man you can trust. When the chips are down, you can come *to me*," he said earnestly. "I'm here."

As if he'd let her suffer in any way if he could help her out. He caught her hands and tugged her closer. He wrapped his arms around her and looked down into her face hopefully.

"Your brother and his wife are coming back," she said. "It won't be the same. Not only that, I'm your employee—"

"You're a whole lot more than my employee!" he said. "And you know it. Don't downplay this. I love you!"

The words were out before he could think

better of them, but he knew they were true. She blinked at him, her lips parted as if she was about to speak, but no words came out. So he did the only thing he could think of, and he pulled her into a kiss. His lips came down over hers, and she melted against him as all those pent-up hopes he'd been afraid to even look at came surging up to the surface. He loved her. He wanted to take care of her, and help her find a solution. This could not be a goodbye!

When he pulled back, he looked down at her face—her lips plumped from his kiss, her eyes a little bleary.

"Do you really mean that?" she whispered.

"Yes," he said. "I really do. I know this is fast, and crazy, and totally unplanned, but there's something really special between us. I've been trying to avoid feeling it, but I've fallen for you."

"Me, too…" Tears welled in her eyes.

"Yeah?" He smiled hopefully. "So this is mutual…"

"I love you, too," she said. "I feel things with you I shouldn't be feeling—"

"Why not?" he pressed. "Why not let your-

self feel it? I'm right here. I'm not going anywhere. You can trust me."

"Because I'm not making choices about
the rest of my life—about where to have my
baby, how to raise this child—based on something this new! I jumped in with Chaney, and
that was the stupidest thing I could have ever
done."

"I'm not Chaney," he said gruffly.

"I know…but I'm still the same woman
who made that mistake, and I now have a
child who will be affected by every choice I
make. I'm sorry, Wilder, but I can't just see
how this goes. If I weren't pregnant, you'd be
worth the risk, but with a baby in the mix…"

The frustrating part was, Wilder completely understood. They'd just met. They'd
started to feel some powerful emotions, and
they were drawn to each other, but this was
brand-new. He'd gone through a divorce. He
knew that just loving someone wasn't always
enough.

"I get it," he said. "Besides, the community
would never see what we saw. They'd see me
as getting in the way of your family's hopes…
and maybe even getting in the way of yours."

"I'm putting mine aside for the time being,"

she said. "But you're right. If you want to be part of the farming community around here—really part of it—you can't be seen to be meddling in an Amish family. I wish it were different, but that's how things are out here."

"I'd risk it for you," he said.

"Would your brother?" she countered. "We're both responsible for more than just ourselves. We have people who depend on us—who we owe something to. If this were anyone else and you were watching from the outside, you'd say it was better for them to part ways."

"I probably would," he admitted. His eyes stung and he blinked a few times. "I just wish you wouldn't put all your hopes aside—" His voice caught.

Sue didn't answer, and he felt his chest tighten. She was going back, and if he hadn't fallen in love with her, he'd see the benefit of her going home to her family… He'd see the benefit of him building his reputation here in the farming community, too. But now, all he could see was a long, drab life without her rolling out in front of him.

"I guess I have to respect that," he said, and

his entire chest felt heavy, like it was filled with concrete, and it made it hard for him to take a deep breath.

"Thank you, Wilder," she whispered, but her voice trembled.

"Will I see you around?" he asked.

She nodded. "I'm sure."

But it would be distanced. What he wouldn't give to see this woman herd some cattle again—riding strong, her ponytail bouncing off her back and her eyes shining. That was where she belonged, and he knew it as certainly as he knew he belonged right at her side—but he couldn't provide that life. She was right—a baby changed everything.

"I'll miss you," he said, touching her cheek.

She nodded, then dropped her gaze. "Let's not make it harder than it has to be. I'm going to head over. I should be there a bit early anyway."

"Okay." He tried to swallow past a lump that rose in his throat, and she stepped away from him. She wrapped a gray shawl around her shoulders, then disappeared outside, pulling the door shut behind her. He looked out the window as she headed across the small field, weaving her way around the first buggy parked there. Then she was gone—out of sight, and Wilder let out a painful breath.

He wanted to cry, but he wouldn't.

"You knew it was coming," he said aloud.

Wollie would be happy—he'd get his sister safely back into his community. The rest of the Amish community, including Enoch, would be happy, too…maybe even Sue would be, eventually.

This was a good thing for them. It was even a good thing for Sue.

Unfortunately, it left him with an unexpected hole in his heart that he was afraid would never fully heal. Was this really the end between them?

CHAPTER SIXTEEN

SUE STEPPED INTO the warm house and joined the other *newehockers* in their teal dresses and gray shawls as they got ready for the wedding service to begin outside in the big tent.

"Sue, you look wonderful," Elaine, one of the other *newehockers*, said, giving her a friendly smile.

"Thanks," she said.

"Does it feel nice to be back in a cape dress?" Elaine asked. "I wore blue jeans during my *Rumspringa*, and they were the most uncomfortable contraptions I've ever pulled on!"

Sue attempted to laugh, but her heart felt tight in her chest.

"How far along are you?" another woman asked, and the women very nicely made her one of the group. Sue knew most of the *newe-hockers*, and there were polite hellos and congratulations on her pregnancy. It seemed to Sue that they'd been filled in on her situation already because she didn't have to explain herself. Outside the kitchen window, she could see the men setting up the church benches for the ceremony.

Sue saw Wilder strolling across the lawn. An Amish man shook his hand, and he stopped to talk. Sue's heart thundered in her chest as she watched him through the glass. Would this be what it would be like for the rest of her days, loving a man she couldn't have?

When it was time for the ceremony to begin, things started to move more quickly. The *newehockers* took their places in the front row, and Sue looked over her shoulder, spotting Wilder sitting in the men's side of the gathering. He looked somber, certainly not like a man celebrating his neighbor's wedding. His apparent misery mirrored her own.

Jane came running into the house, and she caught Sue's hand.

"We match, Aunt Sue!" she said with a beaming smile. "Isn't it great?"

"Yah," Sue said, forcing a smile. "You look very pretty."

"And I get to stay the night with *Mammi*. And she says we can stay up late, way after bedtime."

Jane leaned into Sue's arm, and Sue squeezed her hand.

"It's a very happy day, Jane," she said. "Very happy."

Just tell her heart that.

For the rest of the service he was there—she could almost feel his presence—as she listened to the familiar vows as Wollie and Jerusha pledged themselves to each other.

Wollie, do you take Jerusha to be your wife, your helpmeet, and the mother of your children? Do you vow to protect her, honor her, and provide for her all the days of your life?

Wollie and Jerusha didn't touch each other, staying a proper three feet apart, but Wollie's gaze was locked on Jerusha as if she was his lifeline, and she stood there, her cheeks pink from the excitement of the moment, and her hands clasped in front of her... She wore her blue dress with a white apron, the dress that Jerusha would wear every service Sunday. She'd take meticulous care of it, and when it started to wear out, she'd change to a different dress for service Sundays, because this

particular blue wedding dress must be kept
for the day of her funeral when she'd be buried in it.

It was a beautiful tradition…but also one
that relied upon a woman getting married.
Sue was reminded afresh of just how much
her upbringing had been focused on point-
ing the young people toward pairing up and
taking vows.

Sue wasn't going to apologize for wanting that anymore. She wanted marriage—a
husband of her own, a home they shared together, kids to raise, love, and to get in the
way. She was raised wanting a family, and
watching her brother get married, she knew
that she wanted this for herself just as pow-
erfully as ever.

There was a time when Sue had dreamed of
an Amish wedding exactly like this one, but
over the years, her hopes had matured. Her
mother was right that she couldn't undo her
upbringing, and she no longer had her hopes
pinned on an Amish wedding. But she was
Amish born, Amish raised, and it was that
upbringing that had programmed all of these
marital dreams of her own. Maybe she was
crazy to think she could realize those hopes

with a handsome *Englisher* man like Wilder who could fill up her heart so easily...

Sue turned once more, glancing over her shoulder as quickly as she could, and she spotted Wilder right away. His eyes weren't on the wedding—he was watching her, and his gaze was filled with agony. She turned back around, her hands shaking. Her eyes kept misting with tears that she held back with all the strength she had in her.

The service finally ended, Wollie and Jerusha going back down the center aisle together, both smiling happily. People rose to their feet and followed them out, going to wish them a hearty congratulations, and in the hubbub, Sue slipped away.

She murmured some excuses about finding the bathroom and almost ran toward the house. She jogged upstairs to her old bedroom. It was habit—she'd done it without thinking. It was now Jane's room—little girl's dresses hanging on hangers in the open closet, and Jane's shoes in a row across a freshly polished floor. Sue sank onto the edge of the child's bed, and the tears started to fall. She'd been holding them in since she walked away from Wilder's house, and her shoulders shook with the force of her grief. She clamped a hand over her mouth, and squeezed her eyes shut against the hot tears.

Sue loved Wilder... As foolish as it might be, as useless as it was, she loved that man. And she'd have to see him over there living the life she longed for, possibly moving on with another woman who'd get to love him back. It would be better for him, and better for her...if she could only get past what she had started feeling for him.

It was only a couple of weeks! Why couldn't she turn it off?

The door opened with a squeak, and Sue hurriedly wiped her face. Linda came inside, and she shut the door behind her.

"Sue, what's wrong?" Linda sank onto the bed next to her. "Did someone say something, or—"

"No." Sue tried to swallow back the tears and wiped at her face again. "It's not that."

"Then what is it?" her mother asked, putting an arm around her shoulders.

How many times had Sue sat in this very bedroom as her mother comforted her? But Sue wasn't a little girl anymore, or even a teenager.

"I'm going to come home, *Mamm*," she said.

"You are?" Linda brightened. "Oh, Sue! That's wonderful! I've longed for this!" Her mother's face fell. "So why the tears?"

Sue looked at her mother and fresh tears slid down her cheeks. "I have to say good-bye to some things that I wanted very badly."

"Some things, or someone?" her mother asked softly, pulling her closer. "Wilder?"

"How did you know?" Sue whispered.

"I'm not blind," her mother said. "I could see the way you looked at each other. But you chose to come home instead of staying with him."

"How could I stay with him?" Sue shook her head. "I'm pregnant! I'm having a baby! It changes everything. And the Westhouses can't afford to keep me on indefinitely as their ranch hand. If I don't come home, I need a job that will keep me and my child fed and clothed. Plus Wilder has worked hard to gain respect around here. I'd ruin that for him... for *what*? To date a little while until he sees how much responsibility it is to date a single mother? He'd lose everything he worked for here in the community, and I'd be just as alone then as I am now."

"So it can't work," Linda said softly.

"It can't! I had to look at my options, and I think coming home is better for my baby. But if I come back, I can't do it halfway. I can't just use you for the shelter and then skip off again. I have to make a choice and build my life. I'm a grown woman now."

"I've been wanting to hear those words, but the heartbreak—" Her mother shook her head. "I wanted you to come home, Sue, but not like this."

"Pregnant?" Sue asked, sliding a hand over her stomach protectively.

"Do you really think that of me?" Linda took her hand firmly. "This baby is a blessing for me—I promise you that. I wanted you to come home because you wanted this life, not because you couldn't find a way around it!"

"I'm sorry, *Mamm*, I'm not trying to be insulting."

"I'm not insulted."

"I'm sorry all the same…" Sue sucked in a shaky breath. "You raised me well, *Mamm*. I just want to give my child the same kind of stability. I don't know if I can find it out there."

Linda was silent for a moment, gently

smoothing her hand over Sue's, then she said quietly, "I can't believe I'm going to say this, but...maybe you should think about this more."

"What?" Sue blinked. "You don't want me to come back?"

"Oh, I do! I do!" Linda looked earnestly into Sue's face. "And you can stay with us at your uncle Samuel's as long as you need to. I know for a fact my brother wouldn't turn you away. You're my daughter, and you're going to have a baby of your own. We'll find a way to help you. But—" Linda blinked back tears of her own. "I'm your *mamm*, Sue. I know your heart better than anyone, and as your *mamm*, I want to see you happy. I thought coming home would take care of that, but if I was wrong, I'm not going to hold to an idea that isn't working. If you are Amish or *English*, my beautiful girl, you are still mine."

"So what are you saying?" Sue whispered.

"I'm saying, be true to yourself, Sue. Be that glorious, rebellious, strong, independent woman that drives the community to distraction! Ride your horses, rope your cattle, wear those blue jeans—although I could request that you wear some that are just a *smidge* looser…" Linda laughed tearily. "I love you, Sue. And I know you well enough to know that trying to fit back into an Amish life like this isn't going to work."

"What do I do?" Sue whispered. "I'm pregnant!"

"*Yah*, you are…" Linda sucked in a slow breath. "But you're also strong and smart. Like I said before, you're very welcome to stay with me at Uncle Samuel's as long as you need to. But if you come home for good, I want it to be because you truly want it. You need to follow your heart."

"The bishop would be scandalized at you saying that," Sue said with a short laugh.

"The bishop isn't in this room," Linda said seriously. "This is between a mother and her daughter. It's none of the bishop's business."

"I don't know what I'm going to do, *Mamm*," Sue said softly. "I'm scared."

"You don't know what you're going to do *yet*," her mother corrected her. "You'll figure it out. You always do. And whatever you choose, your mother is behind you."

"And Wollie?" Sue asked.

"Your brother loves you more than you know," her mother replied. "Trust in that."

Maybe it would be possible to see where things went with Wilder…maybe she could actually consider dating him! Except, he'd be giving up a respectful relationship with the other farmers.

Still, her heart beat a little faster. She'd never be like the other *Englishers*. But she'd also never be a sweet, patient, satisfied Amish woman, either. Maybe there was a reason she was happiest on horseback, running free and feeling the wind on her face. Maybe she needed to find a way to get back on a horse again…and heaven help her, but in her mind's eye, she had someone riding next to her with a cowboy hat and a warm smile just for her.

Was there a way to find some middle ground where she could embrace her roots and still ride free with Wilder at her side?

"You need to eat," Linda said.

"I am hungry," Sue admitted. She crumpled a sodden tissue in her hand.

"Of course you are," Linda said. "Come down stairs, and I'll get you a sandwich to start. We'll go out and make nice with everyone else once your blood sugar is up again."

Right. The wedding… She still had some obligations to fulfill. She was a *newehocker*, after all, and she wanted her brother to remember this day as happily as possible.

Sue squeezed her mother's hand. "It's nice to be home, *Mamm*."

She couldn't stay. She couldn't go... Where did her roaming heart belong?

THE WEDDING WAS longer than Wilder was used to. Once the vows were said and the ceremony was complete, there were lots of people congratulating the new couple. Some of the local farmers leaned over to explain a few things that were going on, and when Wilder looked up again, Sue had disappeared.

The reception kept the men and women separate, but there were games that brought them all together, and after what felt like an eternity and Sue hadn't returned, he said his goodbyes.

Wollie and Jerusha were occupied with other people, and Wilder slipped away from the chatting, laughing, joyful throng of Amish people and threaded through the buggies toward his own land.

This was going to be Sue's world again, and he could see just how difficult it would be to get time alone with her. The Amish kept things very separate with men and women, and the women with babies and small children were even more separated still. Sue was here somewhere, but she might as well be across the country. If he were Amish, he might actually have a better chance of spending some time with her. She was coming home, and that put him solidly on the other side of the fence.

So was this the end of his time with her? Would she continue working for a few more weeks, or was she going to settle into an Amish life starting now? He wished he knew what to expect, because at least then he could brace himself for it. Because he longed to see her just once more—to hold her close, and if she wouldn't allow that, to just look into her face and see what she was feeling. Because that mattered to him. Would this choice make her happy? If it would, he'd back off. And maybe he'd feel better knowing that she was happy.

The sun was getting low, the shadows long, as he walked toward his house. His mind was still on Sue, though, and he wondered what she was doing back at the wedding, and if she'd miss him at all. He'd promised to be there for her, but she didn't seem to need him now. He should be happy for her. One man couldn't be her answer to everything. She needed her family as well. It was a lesson that the rest of the world needed to learn, too. Community mattered.

But his heart was raw.

As he came onto his property, he spotted that gray pickup truck, and he sighed. Chaney was back. He didn't bother going to the house and headed around to the drive where he found the man leaning against his vehicle, a sour look on his face.

"I thought I told you to stay away," Wilder said. He was in no mood for games. He'd been through enough today. He adjusted the black suspender over one shoulder. It was time to get into his own clothes again, get back to his own life.

"Where's Sue?" Chaney demanded.

"At a wedding," Wilder said.

"Over there?" Chaney jutted his chin in the direction of the Schmidt property with the buggies all parked in neat rows in the field.

"What do you want?" Wilder asked tiredly.

"I want to see her. I brought her stuff."

"Okay, well, you can leave it with me. I'll make sure she gets it," Wilder said.

"Are you dating her now?" Chaney asked.

"No, I'm not," Wilder replied. "Not that it's your business."

"Huh." Chaney didn't seem to believe it. "She's got a way of drawing a guy in. Watch yourself. She seems innocent, but she's not."

Wilder gritted his teeth and eyed the other man irritably. "Don't talk about her, man. Just leave her stuff and go."

"I don't even think I'm the father of that baby," Chaney said, getting out of the truck and heading around to the back. He hauled out two black garbage bags. "I'd need some actual proof."

"Is that how you're going to get around your conscience and not support your own kid?" Wilder asked bluntly.

"Do I even know what she was up to?" Chaney demanded. "I'm not going to be sending money for some kid that might not even be mine."

"Are you really suggesting that Sue was cheating on you?" Wilder's patience was gone now, and he glared at the man in barely concealed rage. "Even I know she's not that kind of person. So you came all the way to drop off a couple of bags of stuff and insult her?"

"It's none of your business," Chaney snapped. "This is between me and Sue. I'll wait to talk to her."

"It's my business now, and you're on my property. Get off of it."

"Or what?" Chaney barked out a laugh. "Look at you in your Amish clothes. I thought the Amish were peaceful. They wouldn't hurt a fly." He was talking in a singsong voice now, and Wilder clenched his fists at his side.

"Don't be deceived," Wilder said, taking off the black felt hat and tossing it onto the gravel a couple of yards away. "I'm not Amish, and I'm perfectly willing and able to remove you from my property. It's up to you what kind of state you're in by the time I get you up to the road."

Chaney's mocking stance changed then. He was several inches shorter than Wilder was, and Wilder had a good twenty or thirty pounds of solid muscle on him. Chaney wasn't going to win if he decided to tangle with him.

For a moment, Chaney stood immobile as if trying to gauge his odds, uncertainty flicking in his belligerent eyes, and when Wilder took a purposeful step toward him, he put his hands up.

"Fine!" he said, stepping around his truck and hauling the driver's side door open. "Fine! I'll go. But tell her not to bother calling me when that baby arrives. It's not mine anyway!"

Wilder cross his arms over his chest and stood there watching the pickup truck as it spun back up the drive toward the road.

If Wilder were an Amish man, he'd have access to the woman he loved…and if he were an Amish man, he'd have his own beliefs holding him back from physically dealing with the likes of Chaney. His hands were still shaking as he shoved them into his pockets. He halfway wished the guy would have given him an opportunity to manhandle him a bit, but whatever.

At least he was gone. And Wilder would be here to face him down as many times as it took if he came back. He turned toward the house, but adrenaline was still pumping, and a new thought was tickling the back of his mind.

The fact that Wilder wasn't Amish was actually a benefit when it came to protecting

Sue. He was willing to step up and do whatever it took to defend her—stuff Amish men couldn't. Or shouldn't. Whatever—Wilder would do it.

He'd spent the last three years trying to build a respectful relationship with his Amish farming neighbors, and that had meant being sensitive to their way of life and not stepping on toes. It meant being Amish in his actions when he dealt with them.

But what if being an *Englisher* was more beneficial to his community than him fitting in with their ways? What if he could leverage the things he brought to the table because he was different?

He might not be Amish, but he had access to the internet, world news and his law enforcement brother. He might not be invited to barn raisings and the like, but Wilder could get large tractors and trucks. There were bound to be times when literal horsepower wasn't going to be enough. The Amish couldn't drive a truck or a tractor, but Wilder sure could.

What if he stopped trying to be like them in their Amish ways, and instead decided to be useful in his own way?

He had their respect as a man of his word and a hard worker. He was a good man, and they knew it. So what if he started leveraging what he could offer them from the *Englisher* world?

Wilder jogged up the steps and headed into the house. He flicked on the lights, his heart hammering hard in his chest.

What if Wilder didn't stop there? What if he showed Sue what he could offer her—starting with his heart and ending in his life-long commitment. He couldn't keep her on as an employee, and he couldn't date her, but he could marry her! Sue wanted to work a ranch—let her work this one by his side as his wife.

Sue wanted marriage and kids, and Wilder had been watching the Amish grow their families for long enough to know that he wanted the same thing. He'd just watched his neighbor marry the woman he loved, and Wilder would feel infinitely lucky if he could do the same. As long as it was with Sue. He didn't want to find *someone*. He'd already found her, and no other woman would do. He wanted a life with Sue Schmidt at his side. He wanted to be the man who protected her, provided for her, and told her she was beautiful for the rest of her life.

If she'd have him…

And that was the sticking point, wasn't it?

CHAPTER SEVENTEEN

SUE WOUND HER way through the crowd of chatting neighbors. Children had fallen asleep on laps and in parents' arms. The older kids were still up and talking—wired at the lateness of the hour. Sue was noticing the children more lately. One day soon she'd have this baby in her arms, and she'd be facing a whole new set of challenges…

Jerusha was already off with her mother and aunts. There were some final bits of advice to give to a newly married woman, and this was their chance to give it. Later on, it would be meddling, and the couple would need privacy to deal with their fledgling marriage. But now, on the wedding day, it was all about community.

Wollie stood with some cousins, chatting and looking a bit shy. She hadn't had a chance to talk to him alone yet, and she stopped in his line of sight and waited for him to notice her. It took a minute, but when his gaze landed on her, he excused himself from the group and came over.

"I just wanted to say congratulations before I head back," Sue said.

"You won't stay longer?" he asked.

"It's late." She shrugged. "And I'm really tired."

"*Yah*. Right." He nodded. "I didn't thank you yet for working miracles with Jane."

"What are aunts for?" Sue said, but tears rose in her eyes, and she blinked them back. She was feeling emotional—her heart still felt so battered. "Where is Jane?"

"*Mamm* took her inside. She's tucked into bed."

"Where are you and Jerusha going tonight?" Sue asked.

"There is a *dawdie hus* on her parents' property. We'll stay there for the night, and then come back to start fresh tomorrow with Jane here," Wollie replied. "*Mamm* will stay here for tonight, and tomorrow we'll get her moved in with Uncle Samuel."

The plans were coming together—a new home was forming here. Weddings changed everything. Sue nodded and dropped her gaze.

"Sue, I'm really glad you came back, even just next door," Wollie said. "I know we always argued a lot, you and me, but I don't want to do that anymore. I want to... I don't know...cooperate. Jerusha says you're really something with Jane, and I figured that I could be that kind of uncle for your baby when it arrives...you know?"

"I'd really like that, Wollie," she said.

"Look, I don't care if you're not Amish right now," he said. "And I don't care if you're a single mother. You're my sister, and I'm going to be here for you. Jerusha agrees with that, by the way."

"Jerusha is good for you," Sue said with a misty smile.

"*Yah*... I think so, too."

"So...am I welcome to come visit sometimes?" she asked. "Even if I'm dressed in blue jeans?"

"*Yah*. You're welcome here, blue jeans and all. You're my sister," he said, his voice suddenly tight. "That doesn't change. I still think you should come back and be Amish, and that you're wrong about being an *Englisher*."

"For the record?" she asked with a wry smile.

"*Yah*, something like that," he said, but a smile toyed at his lips, too. "As long as you're okay with me bringing that up from time to time, come on by."

"Well, I'll give you some space with Jerusha for the next little while, but I'll be working next door for the next few weeks."

"Not too hard, I hope," he said.

"Wilder won't let me lift more than a cat," she said. "Trust me, I'm almost useless over there. I'm just grateful for a paycheck." Sue looked toward the house. The women had come back outside. "Jerusha will be ready for you soon."

Wollie's cheeks pinkened at the mention of his new bride. "I'd better go. I'll see you."

"You certainly will," she said with a smile. "Go!"

Wollie would be just fine, and Sue was happy for him. He had found the right wife to love him, and to love Jane, too. They'd have a good life.

Sue turned toward the Westhouse property, and her brother called after her. "I'll get someone to walk you back!"

"I'm fine," she said, turning to shoot her brother a smile. "Wilder left the lights on."

The moon was full and high, shining silvery light over the short field between the two properties, and she headed out, winding her way through the parked buggies. She pulled her gray shawl closer around her, and it felt good to leave the murmur of happy voices behind her. The wedding had been lovely, but so was solitude.

The evening wasn't too chilly—the breeze had a bit of warmth to it, one last whisper of summer. And somehow she felt more hopeful tonight than she had in a long time. That one word, *yet*, had changed her perspective. She'd figure this out.

Sue ran her hand over her belly, and she could feel a faint movement within—a reassuring little squirm that let her know that her baby was awake.

The lights at the side of the house were blazing cheerily, and she headed in that direction. But she paused when she saw another glow in the backyard. Wilder had started a little bonfire, and she could see his outline in a lawn chair next to it.

"What are you doing out here?" Sue said as she walked up.

"Waiting for you." His voice was a low

rumble. "If you did come back, it would be late. I wanted to make sure you got in safely." He pushed himself to his feet, and she met him over by the warm, fragrant fire. He caught her hand and gave her fingers a squeeze. "Honestly, I didn't know if you were coming back, and if you weren't, I guess I wanted to know that, too."

"My clothes are here," she said weakly.

He chuckled. "If you were going Amish, you wouldn't need your jeans."

"True..." She swallowed. "But I've had a chance to think, and I had a good talk with my mother, and... I still need my jeans."

Wilder looked at her, then cocked his head to the side. "Explain that," he said. "Really thoroughly. You aren't going Amish?"

Sue shook her head. "No, I'm not going to be Amish. I have to be true to myself, too."

"Chaney came by tonight," Wilder said. "He brought your stuff."

"For what it's worth," she said quietly.

"You're a good woman, Sue," Wilder said softly.

"Thanks." She stepped closer to the fire, enjoying the warmth against her legs through the thin dress.

"I've been thinking," Wilder said, and then he paused.

"Yeah?" She looked up at him, and he was looking at her somberly.

"There's more than one way to belong around here," he said slowly. "I've been working hard to prove myself to the Amish, but I'm not ever going to *be* Amish. I think I was mostly trying to prove to myself that I could be the kind of man I wanted to be. I've made too many mistakes in my lifetime, and I'm trying to fly straight." He turned his attention to the fire, his voice low. "The thing is, I have a lot I can offer to this community simply by not being Amish, like the power of a big tractor when someone needs help, or a telephone, or internet access, you know?"

She nodded. "Yeah..."

"And I figure that applies to what I can offer you, too." He swallowed hard and turned back toward her. "I love you, Sue. I just...do. You're amazing, and you make me feel things I've never felt before. I can't offer you a full-time job, but I can offer you my heart. It's yours, if you want it."

Sue blinked up at him, and she put a hand against her throat. "Oh, Wilder..."

"You want a family," he went on. "You want marriage and kids, and all that. And you know, for years I balked at the idea of getting married again. Honestly, the thought of getting married to anyone else kind of freaks me out, but I want all of that with you. It's not scary thinking of vowing to place the rest of my life into your keeping. And if you'll have me, I'll be true to you. I'll be honest, and I'll be devoted, and—" He voiced cracked. "I'll be the best dad your baby could ask for."

"Do you mean that?" she whispered.

"Do you love me?" he asked, agony in his dark gaze.

She nodded. "More than you know, Wilder. But what about the community? Will you be okay if they're mad at you for a while? Because this is going to matter to them…"

"I'm counting on someone getting good and stuck this winter," he said with a slow smile. "And I'm counting on those horses not being quite enough. I'll be the neighbor with the tractor, *and* a handshake they can count on. I know it'll take some adjustment, but I can't just sit here and watch you go on with your life without me. That's torture."

Sue took the *kapp* off and pulled the pins

out of her hair, letting it swing free around her shoulders. "I was miserable at the thought of letting you go. My mother saw straight through me, too. I didn't hide it very well."

"I don't know how much time you need to feel comfortable with the idea of me for the rest of your life," he said with a faint smile. "But I'm here. And I love you. That's not going to change. Do you think...you could see yourself..." He sucked in a wavering breath. "Sue, will you marry me?"

His words came out in a rush, and she could see the rhythm of his heartbeat in his neck. He was nervous—he was holding his breath, and she realized that she was, too. This cowboy with his heart of gold, his best intentions and his protective nature filled her heart up to the brim. She'd take care of him just as well as he took care of her.

"Yes," she whispered.

Wilder pulled her into his arms and his lips came down over hers. This kiss was different from the others—this one was filled with relief and longing, tenderness and happiness. This kiss was like heading in after a long cattle drive and sinking into a soft bed. It was a homecoming.

When Sue pulled back, she looked up into his dark gaze, the firelight flickering over the faint stubble on his chin.

"So when do you want to get married?" he asked.

"You want to set a date now?"

"I think your family might appreciate having this baby born into a married home," he said. "And I'm willing to make that happen for them. Let's take a couple of months to throw something together...and make it official. I don't need longer than that. What about you?"

"I could work with a couple of months," she said, and a smile broke over her face. "You're a good man, Wilder."

"I know this is wedding season for the Amish, and you come with a family, Sue," he said, nodding in the direction of the festivities next door. "You can't separate a woman from the family that raised her. And they're a very big family with some very strong opinions." A smile turned up his lips.

"I'm looking forward to meeting yours, too," she said.

"Conrad and Annabelle will be thrilled to pitch in with the baby. You'll love them. And my mom gets to be a grandma—just try and hold her back." He grinned.

"My family might be harder to please," she said.

"I can cooperate. They're going to be a big part of our life, after all."

"Is that the only reason?"

"Not really." His smile turned sheepish. "I just want to marry you already. What your family wants and what I want kind of match up this time around. I might be less cooperative with them later, but to start out, I'll be an absolute teddy bear."

Sue laughed and tugged him down into another kiss, and her heart swelled with love. She'd marry this man, and she'd work the ranch with him, and go riding with him, and cuddle up under a warm quilt with him after a long day of working together.

She'd come back to Amish Country, and somehow along the way, she'd found her home in this cowboy's arms.

EPILOGUE

WILDER'S COMMUNITY WATCH plan got a whole lot more support once Wollie threw his complete support behind it. He went around to the neighboring farms and talked to their neighbors individually. Wilder couldn't have been more grateful for his soon-to-be brother-in-law's help. But Wollie had a few strong opinions of his own, too. For example, Wollie insisted upon an *eck*. He didn't just suggest it, or recommend it, he cornered Wilder one afternoon when he was brushing down the horses, and he'd downright demanded it.

"This is important," Wollie said. "I'm supporting you here, but you have to show people you respect our ways. You're marrying my sister, and for an Amish wedding, it's not a wedding without an *eck*. You're already getting married in a church in town instead of on a farm, and she's already wearing a white wedding dress instead of blue… But if there was an *eck* for the reception—that would be very nice."

"I'd need help putting it together," Wilder said.

"Well…" Wollie shrugged and looked over Wilder's shoulder with exaggerated nonchalance. "I mean, if you needed help… I've made one before…"

Wilder grinned. "Will you help me make my *eck*, Wollie?"

"*Yah*. Sure. I could do that."

And so for the last two weeks before the wedding, while Sue, Linda and Jerusha dealt with the other details, Wilder put together a decorative corner to commemorate his relationship with Sue. Conrad pitched in, although he wasn't really the creative type. Wilder's *eck* wouldn't be traditionally Amish. He was including a horseshoe for luck, and a brand-new pair of riding boots for Sue—a surprise for her, because she was serious about getting back into the saddle as soon as she was able. Though at seven and a half months pregnant, her boots were remaining solidly on the ground for now.

Sue stayed with her mother at Uncle Samuel's place until the wedding. That was an-

other demand from her family, but Wilder
didn't mind so much. They meant well. They
were looking out for Sue and making sure he
wasn't going to take advantage of her, and he
had no intention of doing that.

It also gave him time to get the guest bedroom ready with a crib, a little white chest of
drawers and a rocking chair. Sue was having a boy. They'd found out at the last ultra-
sound, and Wilder had gotten choked up at
the thought. While the baby wasn't biologically his, this little boy was going to be his
in every way that mattered.

He was going to have a son!

Wilder also bought some new furniture
for his own bedroom—the one they'd share
just as soon as he married her. He brought
in a new chest of drawers, set up a new bed
frame and brought in one of those full-length
mirrors that the woman at the store told him
women liked a whole lot. He even bought a
bunch of new bedding so that things could be
fresh and new for her. Wilder was enjoying
this old-fashioned preparation for bringing a
wife home. Sue deserved his best.

When the wedding day came, he picked up
Sue from her uncle's place, and everyone else

was cramming into some vans the Amish had hired to get down to the church. They'd all done this not so long ago for Conrad's wedding, so they knew the drill.

Sue's bridesmaids were her friend Becky and Jerusha. Her sister-in-law didn't wear a traditional bridesmaid's dress, but she did wear an Amish cape dress of the same pink color. Wilder had Conrad standing with him as his best man, and Wollie, too, as his groomsman of course. Conrad and Annabelle were over the moon excited for Wilder. Conrad had gifted him some cuff links for his wedding day, and Annabelle stood there in a pretty floral dress, beaming like a proud mother.

The wedding ceremony was quite quick. Wilder didn't even remember all that was said. There was a short talk by the minister about love and marriage, but Wilder was too focused on his beautiful bride. She wore a simple white dress that draped over her pregnant curves gracefully, with a long veil. Sue was a gorgeous woman at the best of times, but today she absolutely took his breath away.

The minister asked if he would take her as his wife, and Wilder agreed wholeheartedly.

She gave her "I do," too, and it was done. He kissed her lips chastely—already a shocking thing for the Amish, apparently—and they headed out of the church for a flurry of pictures for his side of the family since the Amish didn't have their photos taken, and then they all headed back to the Schmidt farm for the wedding reception.

The Amish didn't dance, either, and after the games and speeches, a massive meal, and all the festivities were complete, Wilder gathered his bride into his pickup truck and took her back to the hotel where they'd start their honeymoon.

"We need our first dance," Wilder said, and he pulled out his cell phone and selected a nice slow country ballad. Sue stared at him, eyes wide, and then her cheeks started to grow pink.

"Tell me you know how to dance…" he said with a small smile. Funny, this was one thing they hadn't talked about yet. He'd just assumed…

"Nope," she admitted. "Amish don't dance, and I suppose by the time I could have learned, I was too self-conscious. I don't think I can give you a first dance. I have no idea how!"

Embarrassment flushed her cheeks, and Wilder wouldn't have that. She didn't need to be self-conscious around him. He caught her hand and tugged her against him, sliding his arm behind her back. Her pregnant form was pressed against him, and he felt a wriggle from inside. Then Wilder started to rock with her back and forth, his lips a whisper away from her temple. She smelled good, and he shut his eyes, feeling the perfection of the moment.

"See?" he murmured. "It's easy."

"We're married, Wilder," she breathed.

"We're married..." He kissed her temple.

His heart filled with such love for his beautiful bride and the baby on the way. Sitting on the fence was normally considered a bad thing, but he and Sue were going to build their life right there on the fence between two cultures. His life was never going to be the same, but he couldn't wait to see how their life would evolve together.

Anywhere with Sue in his arms was home.

* * * * *

*Don't miss the previous book
in Patricia Johns's
Amish Country Haven
miniseries, available now
from Harlequin Heartwarming:*

A Deputy in Amish Country

COUNTRY LEGACY COLLECTION

19 FREE BOOKS IN ALL!

Cowboys, adventure and romance await you in this new collection! Enjoy superb reading all year long with books by bestselling authors like Diana Palmer, Sasha Summers and Marie Ferrarella!